FALLING STARS

THE LAST SANCTUARY BOOK TWO

KYLA STONE

PAPER MOON PRESS

FALLING STARS

THE LAST SANCTUARY:BOOK TWO

KYLA STONE

Falling Stars

Printed in the United States of America

Cover design by Deranged Doctor Designs

Book formatting by Vellum

First Printed in 2017

ISBN 978-1-945410-13-0

Paper Moon Press

Atlanta, Georgia

www.PaperMoonPress.com

 Created with Vellum

To my children, Ella and Caleb.
You are my everything.

ALSO BY KYLA STONE

1

AMELIA

Amelia Black thought she knew how to survive. She was wrong.

The world had changed drastically in only a few short weeks. She didn't yet know how—the unknown possibilities flickered constantly in her mind.

So many questions, and she didn't have the answers to any of them. Until now. Soon, they would see the outside world for the first time in almost six weeks.

Amelia leaned against the wall of the military transport. The hard metal bench beneath her vibrated. People pressed on either side of her.

The truck slowed, bumping over potholes and ruts in the road.

"What now?" her brother Silas asked. He lounged on the bench across from her, his legs draped over a plastic-wrapped cardboard box labeled 'Medical Supplies: Syringes'. Dozens of similar boxes were stacked along the front end of the truck and secured with rubber straps.

There were no windows. Air conditioning piped through a vent near the front, but the air still felt hot and stuffy. They'd been riding for hours since departing the naval base in Jacksonville, Florida, early that morning.

The brakes squealed as the truck rumbled to a halt.

"What's going on?" Amelia asked, though she didn't expect an answer.

Their convoy included ten transport trucks: four filled with medical supplies, two filled with canned goods, MREs, and bottled water, and four for transporting civilians.

Four camouflaged military vehicles took up the front and rear of the convoy, the soldiers decked out with combat gear and pulse guns.

"How much longer?" eight-year-old Benjie asked beside her.

Willow Bahaghari squeezed her brother's hand and grinned. But her grin was forced, her eyes tired. She pushed her thick black hair behind her ears. "It's probably just something blocking the road. This will all be over soon, I promise."

Amelia sighed. If only that were true. It still felt strange not to be quarantined, trapped in the same small space day after day, surrounded by the white walls of a medical tent.

They'd been quarantined for almost a month—five days on the naval ship that rescued them from the sinking *Grand Voyager*, then another twenty-one days once they'd arrived at Mayport Naval Station in Jacksonville.

A few of the most high-value government officials and powerful CEOs had been airlifted to an undisclosed location the day they'd cleared quarantine. The rest of the one hundred and thirty-six survivors waited five more days for a supply transport to take them to Fort Campbell in Kentucky, a military base relocating the survivors of the Hydra virus.

"Can I have one of those?" Benjie pointed at the CDC epidemiologist sitting on Amelia's other side. Dr. Martinez wore a bulky yellow hazmat suit, every inch of her covered by the suit, gloves, and a helmet sealed at the neck.

Dr. Martinez had taken bloodwork from them every day for the last three weeks. She was in her mid-forties and spoke little, her expression always grim. She folded her hands in her lap. "Personal

Protection Equipment will be issued as needed when you reach your relocation destination."

Benjie scrunched up his face. He was cute, with brown skin, large dark eyes, and black hair sticking up all over his head. "I don't want a new home. I like my old one."

Amelia's gut tightened. She agreed with him. She missed her own sleep pod and her light-filled studio, where she practiced the violin for three hours every day.

But the world had changed drastically in the six weeks since they boarded the *Grand Voyager*—that much was clear.

She despised all this not-knowing. What was out there? What was happening? How many people were sick? Why wouldn't they tell the truth?

"Why can't I go home?" Benjie asked again.

Willow squeezed his hand. "Benjie, hush."

Dr. Martinez pressed her lips together behind her helmet. "They'll explain more once you reach your destination. Until then, that information is classified."

Benjie sighed and clasped his arms around his ratty backpack. "That's what everyone says."

Dr. Martinez hesitated. "I am sorry."

Willow shifted uncomfortably. "I've gotta pee," she said under her breath. "How long 'til we get to wherever the hell we're going?"

Amelia shrugged. "I don't know."

"It'll take forever at this rate." Willow gestured at the walls of the transport. "What do you think it's like out there?"

"Your guess is as good as mine." Amelia didn't know how bad it was. None of them did.

The *Grand Voyager* survivors were all anxious and antsy, desperate to return to their homes, find their families, and figure out what the hell had happened.

Amelia knew what her mother would say. *At least we have each other.* Amelia had her mother and brother, which was more than most people.

3

Willow had lost her mother and sister. Willow's friend, Finn Elling-ton-Fletcher, a giant black kid with a gap-toothed smile and a penchant for goofy humor, had lost his father. Others lost their entire families, gunned down by the terrorists, burned in the explosions, or trapped and drowned as the ship sank, consumed in smoke and flames and terror.

"I thought you might have a higher clearance or whatever," Willow continued. "Seeing as you're the daughter of Declan Black."

The world knew her father as the founder and CEO of BioGen Technologies as well as the chairman of the Unity Coalition, a conglomerate of powerful biotech, communications, and defense corporations. BioGen had manufactured and distributed the universal flu vaccine to combat the raging bat-flu epidemic.

Only a few people still living knew the truth.

Her father had also designed the Hydra Virus, releasing it as an act of bioterrorism in a calculated attempt to pass his rights-reducing, citizen-tracking Safe and Secure Act. The new president blamed the attack on the domestic terrorist group, the New Patriots. Consumed by fear, the government had passed the Safe and Secure Act in an emergency session, just as her father predicted.

But the plan backfired. The virus, meant to kill one hundred thousand people deliberately culled from the disposable poor, mutated instead. It underwent reassortment, recombining with the virulent bat-flu to create a deadly, highly contagious supervirus.

Declan Black—though not the mastermind—had designed and implemented the entire thing.

An international terrorist syndicate had taken her father hostage. Was he still alive? Did she even care?

She did, in spite of everything.

She rubbed the diamond-studded charm bracelet on her left wrist, the one he'd bought for her thirteenth birthday. Part of her wanted to rip it off and throw it away, but for some reason, she couldn't. Even though he'd betrayed her, betrayed them all.

"No," she said finally. "I don't know anything."

Willow shot her a dubious look, shrugged, and turned back to her brother. "Suit yourself."

The truck started again, jolting forward. Amelia's shoulder bumped the wall. She rubbed her shoulder and scanned the people in the transport—Enrique López, the Mexican-American senator from New York; Tyler Horne, the hotshot inventor of the RFID microchip VitaliChip; her brother Silas and her mother, Elise; and Micah Ramos Rivera, Gabriel's brother.

Gabriel Ramos Rivera rode in the first transport truck ahead of them, a prisoner in handcuffs guarded by a half-dozen soldiers and her father's former head of security, Ed Jericho.

Gabriel. The guy she fell for against her better judgment. The enigmatic, brooding Puerto Rican hothead with the bronze skin, dark smoldering eyes, and irresistible smile.

The ruthless rebel and New Patriot who'd hijacked the *Grand Voyager*, taken her hostage, and betrayed her—who willingly and knowingly gave her up to Kane, a psychopathic terrorist who'd enjoyed killing. Who took pleasure in others' pain. Who'd taken pleasure in her own.

Kane and his rough, scrabbling hands, his beady eyes, his vicious leer as he hovered over her. That asshole tried to break her. He almost succeeded.

Still, he invaded her nightmares every night. She always woke up gasping, her heart a wild, frantic thing in her chest, her thoughts a tangled knot of terror. Amelia closed her eyes, shoving those thoughts out of her head.

The truck slammed to a stop. Amelia crashed into Benjie and nearly knocked him off the bench. Across from her, Micah and Silas jolted awake, gripping the bench to keep their balance.

Outside the truck, someone shouted.

"What was that?" Benjie asked, eyes wide. Amelia and Willow exchanged nervous glances. Whatever it was didn't sound good.

Dr. Martinez clutched her hands together in front of her chest. "I'm sure it's fine. Just a routine checkpoint." But her voice quavered.

Gunfire exploded outside the truck, somewhere to Amelia's right. Shouting filled the air. "Get down!" Someone screamed.

Her heart squeezed, her breath stilling in her chest. Why had they stopped? Why were the soldiers shooting? What was happening?

Tyler Horne leapt to his feet, his perfectly coiffed blonde hair matted against his head. "We're being attacked, aren't we?"

Dr. Martinez said nothing as more shouting filled the air. Something struck the side of the truck. The wall shuddered. Amelia jerked forward.

"Tell us the truth, damn it!" Horne took an aggressive step toward the doctor.

Senator López stood and blocked Horne with his outstretched hand. "Let's stay calm. Panic won't help anything."

A bullet punctured the left side of the transport above Horne's head.

The passengers screamed and ducked, scrambling off the benches along the walls and crouching low. Amelia covered her head with her arms, the hairs on her neck standing on end.

Beside her, Willow pushed Benjie down and covered his body with her own. "Stay down!"

More shots rang out. Loud bangs and thumps shuddered the truck, as if people were shoving it from both sides. Maybe they were.

Angry shouts filled the air. It sounded like they'd surrounded the truck. The back doors clanged and jerked, but they didn't open. They were locked from the inside.

"They want the supplies, don't they?" Micah adjusted his glasses nervously. His brown eyes were huge in his boyish face, his dark wavy hair damp on his forehead.

"Why the hell won't you say something?" Willow asked Dr. Martinez, her voice rising. "*This* can't be classified, too!"

"Yes," Dr. Martinez admitted, fear and defeat in her voice. "It must be an ambush. The roads are—dangerous. There are no hospitals, no stores. People are desperate."

Amelia's mind couldn't focus on the words. No hospitals? That didn't make sense.

Another bullet punched through the transport walls like they were butter. The attackers were using armor-piercing rounds. The next stray bullet would hit someone. "Maybe we should give them what they want."

"She's right," Silas said. He had their father's intensity, the same sinewy frame and lean, wolfish face. "Open the doors."

Horne pointed his finger at Silas. "You're insane if you think you're going to let them in here. They're shooting people!"

Silas bristled, his smoke-gray eyes glittering. "You're not in charge here."

"Give them the supplies, and they'll stop shooting," Micah said.

"You don't understand." Dr. Martinez twisted her hands. "We need those supplies for research and medical personnel at the base. We can't just give them—"

"Screw this." Silas leapt to his feet, crouching low and lurching over cowering bodies to reach the back doors.

Micah followed close behind. The truck rocked and they stumbled, righting themselves and lunging for the doors before anyone could stop them.

"Don't open that door! You aren't protected!" Dr. Martinez rose to her feet just as another bullet punched through the wall inches from her head. She shrieked and dropped to the floor.

Amelia craned her neck to watch Micah and Silas wrestle with the doors' locking mechanism. Her knees ached from kneeling on the metal floor. A rivet scraped her shin, ripping a hole in her khaki cargo pants. The shouts and screams from outside the truck echoed in her ears.

A chill ran down her spine. Opening the doors might be a terrible idea, but they had to do something. They were sitting ducks, just waiting for the next bullet to kill somebody.

Someone gripped her arm. Amelia glanced up and stared at Dr.

Martinez. Her mouth pressed into a grim line, her eyes hard and unreadable. "Whatever you do, don't touch anyone."

"How bad is it?" Amelia asked.

Dr. Martinez shook her head. "I wanted to tell all of you right away, but my superiors were concerned with suicide attempts and panicked rebellion. They thought you wouldn't sit meekly in quarantine if you knew..."

Her voice trailed off as an ear-piecing shriek drowned her out. Amelia's blood turned to ice. "If we knew what? Tell me!"

Someone shouted as the back doors swung open. Daylight poured into the transport. The attackers yanked Micah and Silas from the truck. Four of them scrambled inside, black streaks across their cheeks and foreheads, assault rifles flailing.

Terror gripped Amelia. She couldn't focus on the doctor's words. Would these people actually kill them? What had they done to Silas and Micah? Was her brother hurt? Was he—

"It's airborne, passed through coughing and sneezing," Dr. Martinez said hastily, her words tripping over each other. She squeezed Amelia's arm with her gloved fingers. "It lives on non-organic surfaces for twenty-four hours, organic surfaces for up to two weeks. Always wear gloves and protective gear—"

An attacker with long red hair bound in a ponytail reached them and lunged for the doctor. The attacker wasn't a man but a tall, muscular woman, her face contorted in rage.

She seized Dr. Martinez by the throat, lifting her to her feet with one hand. She thrust the muzzle of her gun against the doctor's stomach.

"You people!" she spat. "You just left us to die!"

Amelia watched in shock, unable to move.

"Amelia!" Her mother moved to her, gripping her arm. "Go! Go!"

Amelia, Willow, and Benjie scooted from their seats and scrambled after her mother, weaving around the legs of a dozen attackers as they leapt onto the truck. They were just people, not soldiers. Men and women, some with combat gear, some only in dark clothes. Their faces were desperate and angry, their eyes blazing dangerously.

Amelia flinched as someone kneed her in the ribs. Hands scrabbled over her, scratching at her arms. Someone else seized her Smart-Flex and tried to rip it off her wrist.

"Let go!" She jerked free and kept moving, stumbling toward the back of the truck. The rest of the attackers ignored her. They were focused on the boxes of medical supplies.

The sound of a gunshot ricocheted inside the truck. Dr. Martinez moaned.

Amelia twisted in her mother's grasp, trying to see what happened. But the icy dread in her gut told her she already knew. The woman with the ponytail had shot the doctor for no reason.

They ran for the wide-open doors.

2

MICAH

The second the door flew open, angry hands grabbed Micah Ramos Rivera and jerked him from the transport truck. He fell, his spine and the back of his head cracking hard against the pavement, skewing his glasses and knocking the breath from his lungs.

For an agonizing moment, he tried unsuccessfully to suck in air as he stared helplessly up at a tangle of lunging, shoving bodies. Someone stomped on his hand. A sharp kick to his ribs sent pain exploding through his side.

He rolled to the right until he slid beneath the truck. He gasped for air, half-expecting someone to grab him, drag him out, and do whatever damage they intended. But as soon as he hid out of sight, the attackers forgot him. They scrambled into the truck, shouting and screaming.

His brain screamed for oxygen. His heart thundered in his chest. He craned his neck, scanning for Silas. He couldn't see him, only an army of legs, the attackers dirty and ragged, the soldiers' uniforms crisply creased. Screams and gunshots filled the air. Several bodies were on the ground, some unmoving, a few groaning as they tried to drag themselves to their feet.

He sucked in his first ragged breath, but there was no time to recover. He could wait here in relative safety for the military to regain control and fend off the attackers. Unless the attackers were stronger. They had their own guns. Maybe they would win—and then what? Would they kill everyone in the transports, just for spite? It was possible. Anything was possible.

He didn't know the state of the new world, since they'd been locked up in quarantine for weeks, but he knew the old one. The old world was plenty bad enough. There were gangs of killers who would as soon slit your throat as smile at you. If these attackers were desperate enough to attack an armed transport, they were desperate enough to do just about anything.

He couldn't stay here. Amelia and Willow were still in the truck. His brother Gabriel was trapped in the other transport, along with Nadira and Celeste and the others. He had to help them. He was no fighter, but he'd do whatever he could.

Micah rolled onto his stomach with a gasp. Pain lanced his side. He felt his ribs gingerly, but he couldn't tell if anything was cracked. Nadira might know, but there wasn't time for that now. He scanned either side, searching for an opening in the raging battle. There didn't seem to be anyone at the front of the truck.

He adjusted his glasses, took a breath, then crawled on his belly, ducking his head and using his arms to propel him forward, the bare skin of his elbows scraping against the pavement. He inched behind the right wheel and looked out.

A thick copse of trees lined the shoulder of the highway. Ahead and to his left, an SUV had flipped on its side, its windows shattered, a bullet hole puncturing the bumper through a faded sticker that read "Home Sweet Home" below a photo of palm trees and sand.

Further along the shoulder, dozens—no hundreds—of vehicles were pushed into the middle of the road in a haphazard jumble, some tipped, others turned sideways, still others with their doors hanging open.

All of them empty. Micah shivered. They reminded him of dead animal carcasses.

A dozen yards away, a soldier shot an attacker point blank with a pulse gun. The man shuddered, his eyes rolling wildly in his head, before crumpling to the ground.

A drone sailed over a group of six people prying open the doors of the second transport with crowbars, shooting rapid-fire into them. Three fell, dropping their guns as red bloomed across their backs. Two more attackers ran at the drone from behind, threw an electric net over it, and brought it down.

The second transport door burst open. The attackers yelled and hurled themselves inside, leaving their fallen comrades. One of the rifles lay only a few yards in front of Micah. So tantalizingly close.

He pulled himself out from beneath the truck and blinked against the harsh sunlight. The air smelled burnt, singed with bullets and seared flesh from pulse guns.

He winced against the pain as he crawled across the hot pavement and grabbed the gun. His hand ached in protest as he wrapped his fingers around the rifle's stock and jumped to his feet.

A gunshot blasted far too close. He whipped around, raising the barrel, his blood roaring inside his own head.

Three dozen people were pushing the soldiers back, covering the rest of their group as they unloaded boxes of supplies. There were so many of them, over a hundred compared to the dozen soldiers. They were men and women, young and old. They all had weapons.

Several of his own people sprinted for the woods. He recognized Horne and Senator López, Amelia and her mother, Elise. Willow dragged her brother by his arm. Silas ran after them. He grabbed a rifle of his own and covered them as they fled.

They were safe. At least, they were safer than he was at present. Micah turned his attention to the second transport. His heart constricted in his chest. His brother was a traitor and a terrorist, but he was still his brother.

Just us. Always. The phrase they always used with each other echoed painfully through his mind. Micah both loved and hated him.

Sometimes he thought his own emotions would tear him into pieces. But however conflicted he felt, he couldn't stand by and let him die.

He spotted Jericho inside the transport, struggling to reach the doors from within as attackers poured inside. In front of him, a man dressed in black aimed a rifle at a soldier trying to protect the transport. Micah raced forward and slammed the stock of his gun against the man's head from behind. He dropped to his knees. Micah struck him again to make sure he was out of play, then leapt over his body and dashed toward the transport.

Another soldier wrestled with an attacker a few feet from the door. Both their guns were on the ground, but the soldier pressed a knife to the throat of the attacker, a skinny man with matted gray hair and a respirator mask slung over his face.

A box of medical supplies labeled 'antibiotics' toppled on its side at his feet. Before the soldier slit the man's throat, a second attacker darted in from behind and stabbed the soldier in the back.

"No!" A flashback of the *Grand Voyager* roared through his brain— dead bodies everywhere, shattered glass glinting in the blood pooling across the shiny marble floors, the terrorists mowing down innocent people, the rat-a-tat of gunfire exploding in his ears.

The gray-haired man stumbled back. The soldier fell face-first onto the pavement and didn't move. Micah swung his rifle up and pointed it at the second attacker. These people were murderers. They were terrorists. They were—

A kid stared back at him. Thin and gangly, he couldn't have been older than thirteen. His green eyes glimmered with terror above the mask covering his mouth and nose.

The gray-haired man didn't run. He stepped in front of the kid. "Please." His voice came out muffled behind his respirator.

The gun shook in Micah's hands. Why was a kid attacking an armed convoy? But he knew. He recognized the desperation in the kid's eyes, the same reckless hunger reflected in the old man's. He'd seen that look a hundred times in his old neighborhood, a slum crumbling into crime, drug addiction, and chaos. They were hungry enough, angry enough, needy enough.

They weren't terrorists. They were desperate people willing to do desperate things.

He couldn't do it. He couldn't shoot an old man and a kid. He lowered the muzzle. "Go."

The man grabbed the medical box and ran, the kid on his heels.

Micah stared after them for a moment, the sounds of gunfire fading around him. How bad was it out there, to attack an armed convoy for a box of antibiotics?

A bullet whizzed past him. No time to think about that now. No time to think about anything but saving his people in the second transport. Saving Gabriel, who out of everyone didn't deserve to be saved. But Micah couldn't help himself.

He ran for the transport.

3

GABRIEL

Gabriel Ramos Rivera wished for death every single hour of every single day. He deserved death for the sins he'd committed. Death was coming for him. Death in the form of a firing squad; Jericho promised him that.

He survived the last eighteen days as a captive in quarantine in a stupor. The interrogations were brutal. The deprivation, waterboarding, the chemical-assisted questions repeated over and over, hour after hour. His captors always dressed in contamination suits. In their masks, they appeared like faceless monsters.

He couldn't blame them. As a rebel, he'd known the risks if he were caught. He went in with eyes wide open. Anything was worth bringing the corrupt elite to their knees. Any risk, any sacrifice. But he'd been wrong.

He hardly noticed when the transport lurched to a stop. Even the first pops of gunfire seemed like a distant dream, just another part of the waking nightmare trapped inside his own tortured mind, where he replayed the horrors of the *Grand Voyager* again and again.

When the transport walls began to shake with pounding fists and the first screams filtered through, he came to his senses with a jolt. The convoy was under attack.

The two soldiers guarding Gabriel leapt to their feet. Jericho joined them. Within a few moments, the attackers jammed the doors open, and the soldiers shot into a crowd of two dozen people.

Three bullets punched through the transport in rapid succession. One of the *Grand Voyager* survivors fell with a grunt. The rest of the survivors screamed, spilling from their seats and dropping to the floor.

Gabriel stared up at the twin beams of sunlight pouring through the bullet holes. Was this finally it? Would a stray bullet find him and end his misery?

Jericho stalked back to Gabriel, his face hard as obsidian. Broad-shouldered and muscular, he exuded confident strength. He rubbed his square, stubbled jaw, his brown skin filmed with a sheen of sweat. "Let's go. We need to get off this damn truck."

He yanked on his handcuffs. "I'm a prisoner, remember? The guards will shoot me if I try to escape."

Jericho's lip curled. "They're too busy shooting everybody else. We're not staying in this metal death-box a second longer."

"Leave me, then," he growled. "Let me die."

"You'll die soon enough." Jericho grunted as he jerked Gabriel to his feet. "But not like this."

Jericho shoved Gabriel in front of him. He stumbled over the crouched bodies of the others. Someone grabbed his pantleg. He recognized Celeste Kingsley-Yates, the tall, spoiled black girl with the mass of springy, cranberry-red coils. She was pretty as a model, but now her face was ashen, her lips pulled back in a grimace of terror. "Don't leave me!"

"Follow us," Jericho said. "Your best chance is to get to the woods and wait out the gunfight."

Celeste nodded and crouched behind him. Another woman, Meredith Jackson-Cooper, cowered behind her. Once upon a time, she'd been a corrupt CEO of a big pharma company, with a helmet of poofy yellow hair and a smile stretched taut as a rubber band. Now she was just a shaking, terrified woman.

He suppressed the urge to spit on her. His remorse for his crimes had done nothing to nullify his towering hatred of the corrupt, greedy elite.

Jericho exchanged a few words with the soldier guarding the front doors. His pulse gun pushed back the crowd of attackers momentarily. "I'll cover you!" the soldier said.

Jericho gestured with one hand. With his other hand, he shoved Gabriel out of the transport. He stumbled, falling to his knees. Pain sliced through his knee caps. A moment later, Jericho dropped to the ground and hauled Gabriel to his feet. "Go!" he yelled.

Micah rushed to Jericho's side. He felt his brother's presence like a buzzing pain beneath the surface of his skin. Micah didn't even look at him.

"I'm with you!" he called to Jericho.

Bullets whizzed over his head. Everyone shouted and screamed in the chaos. Soldiers and attackers battled around the transports. One of the transports ahead of them managed to barrel through the car blockade and took off, a dozen men chasing it.

For half a second, he thought the attackers might be another New Patriots chapter—they would rescue him, everything would change—but no, they were just a ragtag mass of angry civilians with weapons.

Several bodies sprawled on the ground. Blood streaked the grass. He nearly slipped as Jericho pushed him.

Two attackers ran straight at them, shouting and pointing assault rifles. Without hesitation, Jericho spun toward the attackers. He reached them before they could react and alter their target. Jericho slammed his fist into the nose of the first one, hurled himself at the second and wrestled his gun away from him as they both went tumbling.

Gabriel watched numbly, his yearning for death and an instinctive desire for self-preservation warring within him. Before he could decide either way, Jericho popped up with an assault rifle in his hands. Both attackers were slumped on the ground, unconscious.

Jericho gestured with the muzzle of the rifle, his black eyes flashing. "Look alive!"

Celeste and Meredith dashed past him. Micah stayed by his side, his gun swinging wildly. Gabriel followed, his arms uncomfortably bound in front of him with the handcuffs. He tensed for another attack, maybe a bullet to the brain.

Both the attackers and the soldiers were otherwise occupied. No bullets or pulse lasers whizzed past them. He and Micah ran into the woods with the others.

Jericho stopped them fifty yards into the tree line. They paused in the center of a small clearing surrounded by towering pine and oak trees. Dead leaves and pine needles littered the ground. The scent of sap filled his nostrils.

Celeste leaned against a tree trunk, gasping for breath, tears streaking her sculpted cheeks. Meredith stood beside her, her arms wrapped around herself, her face a mask of horror. The Middle-Eastern girl, Nadira, and the arrogant bastard Tyler Horne trailed behind them.

Gabriel didn't see Amelia. She was trapped in the first transport. As long as she and Micah were safe, he didn't care about anyone else.

"Are you sure fleeing into the woods is the wisest choice?" Horne held his side. A bit of blood smeared his temple. "We're moving *away* from the soldiers who're supposed to protect us."

"I'm going back for the others." Jericho ignored him and turned to Micah. "Move in deeper. I'll find you."

"Shouldn't I go with you?" Micah asked.

The sound of Micah's voice sent a spear of pain through Gabriel. He'd gone eighteen days without seeing or hearing his brother. Micah was the same as he remembered, maybe a bit taller, his face still boyish, tousled black hair falling into his eyes.

His brother hated him now, loathed him. And for good reason. He glanced at the leaf-strewn ground, unable to meet Micah's reproachful gaze.

"I need you to lead them." Jericho's tone sharpened. "Is that going to be a problem?"

Without a moment's hesitation, Micah answered. "No, sir."

Jericho took off while Micah led them deeper into the forest. Gabriel didn't refuse or even speak. He walked obediently behind his brother. A few moments later, several people crashed through the forest. Elise Black, the senator Enrique López, a huge black kid he didn't recognize, and Willow and her brother broke through the trees.

"Amelia," Gabriel croaked before he could stop himself.

"Don't you dare say her name," Micah spat, so much anger in his voice that Gabriel flinched. Where was the kind-hearted boy who'd been utterly loyal? He was gone, along with everything else.

"She's coming." Elise Black breathed hard, her hands on her stomach. "Silas is with her."

The sound of gunshots faded. For a long moment, the group stared at each other, straining their ears for any sound. There were only the insects trilling in the underbrush, a few birds chirping high in the trees.

"Is it over?" Micah asked.

"They overwhelmed the convoy," Willow said. "There were too damn many of them."

Jericho returned, winding through the trees, leading Amelia, Silas, and several others. He cradled two assault rifles and four handguns in his arms—all stolen from the fallen attackers. He hadn't managed to snag any of the military-grade pulse guns that were illegal for citizens. "Who here can handle a gun?"

He handed a rifle to Silas and a handgun to Micah. "I'll take one," Willow piped up. Holding her hands out imploringly, she looked like a little kid.

"I don't think so." Jericho handed one to Amelia's mother instead. "You know what to do."

Horne gestured for one. "I'll take one of those off your hands."

Jericho hesitated. "You know how to shoot?"

"Of course!" Horne grabbed a pistol before Jericho could protest further and tucked it into his belt. He'd probably never shot anything more dangerous than a pheasant. Gabriel clenched his jaw and turned away in disgust.

His gaze landed on Amelia. Her face was as beautiful as he remembered, with her finely carved cheekbones, delicate features, and skin as pale as ivory. Her long white-blond hair hung to her waist in a practical braid, stray tendrils sticking to her damp forehead.

She glanced at him, caught his gaze, then flicked her ice-blue eyes away, her expression hardening. What else did he expect? Everyone despised him. He was the terrorist, the one who'd murdered their friends and family members and sank their ship, the one who struck horror into the most callused of hearts. He was the embodiment of every secret fear.

"Where are the others?" There were a hundred and thirty-six survivors; only twenty-five or so huddled in the woods.

Jericho shook his head. "They either ran in the opposite direction or never made it off the other transports. A couple of the trucks got away."

"What do we do now?" Senator López wiped his forehead with a handkerchief and ran a hand through his thick, silver hair. "Head back to the transport and radio the base for help?"

"They lined up the last soldiers and executed them," Silas said flatly. Though he was Amelia's brother, they looked nothing alike. Silas was lean, wiry, and darker-haired, like his mother, but with the sullen petulance and cruel gray eyes of his father—the Unity Coalition chairman and sociopathic mastermind, Declan Black.

Jericho nodded. "The only thing heading back to the transport will get you is a bullet to the head."

Meredith moaned. "Those monsters! They're barbarians! Where in the world are the police?"

"Gone," Jericho said.

Gabriel watched him closely. The man didn't appear surprised or panicked. Who knew what atrocities he'd seen—or took part of—as Declan Black's head of security.

Amelia poked at her gold-plated, jewel-studded SmartFlex. "It still doesn't work. No signal. We can't call anyone."

Meredith gestured wildly at the trees. "Then what exactly are we supposed to *do*?"

"We wait here for the military to come looking for their transport," Horne said.

López nodded. "Good idea."

Gabriel shook his head but didn't speak. They were both idiots. These coddled elites had no clue how to survive in the real world.

Horne crossed his arms over his chest. "I'm sure the soldiers reported the attack before they were killed."

"I'm sure they did," Jericho said. "But we aren't staying here. Those hostiles didn't care about us while they were focused on the supplies. They might now."

"Then what do you suggest?" Horne's voice was even, but the corner of his lip twitched, revealing the tiniest sneer. He disliked Jericho. Or maybe he disliked not being the smartest asshole in the room for once.

Jericho tucked a handgun into his belt and shouldered the rifle. "We head east a few miles and await the next transport from a safe position in the woods. We'll flag them down before they reach the ambush point and go from there."

"Are you kidding me?" Celeste swiped a centipede off the leg of her pants. "Through the *woods*? When the road is right there?"

"Did you not see what just happened?" Silas glowered at her. "Or were you too busy staring at yourself in a mirror?"

Celeste frowned, opening her mouth as if to complain further, but then seemed to think better of it. She pushed herself off the tree. "Fine. The woods it is."

Meredith's lip curled, but she said nothing. She smoothed her blonde hair, glancing at the trees around her in obvious distaste, like they might leap out and bite her, or worse, ruin her manicure. Gabriel gritted his teeth in disgust.

"We'll follow you, Jericho," López said. "You seem to know what you're doing."

"Move." Jericho shoved Gabriel in the small of his back.

He took the lead, gingerly stepping over tree roots and winding between massive tree trunks. Small branches scratched his face, since he couldn't use his hands to deflect them. He didn't complain. He didn't say anything.

The image playing in his head over and over wasn't of the transport ambush they just survived. He kept seeing that rain-slicked night, the storm crashing against the ship, flames leaping high in the night sky as he stumbled on the deck of the Grand Voyager, wet with rain and blood. Handcuffs had bitten into his wrists just as they did now. The panicked crowd shoved and thrashed against him as the deck heaved and bullets rained down from above.

He saw the little girl again and again, how she crumpled on the deck in her bright yellow bathrobe. She'd been so small, only five or six, younger and smaller than the boy in their group now.

He saw her in his dreams and his nightmares, in every waking moment. Her black hair spread around her tiny face, her rosebud mouth slack, her eyes dull and staring. Always staring straight at him, accusing him with their terrible vacancy.

He was a terrorist. And he had killed her.

4

WILLOW

Seventeen-year-old Willow trudged through the woods, keeping her grip on Benjie's hand. She already lost one sibling. She sure as hell wasn't going to lose another.

When they were trapped in the transport with no escape, she nearly hyperventilated with terror. *He's safe*, she told herself over and over. Benjie was safe, and she'd do damn near anything to keep him that way.

"Hey, you." Finn fell into step beside her. "For a second, I saw my own death flash before my eyes. I thought I'd be done with that by now, you know?"

"Would you prefer peeing yourself?" she quipped, though her hands were still trembling slightly. She glanced up at him.

At 6'6", he towered over her tiny 5'0" frame. She was short but thick, where Finn was huge all over, with broad shoulders, a meaty chest, and tree-trunk arms and thighs. Shadows dappled his medium-brown skin, his cheeks breaking into that mischievous smile she'd come to adore. He was always good-natured, even after weeks of being confined in quarantine or repeatedly getting shot at.

Though they'd only known each other for several weeks, surviving both the *Grand Voyager* and the hours-a-day they spent in quarantine together solidified their friendship. On the first day of quarantine, Finn settled his bulk in their little corner and never left.

Finn winked at Benjie. "You promised you wouldn't tell anyone."

Benjie managed a giggle. Finn's kindness and humor did wonders for him, somehow easing the trauma he'd endured. Benjie tried to wriggle out of Willow's grasp and reached for Finn instead.

"Nice try." Willow tightened her grip. "You think I'm letting go of you for even a second?"

Benjie pushed between them and slipped his free hand into Finn's. His entire arm looked like a twig next to Finn's. "I can do both. Right, Finn?"

Willow rolled her eyes. "Always the negotiator. And it's Mister Finn to you. Remember to show respect." Now that her mom was gone, the burden of raising Benjie was on Willow's shoulders. *They're your responsibility. Take care of them.* Her mom's words echoed in her mind. She'd do her best to make her mom proud. It was the least she could do.

They walked for another hour. A spider's web tangled in her hair. Benjie tripped on a root and scraped his palms. Birds twittered in the branches above them. Yellow leaves and pine needles crunched beneath their feet.

It was better than eighteen days stuck in a windowless tent with nothing to do, sitting around waiting to find out whether you'd contracted a deadly disease. And it was a far cry better than being trapped and shot at like sardines in a can—which tasted awful, though her *lola* loved them.

Jericho led them to the edge of the tree line, still far enough in to avoid being seen, but close enough to scout any incoming traffic on the highway, which was eerily empty.

"Did you hear any cars while we were in the woods?" Willow asked.

He shrugged his massive shoulders. "Nope."

The majority of vehicles were electric, but if you listened for it, you could still hear their signature hum. "That's weird, right?"

"Yeah." He rustled Benjie's hair. "I'd say that's weird."

They found a spot clear of roots and sat down. Nadira and Micah sat next to them, with Amelia, Silas, and Amelia's mother, Elise, leaning against several tree trunks a few yards away. A group of adults —Horne, Meredith, Lopez, and several others, all rich elites with imperious attitudes who'd done nothing but complain since their first night in quarantine—remained standing, huddled in a circle and whispering urgently.

Jericho stood off to the side, guarding his terrorist prisoner, Gabriel.

Jericho should just kill him and be done with it. She knew it was a dark thought, but she couldn't help it. He didn't need a trial. Everyone here knew he and his rebel terrorists had released the Hydra Virus, which murdered over one hundred thousand people before mutating to kill millions more. He'd slaughtered hundreds on the *Grand Voyager*.

Her mom was dead because of that monster. And her beautiful, spunky little sister Zia, with her pixie hair dyed turquoise, her zany outfits, and her crazy, infectious laugh.

Not all the blame rested with the terrorists, though. She swallowed a lump in her throat.

Willow was supposed to watch Zia. Willow was supposed to be the responsible big sister—*Ate*, as her Filipina mother always called her. But she hadn't been responsible. She abandoned Zia on purpose, left her thirteen-year-old sister crying and upset and alone. Her last words to Zia haunted her every waking moment. *Don't you get it? I don't want you around!*

Willow flinched and shoved the memory out of her head. She couldn't think about that now. She'd never escape it. Her guilt would stay with her no matter where she went or what she did, like a scar, or a scarlet letter tattooed on her forehead.

The sun disappeared behind a cloud, casting the forest in dark shadows. A twig cracked. Something moved back there, something bigger than a squirrel. The buzz of insects grew louder. She slapped a mosquito from her upper arm.

How long had they sat here? It felt like hours. Willow kept wanting to check her SmartFlex for the time. Though her version had been old and crappy, it still performed all the basic functions. But the terrorists stole it, along with her family.

"I'm thirsty." Benjie shuffled and reshuffled a favorite set of cards kept inside his rumpled backpack.

"Here." Nadira tucked a strand of black hair inside her hijab and handed him a half-full water bottle she'd somehow managed to bring with her from the transport.

"Don't take too much." Willow nodded in thanks to Nadira, who smiled warmly. Her heavy, expressive brows and strong nose gave her a regal look, but she was a quiet girl, soft-spoken and genuinely kind. Willow had liked her since they'd first met in the Kid Zone of the *Grand Voyager,* when Nadira convinced her to spare the life of one of the terrorists.

After a while, Nadira rose and slipped between the trees, out of sight. In quarantine, she walked to the same corner five times a day, knelt on a small rug one of the doctors gave her, and prayed facing Mecca.

A few of the older survivors grumbled a bit, but most people didn't care. These days, terrorists looked like everyone. Willow didn't believe in Islam or any other religion, but she wouldn't begrudge anyone what they needed to survive.

The whirring sound of several electric engines reached them just as Nadira returned from the woods, a few pine needles still stuck to her pant legs. Micah, Silas, and Horne leapt to their feet. No one else got up. The strangely empty highway littered with abandoned cars weirded everyone out.

The three guys followed Jericho to the shoulder of the highway. Through the trees, Willow made out a military transport heading toward them. Four transport trucks were led by an armored hummer, just as Jericho predicted.

She stood up, relief flooding through her. She didn't want to complain in front of Benjie, but hunger gnawed at her belly. Exhausted from the terror of the ambush, she just wanted to eat a good meal—preferably real food over tasteless prefab, but she'd take anything right now. She longed to lie down and sleep for a long, long time.

Jericho, Micah, and Silas stepped onto the road, waving their arms. The armored hummer blared its horn but didn't slow down. Instead, it sped up. She couldn't discern the driver and passenger, but she recognized the distinctive gray muzzle of a pulse gun poking through the opened window.

"They're not stopping," she whispered. "Why aren't they stopping?" She squeezed Benjie's hand. Beside her, Finn grabbed her brother's other hand.

Jericho waved harder, yelling for them to stop. They didn't. Jericho, Micah, and Silas stumbled backward off the road at the last second. The military transport roared past them.

Willow stared, her heart sinking into her stomach.

"What just happened?" Celeste demanded.

"They left us behind!" Meredith sputtered. "They can't do that! Don't they know who we are? We have a senator with us! I am a prestigious CEO! They can't leave us!"

"They did," Willow said numbly.

Jericho and the others stalked back to the group. Horne's face reddened with rage. "They flicked us off. Can you imagine? General Thorton himself will hear about this."

"They can't discern us from any other civilian." Amelia's mother, Elise, exchanged a glance with Jericho. "We're nothing to them."

"She's right," Jericho said heavily.

"I don't care," Horne sputtered. "I'll take this to the highest chain of command. When we get back—"

"We're on our own," Willow said. Her voice didn't sound like herself. That old familiar fear crept up her throat. They were lost in the woods in the middle of nowhere. The only other people they'd seen were the crazy attackers who'd just tried to kill them. The woods took on an ominous look, the air colder, the branches sharper, the shadows deepening, hiding who-knows-what.

"We need to follow the first rule of survival," Jericho said. "Seek shelter."

"We shouldn't leave the highway," Meredith said. "Who knows what's out there?"

"What do you suggest?" Silas raised his brows contemptuously. "Just sit here and hope the next military vehicle that passes will take pity on us? I'm pretty sure they're lumping all civilians with those psychos we met this morning."

"We should go back to the base," Celeste said. "We know it's safe. They know us."

"They transferred us because they don't have the room or the supplies to house civilians," Willow said with a calmness she didn't feel. "Besides, we traveled all day. Jacksonville must be four or five hundred miles back."

Meredith paled. "Regardless. That transport could have come from any base. General Thorton will send an emergency team for us. We simply need to wait."

"You'll make yourself a juicier target for whoever comes along," Jericho said.

"What about the closest city?" Nadira twisted her hands in front of her lap. "We find the police, the local government, whoever we can. Then we can find our families and go home."

Willow shivered. Her *lola*, her grandmother, lived in Newark. She missed the smell of *pancit* and the sound of the Filipino channel always in the background, her grandmother chiding her to take her shoes off inside the house and do her homework.

But was she okay? Did she get sick? What about her best friend, Rihanna? The last time Willow talked to her, she'd been burning with fever. That was five weeks ago. What had happened to everyone she knew while she was locked up in quarantine? She missed her family and friends with a fierceness that surprised her. "I want to go home."

"We should find a closer military base first," Micah said. "We don't know what's happening in the cities or how dangerous they are."

Jericho tapped his SmartFlex. "Current location." Even without a signal, the GPS still worked. The satellites weren't connected to internet or signal towers. "We're just north of Macon, Georgia. The nearest base is Robins Air Force Base, about thirty miles south of here."

Celeste scowled. "You expect us to walk thirty miles? Are you insane?"

"That's not an option," Senator López said quietly.

Willow glanced at him. He had the highest clearance of anyone in the group. A chill ran through her. "Why not?"

"After I cleared quarantine, I received a security update from General Thorton. They were going to send me and the other surviving government officials to Mount Weather to join President Sloane." Senator López wiped his face. The color leached out of his tanned skin, the lines around his eyes and mouth deepening. "We were scheduled to leave yesterday, when the latest reports came in from Mount Weather. It has been compromised."

"What the hell does that mean?" Horne huffed. "Speak clearly, man."

Willow's gut tightened. She felt sick. If a top-security base was compromised . . . he didn't want to complete that thought. "The Hydra Virus."

López nodded slowly, like his head was too heavy for his neck. "Something about a tainted medical instrument that came in with the research supplies from a nearby hospital. I don't have any other details."

"What about President Sloane?" Elise asked. "The continuity of government?"

"I don't know."

"What does that have to do with us?" Willow asked.

"In the same conversation, General Thorton stated that they'd lost over half of their military bases. Fort Bragg in North Carolina. MacDill, Fort Hood, West Point. I saw the list. Robins was on it, too."

"That's impossible." Meredith sniffed. "You must be misinformed."

López frowned. "I assure you—"

"Was Fort Benning on the list? It's a hundred miles west of here." Jericho swiped the GPS holo.

"Not that I am aware of."

"Good," Jericho said, his voice hard. "That's our new destination. We can't stay here arguing uselessly. We have less than three hours until darkness falls. Unless you fancy bedding down in the leaves for the night, we need to move."

"There's a town here, just off I-75." Silas pointed at the holo map flickering over Jericho's SmartFlex.

Jericho nodded. "Shelter first. Let's go."

Meredith's unnaturally smooth skin wrinkled strangely as she scowled. "And why, pray tell, should we listen to you?"

"He's the guy who knows how to use a gun," Silas said. "So shut up and move your ass."

Meredith's mouth tightened. "Where are your manners, young man? If your father could hear you now—"

Silas spit on the ground and wiped his mouth. "Thank God for the apocalypse, then."

López cleared his throat. "We appreciate your service back there, Jericho. We do. However, it seems like the definition of insanity to wander off to some god-forsaken place when we know that General Thorton will send reinforcements for us. How will they find us without communications? We need to stay right here."

"No," Jericho said. "It's too dangerous."

Meredith gazed at Jericho like he was some sort of cockroach, her lip curled. "You're nothing but a glorified bodyguard. Who put you in charge?"

"I did," Jericho said simply. "This is no democracy. Follow my lead or go. I protect my own, but I can't protect idiots."

Meredith's face reddened. She raised herself to her full height. "Do you know who the hell you're talking to?"

Jericho shrugged. "I don't care. Your money and shiny titles don't mean shit now."

Silas chortled. Willow couldn't help it; she grinned. It felt good to see these smug, pretentious elites put in their place. Jericho was a true badass.

Meredith shot López a baleful look. "This is entirely unacceptable."

"I agree with Meredith," López said. "We can't risk missing our rescue. I'm sorry, but we're going to have to part ways."

"I don't think we should separate," Micah said. "We're stronger together."

"Speak for yourself." Willow could do without them just fine. Amelia would stay with Jericho, which meant Micah would, too. It wasn't even a question in her mind. She and Benjie were safer with Jericho over a bunch of stuffy, clueless elites any day of the week. This wasn't a company board room or a fashion runway. This was the real world. And in the real world, you had to be strong. You had to know how to make the hard choices.

Meredith gestured at López. "Who else is with us?"

"Not me," Willow said, not that anyone cared.

Six others, all adults—all elites, or former elites—crossed the clearing and went with Meredith. Celeste hesitated, her eyes flicking between Jericho and Meredith.

"Celeste!" Meredith said. "Are you mad? Come with us."

Celeste shook her head, a few copper coils falling into her face. Her simpering, syrupy sweetness was gone. She was shaking, suddenly unsure of herself, the same hesitant expression on her face Willow remembered from the *Grand Voyager*, when they'd cowered beneath the bridge, soaking wet and terrified. "I—I can't sleep out here. I'm going with them."

Meredith sniffed and patted her glossy blonde hair. She turned to Amelia's mom. "Elise? Surely, you have more sense than this."

Elise shook her head. "Our family has trusted Jericho with our security for six years. I'm in no position to stop now."

"What about you, Horne?" Senator López asked.

Horne's gaze darted to Jericho's stacked physique and the assortment of guns and knives he'd stashed on his person. "As much as I hate to say it, Jericho has the training, experience, and expertise to keep us alive. My odds are better with him."

Meredith seemed to take the rejection as a slight. She jutted her chin imperiously. "Suit yourselves."

Senator López turned to Elise and held out his hand. "Sorry, dear, but I'm going to need to take that gun off you."

Elise stepped back, frowning. "What? Why?"

"It's only fair that we split our resources," Meredith said sweetly.

Silas's face contorted. His hand rested on his holster. "If you think—"

"Just give it to them," Micah said. "It's not worth it."

"What he said." Meredith gave a cold smile. "There's no need to make things difficult."

"Two guns," Jericho said. Even Meredith was smart enough to know when to push her luck—and when not to. Elise and Micah sighed and handed over their guns.

Meredith smiled triumphantly. "Good luck," she said, though her tone implied the opposite. Then she strode into the trees, headed toward the road. Senator López and eight other people followed her.

"Stay off the highway!" Jericho called after them. Meredith lifted her middle finger.

"How quickly the cultured aristocrats lose their manners," Finn murmured beside her.

Willow rolled her eyes. "Good riddance."

Their group had shrunk to twelve—Willow, Benjie, Finn, Amelia, Silas, Micah, Jericho, Elise, Horne, Celeste, Nadira, and the prisoner, Gabriel. Willow wouldn't have minded losing a few more. Celeste was a whiny, spoiled princess who complained all the time, and Horne was a smarmy, conceited idiot who might get them all killed.

This little adventure couldn't be over soon enough—if they survived it.

5

AMELIA

A melia watched the discussion as if from a distance. Everything seemed so surreal.

Six weeks ago, she had been at home in Manhattan, training for Juilliard four hours a day. Four weeks ago, she had been a hostage on a burning cruise ship. Two weeks ago, she had been stuck in quarantine on a naval base in Florida. And today, she was lost in the woods somewhere in Georgia, hurled into a harsh new world she barely recognized.

As soon as Meredith and the others marched off toward the highway, Horne wheeled on Jericho. "What about him?" he snarled, his perfect features contorting as he gestured at Gabriel.

Amelia's stomach curdled at the mention of Gabriel. He sat handcuffed against a tree. Her eyes met his, as dark and full of shadows as she remembered.

A memory struck her—his head bent over her, dark curls falling into his eyes as his lips brushed hers, butterflies exploding in her stomach. And then later, his strong calloused hands massaging her swollen fingers, his eyes filled with silent regret for how he'd hurt her. His eyes were filled with that same pained regret now.

She tore her gaze away.

"He's my prisoner," Jericho said tersely. "We take him with us."

Horne planted his feet, fisting his hands on his hips. "So we're gonna be responsible for feeding him? *Sheltering* him?"

"I'm not sleeping anywhere near that monster," Celeste said. "He could kill us all in his sleep!"

"The girl is right," Horne said. "We know he's guilty. Just put a bullet in his head now and call it a day."

"If you shoot him," Jericho said, his face as placid as ever, "I will slap cuffs on you and turn you in for murder."

Horne's mouth contorted. "You've got to be kidding me."

Jericho's hand moved to the rifle slung over his shoulder. "Do I look like I'm joking?"

"He's right," Gabriel said. "Just shoot me."

"Give me a gun," Silas said with a smirk, "and I'd be happy to."

"Killing a man who can't fight back is murder," Micah said.

Silas whirled on him. "So you *are* on his side. I guess it's to be expected, seeing as you're brothers. Are you a terrorist, just like him? Should we find another pair of handcuffs for you?"

Amelia listened to them argue with growing dread. She had as much reason to hate Gabriel as anyone. And yet, she couldn't hate him completely. She'd seen his pain, his vulnerability. For a brief moment, she'd seen his truest, best self.

He'd betrayed her, but before that, he'd shown her a new way to think, a new way to be. When she thought of him, she felt anger, grief, loss, and over it all, a deep, wrenching pain. But she didn't feel hate. Despite everything he'd done, a part of her didn't want him to die.

When Jericho spoke, his voice was iron. "This man is a terrorist and an enemy of the state, responsible for the sinking of the *Grand Voyager* and the release of the Hydra Virus bioweapon. He will stand trial for his crimes, he will be convicted, and the American people *will* see justice done. Until then, anyone who lays a single finger upon him answers to me."

Only Amelia, Silas, and their mother knew Gabriel didn't commit the bioweapon attack. Still, he was guilty enough. But Jericho wouldn't let the others kill him. He would live, for now.

Relief filled her, followed by a pang of shame. She *should* want him dead, like she'd wanted Kane dead. But she didn't.

"Are we clear?" Jericho asked tersely.

For a long moment, no one spoke. "We're clear," Willow said. Horne just shook his head, alternatively glaring at Jericho and Gabriel.

"We've wasted too much time." Jericho gestured through a copse of trees to the west. "Let's go."

"Sounds good to me," Willow said.

A shifting, crackling sound came from the underbrush behind them.

"Something's moving out there." Nadira hugged herself as she peered into the shadows.

"I heard it, too," Willow said.

Silas sneered. "You scared of the big bad woods, little girl? Afraid you'll be attacked by a skunk? Terrified of the raccoons and squirrels?"

Willow tightened her grip on Benjie's hand. "More like bears and wolves."

"Silas—" Amelia said, a warning in her voice. She recognized the cruel flare in her brother's eyes.

But he ignored her. "Now you're just fear-mongering. That Quran-thumper did her prayer-rug thing and managed to not get eaten."

"Don't listen to him," Amelia said to Nadira. "He doesn't know how to act civilized."

Silas clutched his chest. "You wound my delicate heart."

"You have a heart?" Willow snapped.

"It's okay." Nadira touched her pale blue hijab.

"It's not okay," Willow said. "What exactly is your problem?"

Silas's lip curled. "Where do you want to start?"

Willow stared at him coldly. "Why are you always such an asshole?"

"At least he's an equal opportunity asshole," Amelia said before her brother could respond. It was true. Her brother wasn't so much racist or bigoted as a misanthrope. He simply hated everyone.

Silas's eyes went hard. He'd keep insulting everyone until they all despised him, and he wouldn't stop even then. Amelia needed to diffuse the tension. She grabbed his arm. "Walk with me. I'm feeling dizzy."

"Are you okay?" Her mother pressed her hand to Amelia's forehead. "Do you need—"

"I'm fine."

"Amelia—" Her brows lowered in concern. Even in loose army fatigues and no make-up, her mother exuded grace and beauty, with her high cheekbones, perfectly arched brows, and dark curls tumbling over her slim shoulders.

"I said I'm fine." She jerked out of her mother's cloying reach. She didn't want anyone knowing about the pills, or the pouch with her last auto injector that looked like an EpiPen but wasn't. She had kept her epilepsy a secret her entire life.

She didn't plan on changing that now. She didn't know what kind of world awaited them, but it was likely one that would brook even less weakness than the one she knew—the harsh, unforgiving world of her father.

Whatever happened next, she couldn't be weak. Not anymore.

Jericho marched off into the woods. Horne and Celeste huffed and moaned, but they followed the rest of the group, Celeste grumbling something about ticks and mosquitoes.

Silas fell into step beside Amelia with a huff. She pushed through the underbrush, thorns snagging at the bare skin of her arms. Deeper beneath the forest canopy, the sunlight grew dim. Amelia straightened her shoulders, warding off a shiver.

Silas picked up a large stick and whacked it against the trunk of a gnarled oak. "Did that tree offend you, too?" Amelia snapped. "I'm fairly certain they don't bite."

He shrugged and flashed her an insolent smile. "I just like to hit things."

"Could you please try to be a bit more kind?"

"Why?"

"Because we need to work together to survive, that's why. And it's what good people do."

"Who says I want to be good?"

Amelia sighed. "Being a jerk isn't something to be proud of."

He smirked and whacked another tree. "It is if you do it well."

"What would it take for you to be nice to people?"

"I dunno. A lobotomy, maybe."

"Fine. I give up." Her brother was sharp and prickly with everyone, always sarcastic, often cruel. She used to be exempt, but not anymore. They'd drifted apart for years, so much that she feared the breach stretched too far to cross.

But after the terrorist attack on the *Grand Voyager*, he proved he still loved her. She'd seen it in the desperation written across his face when he and Micah broke into the captain's quarters during Kane's attack—right after she stabbed him in the eyeball with a syringe.

She never dreamed about the part when she rescued herself, when Silas came for her. It was the nightmares that haunted her: the gut-wrenching fear, Kane looming over her, his viper eyes as he hurt her again and again.

She shook the dark thoughts from her head. The sun shone through the leaves, the birds were chirping. She couldn't let the nightmares control her waking life the way they ruled her sleep.

"Please don't say anything about this." She gestured at her cargo pocket where Silas knew she kept her pouch and the bottle of remaining pills.

He rolled his eyes. "I'll make sure to keep it to myself the next time epilepsy comes up in general conversation."

"Be quiet, would you? I'm serious. Horne and the others would leave me behind in a heartbeat if they thought I was a liability, just like —" *Just like Gabriel.* But she couldn't bring herself to say his name aloud.

Silas whacked another tree. "Who cares about any of them? Jericho won't leave you. He's all we need."

"Maybe," Amelia allowed. "But still."

She didn't tell him she only had two weeks left of her epilepsy medication, only fourteen of the illegal pills that kept her alive, that kept her brain from turning to mush—pills illegally created for her by Declan Black, her stepfather. After that, she had nothing but the last emergency auto-injector.

After that, the next seizure she suffered could be the one that killed her.

Her mother came up on their other side, stepping nimbly over a fallen branch. She touched Amelia's shoulder. "We need to talk."

I'm pretty sure we don't. But Amelia's manners were bred deep. She couldn't simply abandon her upbringing, no matter how angry her mother made her. "Can it wait, please?"

Her mother sighed. "I think you should cut off your hair."

"What?" She looked sharply at her mother, eyes widening. She nearly walked right into a tree.

"We don't know what—or who—waits ahead of us," her mother said in a low voice. "We aren't protected out here, Amelia, not like at home. Not like it used to be."

She remembered the CDC doctor's frantic face, her fingers digging into Amelia's upper arm. And all those people, their hungry faces and desperate anger as they grabbed at her. She shuddered. "I get that."

"No, you don't. You're a beautiful girl, Amelia. Your hair is—it catches the eye. You're used to beauty as a gift. But out here, beauty is a liability. It's dangerous."

Amelia wasn't stupid. For years, her father had used her beauty as a weapon in his arsenal to woo his political allies. Gabriel wanted her beauty. Then he betrayed her. Kane wanted to destroy her for it.

But her hair . . . it was part of her identity. So were her looks, her face. It wasn't vain to simply want to be yourself. She'd spent years of her life checking mirrors to ensure she looked absolutely perfect, just the way her father wanted.

As usual, her mother was overreacting. She'd been cloying and overprotective for her entire life. But Amelia was an adult now. She wouldn't be weak and stupid anymore. "I know, Mother. I'll be careful."

"It's safer if you cut it off. Wear the loosest clothing you can—men's clothes would be best. Dirty your face. And hide your SmartFlex."

Amelia wanted to roll her eyes, but something in her mother's voice stopped her. Still, how would she know anything about how to survive in a harsh world? Amelia knew little of her mother's life before she married Declan Black when Amelia was a baby. Her parents raised her in wealth and luxury. Her mother always wore custom designer dresses and attended lavish balls and extravagant dinners. What made her think she knew anything more than Amelia did?

"You've never had to see the world the way it is. I've protected you from that."

Anger pricked her. The words poured out of her before she could stop them. "Like you protected us from Father?"

Her mother flinched, her hand fluttering to the hollow of her throat. But she didn't back down. "You don't know the whole story, Amelia. Quarantine wasn't the time or place, but—"

"I know enough." Amelia touched her charm bracelet, the diamonds winking even in the shadows. She stepped over a hollow log, smashing several wild mushrooms with her boots. "I know you stayed with that—that monster after you knew what he was—" The old fear swelled in her throat, choking off her words. The fear she lived with her entire life. Fear that made her meek and submissive. Fear that made her weak.

Declan Black had instilled that fear in her. Her stepfather was a hard, cruel man who'd sought power at any cost—even over his own children. He raised Amelia to dread imperfection, to never question him or desire anything that lay outside the boundaries of his own control.

She spent her life desperate to earn his love. But nothing she did was ever good enough. It wasn't until his final rejection on the *Grand*

Voyager's bridge that Amelia truly understood that her father was incapable of love.

In some ways, it freed her. She didn't need to be weak and afraid anymore. But she still felt a burning, bitter anger toward her mother, the woman who stood by, watched her daughter suffer for years, and did nothing.

"We *will* talk." Her mother took her arm and thrust something into her hand. A knife, sheathed in a matte black guard with a leather loop to attach to a belt. Where had she gotten it? From one of the fallen attackers? They weren't allowed weapons on the naval base. "Until then, take this. I'm begging you to do as I ask."

Silas grunted. "Since when has begging done you any good?"

A flash of hurt crossed their mother's face. Amelia's throat went dry. Guilt pierced her. No matter how angry she felt, she didn't like to see her mother in pain.

"You coming, sister?" Silas quickened his step, and Amelia hurried to follow, leaving her mother—and her guilt—behind.

Silas glanced at the blade in her hand. "You should keep the knife."

She attached the sheath to her belt. She liked knowing it was there, just in case. She slid her SmartFlex off her arm and stuffed it into one of her cargo pockets. "Fine. But I'm not cutting off my hair."

He cocked his eyebrow at her, a slow, hard grin spreading across his face. "Good."

She wasn't giving in to them, to anyone. She wasn't changing herself for anyone else, not again. Maybe someday, if she was strong enough, hard enough, the nightmares would fade. Maybe someday, she would finally defeat the fear curled deep inside her.

6

MICAH

"So, do we just walk right up to them?" Micah stood with Jericho, Silas, and Horne. In front of them, the I-75 exit ramp stretched down into a small town. A few stores, a gas station, a tiny hotel, and several smaller roads branched off into clusters of small, hunched houses.

"They don't look too friendly," Silas said sourly, slouching against a tree.

At the bottom of the ramp, six sheriff cars blocked the road. It'd be impossible to plow through, even if they had a vehicle. A guardian drone hovered over two cops lounging against the bumper of one of the cars, smoking cigars. Rifles were slung over their shoulders. There were no cop-bots as far as Micah could see.

He was used to state and city checkpoints. They'd been everywhere for years: attempts to stop the domestic terrorist groups and prevent openly sick individuals from spreading the flu and other diseases that seemed to get more contagious every year.

You had to scan your SmartFlex at each checkpoint, cataloging your ID, last well visit from a doctor, and criminal and political background. But he'd never seen a checkpoint at the town level, especially one as small as this. It had a population of less than five thousand.

"We'll go around and sneak in another way," Jericho said.

"Nonsense." Horne mopped his brow with his handkerchief. "They're officers of the law, not armed bandits or terrorists. We'll go down and speak to them, man-to-man."

Horne's idea seemed reasonable. They were cops, after all. Public defenders, community leaders. The good guys, supposedly.

Micah's stomach rumbled. His mouth was dry, his throat beginning to ache. If they had food down there, he was all in. "I think we should check it out."

Jericho squinted, shielding his eyes. "They might be hostile."

"This isn't backwoods Africa, man." Horne clapped Jericho on the shoulder.

Jericho stiffened, his eyes going hard. Micah thought he might slap Horne's hand away. His jaw muscles twitched as he glowered at Horne for a tense moment. Finally, he spoke in a low, restrained voice. "I'd prefer not to be touched."

"Whatever you say, soldier boy." Horne removed his hand and made a show of wiping it on his own shirt. "Do what you want. I'm negotiating food and shelter." He took off down the hill, his arms waving.

"We're not letting that simpering pansy take charge, are we?" Silas asked. Without waiting for a response, he jogged after him. Jericho sighed and gestured for the others.

By the time they reached the checkpoint, both officers had their weapons pointed at the group. "Halt!" the first one, a portly Asian man, said when they were still a dozen yards away.

"No closer!" The second officer was Latino and in his mid-fifties, with gray striping his goatee and sunglasses masking his eyes. Both officers wore gloves, with surgical masks around their necks and goggles perched on their foreheads.

"We mean no ill will," Horne said. "I'm Tyler Horne, founder and chief executive officer of Vitalichip Industries."

The portly one merely raised his eyebrows.

"We need food, shelter, and access to communications," Horne said. "I see you have a lovely hotel down the road. We just need a place to stay for the night and to contact our base to come get us."

"None of you are military." The guy with the shades spat tobacco on the ground.

"Like I said, I'm a chief exec—"

"No offense, *Executive*, but you could be the king of Timbuktu for all I care. No one gets into our town."

"All we're asking for is some hospitality." Micah adjusted his glasses.

"Keep your hands in the air!" Shades barked, whipping his gun toward Micah.

Micah jerked his hands up, heat flushing his cheeks. "We aren't dangerous."

The portly one smirked. "Everyone is dangerous these days, son. And hospitality is what gets people killed."

Micah exchanged a nervous look with Finn, who stood closest to him. He was starting to get a bad feeling about all this.

"Come on now," Horne pushed. "Let's be civilized about this. We're willing to pay."

Shades stood up and took a step toward them. The drone buzzed menacingly over his head. "I don't know what rock ya'll have been hidin' under, but the world's fallen to hell and we're protecting our own. This town is sealed."

Horne scowled. "You can't keep us out."

Both officers turned toward Horne, their expressions darkening. These guys weren't playing around. Micah wanted to tell Horne to shut up. He was too arrogant, too aggressive. He just pissed the cops off. Horne would escalate things if they weren't careful.

Micah took a step forward. The officers' attention swiveled to him. "We'll go now," he said in a placating, soothing voice. "But can you give us any suggestions on where to go?"

"Stay the hell back!" Shades snarled.

The other officer took a puff of his cigar and blew out the smoke.

"Try five exits down, Mayfield. Our scouts say it was infiltrated a few weeks back. The Headhunters have it now."

The way he said *Headhunters* made Micah's gut twist. "Who?"

Before they could respond, Benjie sneezed.

Both officers flinched. They yanked their masks up over their faces. "Git now," Shades said, "before I've gotta do something nobody wants."

"How bad is it out there?" Micah asked.

But they weren't interested in talking anymore. The drone whined as it swooped from behind the officers and hovered menacingly over Micah's head.

"Time to go," Jericho said. "Now."

———

By the time they made it to the Mayfield exit, everyone was tired, hungry, and thirsty. The sun banked low over the horizon, flares of red, violet, and orange tingeing the clouds over the trees.

Micah walked with Willow, Benjie, Nadira, and Finn. Amelia walked beside them but a little apart, and Gabriel was up front with Jericho, Elise, and Silas. Celeste trailed behind, muttering complaints and curses over blisters.

Abandoned cars littered the exit ramp, forcing them to walk along the shoulder. At the checkpoint, a temporary plasma fence blocked the road. Several cars parked across the road behind it. Three cop-bots slumped against a state patrol car, their charges long exhausted.

The checkpoint was abandoned.

Micah stopped and stared, his stomach knotting. What happened here? If the country was under martial law, where were all the soldiers? The National Guard? Shouldn't they be protecting people? He knew what Gabriel would say. *The military protects the elite, and the elite protect their own.*

"I'm scared," Benjie whispered.

"This place gives me the creeps." Celeste limped as she joined the rest of the group.

Willow squeezed Benjie's hand. "There's nothing to be scared of. Let's go get some grub, okay?"

"How about some prefab hamburgers?" Finn grinned down at Benjie. "Fancy some cardboard for dinner?"

Benjie managed to grin back. "Eww. Gross, Mister Finn."

"At this point, I'd happily take cardboard," Micah said. "I'd sleep in a cardboard box if it gets us off this road."

"Speak for yourself." Celeste sniffed. "I certainly will not."

"I'm sure it will be fine." Nadira pressed her hands against her stomach. She sounded like she was trying to convince herself. "Everything will work out."

They followed Jericho around the checkpoint, weaving between the cars, and into the eerily quiet town. Here, too, vehicles were parked in the streets. There was no movement, no life.

A gas station and a couple of fast food restaurants huddled to the right. To the left, more stores and a motel, Save More Inn, the ancient sign hanging half-off the building. The roads were pitted and pocked with pot holes. Everything was dated and fast falling into disrepair. It looked like a holoplex horror movie set.

"We shouldn't be out after dark." Micah glanced around, half-expecting some monstrous creature to leap out at him.

"You can say that again," Finn said.

"Great," Silas said. "We're stuck in the ass-end of nowhere."

"Why do these towns look like they got stuck in a time warp from fifty years ago?" Celeste sniffed. "Where are the holo ads? The auto-transports? The sani-bots to clean up all this trash and maintain everything?"

"Progress left them behind," Micah said in a low voice, recalling Gabriel's rants against the state of things. The rich elites only saw what they wanted to see. People like Horne, Celeste, and Amelia had probably flown by private jet wherever they needed to go, never stepping foot in the world the rest of them were forced to live in. "What're people supposed to do with little money and no jobs? Outside the major cities, more than half of America looks exactly like this."

"That's awful," Amelia said, genuine compassion in her voice.

Celeste only looked around in distaste. "Where are we going to sleep?"

"Check out the hotel," Jericho called back to them.

They made their way to the sagging building, its brick-red paint peeled in several places, the parking lot weed-infested and riddled with cracks.

Willow cupped her hands and peered through the entrance window. "This place is a dump."

Finn waggled his eyebrows. "What if this is the zombie apocalypse?"

"Zombies eat brains," Willow retorted. "You're safe."

Benjie giggled. "What about me?"

"They'd definitely eat you first." Finn grinned, revealing the gap between his teeth.

Nadira turned to Micah. "Shall we check this place out?" She winked at Benjie. "All this zombie talk is making me nervous."

Micah rubbed his gloved hands together, praying they'd be enough to protect him from the virus. It didn't seem like enough—just two layers of flimsy, rubbery plastic between him and a deadly contagion. He shivered as he yanked on the front door, expecting it to be locked, but the door swung open soundlessly.

Inside, heavy shadows draped over everything. Micah blinked, adjusting to the darkness. There was a check-in desk, a small lobby with worn upholstered chairs, an old-model holoscreen with an Area Attractions slot to scan your SmartFlex and receive all the coupons, maps, and information you wanted on the area's entertainment and restaurants. Not that there was much here to see.

"Help me clear the rooms first," Jericho ordered.

The rooms were all locked with old model sensors, but the doors themselves were cheap prefab wood. Micah and Silas kicked them in just as they had on the *Grand Voyager* when they rescued Amelia. Rather, she'd rescued herself. They just found her.

Micah still disliked Silas as much as that first day. He was cocky and elitist and cruel. But Jericho taught Silas to fight and use a gun, and he was damn good at it. Those were skills they all needed now, whether they liked it or not.

The first three rooms were clear and quickly claimed. Horne took the first room. He leaned against the doorframe and flashed Celeste a haughty grin. "You can share with me, Celeste. I'll keep you safe."

Celeste crossed her arms over her chest. "I'm not into dudes. And if I was, it wouldn't be an arrogant douche bag like you."

Finn chuckled. "Well played."

"Shut up." Celeste rolled her eyes. But as she turned away, Micah caught the slow, satisfied smirk spreading across her face.

Horne's expression darkened. He raked his hand through his dyed blonde hair, the roots beginning to show. "I was only attempting to act like a gentleman."

"Maybe acting isn't your strong suit," Willow said.

Horne swept into his room with a huff and slammed the door.

"Well, he's a bit of an ego goblin, now isn't he?" Finn said.

Willow snorted. "A bit? That's the understatement of the year."

"He was trying to be nice," Nadira said. "I know we're all hungry and stressed, but I think we can give each other the benefit of the doubt, can't we? We're all in this together."

"She's right." Micah glanced at Willow and Celeste. "I think we can all try to be a little nicer."

"Tell that to Horne and Silas," Willow muttered, but she nodded grudgingly.

She, Finn, and Benjie took the second available room, and Elise took the third. Silas, Amelia, and Jericho were further down the darkened hall, searching rooms on the opposite end.

Micah paused at the next door. He opened it with three swift kicks. The fourth room contained two bodies.

He froze, staring in horror at the bed. A man and a woman lay facing each other, their features masks of pain and fear. Their limbs were flung in awkward positions, as if they'd died writhing in agony. Rust-brown blood stained their noses, mouths, and ran like tears from the corners of their eyes. The room stank of sweat and sickness.

Micah stumbled back. This was the Hydra Virus? They made it sound like a flu. But this was no flu. His stomach wrenched and he doubled over, gagging.

"Don't touch anything!" Amelia came up behind him. "Don't go in there. Seal the door."

She handed him a water bottle. "The room mini-fridges were ransacked, but we found a storage room in the back with a few unopened boxes."

Micah gulped down the water, still shaking. "This is bad. Very bad." He didn't want to believe it. All those days in quarantine, he'd believed the government was cleaning everything up, healing the sick, fixing things.

He should've known better.

Gabriel would call him an idiot. Maybe he was.

7

WILLOW

"Stay right next to me, you understand?" Willow squeezed Benjie's hand.

Benjie clutched his backpack to his chest and nodded. "What about food, Lo Lo?"

Willow's heart ached at the familiar nickname, the one Zia had always used for her, too. "That's what we're looking for today, okay?"

They'd spent a restless night at the motel attempting to sleep next to rooms contaminated by the dead. At first, Finn insisted she have the bed. He took the crappy couch, but the whole thing groaned when he lay down. His long legs hung off the end, and he could barely fit his massive torso on the cushions.

"You're way too enormous for that thing, you big oaf." She shoved him off the couch and forced him into the saggy bed, where at least he sort of fit. She settled on the couch, while Benjie curled up in a thread-bare blanket like a puppy on the floor beside her.

Now, morning light flared through the trees. They still had a hundred-mile journey to Fort Benning, and they needed backpacks, food and water, masks and gloves, medical supplies, and transportation, if they could get it. In a town bursting with abandoned cars, it was supremely ironic that they couldn't steal any of them. DNA-ID locks on the engine button saw to that.

"Let's make it a game," Finn said. "We'll see who can find the most items of food by the end of the day. If I win, you have to tell me the secret to one of your magic tricks."

Benjie's face brightened. "And if I win?"

Finn rubbed his chin. "I'll give you my share of dessert."

"Deal!"

Willow rolled her eyes. Like there was going to be any dessert. But Finn was so eager, so earnest, it was hard not to be drawn into his games. And it was a good distraction for Benjie. "All right, you guys, let's go."

They stood outside the motel front doors. The sky glowered a bleary gray, the morning air crisp and chilly. They broke into groups of two or three, with plans to return to the abandoned checkpoint at noon. Even those without working SmartFlexes could tell when the sun rose to its highest point.

Jericho assigned Willow and Finn the job of searching cars. Many vehicles had shattered windows, their interiors scraped clean of anything but trash and dozens of empty water bottles.

Breaking into cars sounded fun enough, and Finn was good at it. He found a couple of loose bricks around the side of the building. He hurled a brick at the passenger side window. The glass dented.

He gave her brother a turn. Benjie tried a few times before it splintered. A few more throws, and the glass shattered into gummy shards.

They'd searched a few dozen vehicles when they stumbled across the first bodies. Finn broke the front pane of a dusty SUV with darkened windows. He stuck his hand in and released the latch from the inside.

Finn recoiled, stumbling back from the window, thrusting his hand over his mouth and nose. Willow smelled the stench. It was the putrid stink of living things decomposing, liquifying from the inside out and releasing all their gaseous fumes.

"Stay back," she told Benjie. She covered her nose and circled the vehicle, keeping her distance.

Two large men slumped in the front seats, blood staining the masks still over their mouths and streaking from their eyes. The bodies were bloated and discolored, their swollen limbs locked in some writhing dance of agony.

Finn gagged and vomited. Willow's own bile roiled. The stench overpowered her, the sight of the dead revolting—and terrifying. They died in extreme pain. That much was evident. What kind of bio-engineered flu was this? Dread swirled in her stomach.

"What is it, Finn?" Benjie asked in a muffled voice, his hands clasped over his mouth.

"Mister Finn," Willow corrected automatically. "Don't come any closer." She circled to the rear of the SUV. The victims wore masks and gloves, though it hadn't done them much good. Maybe they had more supplies stored somewhere. "Can you break the back window?" she asked Finn.

Finn wiped his mouth and stood up. He flexed one huge arm. "Do you not see these manly muscles?"

"Of course. That's why I asked." She tried to keep her voice bright for Benjie's sake, but inside she wanted to scream.

"You can't get enough of that lovely scent?" He flashed her a crooked smile, but it wavered. He was shaken, too.

"Something like that."

Finn smashed in the back window with the brick. Willow stood on her tiptoes and peered inside, keeping her mouth and nose covered with her hand. The stench made her dizzy. It was the worst thing she'd smelled in her entire life. But it was worth it.

Two backpacks lay in the trunk next to a tarp, a shovel, and a cooler. She climbed on the bumper and reached inside.

"What are you doing?" Finn asked.

"We need the supplies. The only reason no one broke in is because of those bodies. Every other car we search will be scavenged already, at least in this town."

Finn took a reluctant step closer. "What if the virus is on that stuff?"

Willow hesitated, weighing the odds. "Those bodies have been dead for a while. A week at least, maybe more. Amelia said the CDC lady told her twenty-four hours. This stuff was in a separate compartment. We have to take a few risks, Finn. We have a long way to go."

He nodded grudgingly. "Do it quick."

Like if she was speedy enough, the virus wouldn't have time to infiltrate her skin. She plunged her hands in lightning-fast anyway. A little superstition never hurt anybody. She grabbed both backpacks by the loop at their tops and yanked them up and back. She tumbled off the bumper and smacked her butt hard on the pavement.

Benjie laughed out loud.

Finn grinned. "Anybody tell you that you're about as elegant as an elephant on roller skates?"

Benjie giggled as she jumped to her feet and rubbed her butt. She gave an awkward bow. "Hilarious, I know. I'm here all night for your entertainment."

"I'm entertained," Finn said. "Are you entertained, Benjie?"

Her brother nodded, his goofy hair sticking up all over his head. Willow rolled her eyes and unzipped the first pack. Finn hovered anxiously over her shoulder, trying to peer into the bag. "Finn, you're blocking all my light like a towering tree."

He took a step back. "Oops. Sorry. You know what they say. Great men cast long shadows."

"That must be it." She pulled out several bottles of water, a dozen tins and foil packs of various prefab meals, a hunting knife, a digital compass, a roll of duct tape, water purification tablets, two boxes of plastic gloves, and a bag of five N95 respirator masks. No goggles, but good enough.

Her stomach twisted. These people were prepared. They owned bug-out bags and were prepared to get the hell out of dodge. The Hydra Virus snared them anyway. To survive, Willow and her people would have to be better than everyone else, and more prepared. She couldn't let her guard down for a second.

"Jackpot!" She handed out the masks and opened the box and slid on a pair of gloves, then added another pair for good measure. On Benjie, the gloves flopped loosely at the fingers and wrists. Willow taped his wrists with duct tape. "Looks good, kiddo."

She and Finn each shouldered a backpack. The thing had to be half her weight. The bottom bumped against the back of her thighs. Finn choked back a laugh. "You should really see yourself right now."

"Don't say a word," Willow muttered, trying not to collapse or lose her balance. But after a few minutes of clumsy awkwardness, she adjusted to the weight.

Before the cruise, she'd worked for a landscaping company, hefting fifty-pound bags of mulch and fertilizer every day. She was short, but she was strong. Her lack of height gave her a low center of gravity, and the extra chub added balance—or so she told herself.

Benjie flapped his loose gloves at her. "I gotta use the bathroom."

"Can it wait?"

Benjie squirmed uncomfortably. "Nope." Oh, crap. The potty dance.

Willow looked around. They'd scoured the motel parking lot and most of the road leading to the perpendicular main street. Down the street, Amelia and Micah entered a McDonalds.

To her left, Celeste rested beneath a tree on the side of the road. Horne lounged a few feet away, his eyes closed. It figured. They were like two lazy-ass peas in a pod. Elite princesses who weren't used to doing a thing for themselves.

"There should be a bathroom at that gas station." Finn pointed. "Though it looks like there should be a sign: 'use at your own risk'."

They headed toward it, hefting their packs as they weaved through dozens of abandoned, gutted cars, turning right on the main strip. Trash, crumpled leaves, broken glass, pop cans, and scattered papers littered the road. Willow stepped around a dull red splotch that looked an awful lot like blood.

"What's that?" Benjie bent and picked up a stained and ripped green paper. "What's F-E-M-A?"

"Let me see." Willow took the flyer from him and rubbed out the creases. *Anyone exhibiting the following symptoms should immediately make their way to their nearest regional FEMA medical center for treatment.* It included a list of symptoms: runny nose, sneezing, coughing, fever, headache, vomiting, bleeding from orifices. And below that, a list of the closest FEMA centers. "There's a treatment," she said, her voice rising. "A place to go for help."

"Is that where people go to get better?" Benjie asked.

Willow nodded. She folded the flyer and slipped it into her pocket. "We'll give this to Jericho later."

Her gaze snagged on dozens of green slips of paper scattered with the rest of the trash. Maybe a helicopter flew overhead and dropped the flyers, so everyone knew where to go. But the guys in the white SUV hadn't made it.

Is that why people abandoned this town? How many people got sick and fled to the FEMA center, leaving their entire lives behind? She shivered and kept walking.

"Look," Benjie said.

The gas station's windows were shattered. So were the barber's shop and the hardware store. Small holes punctured the walls and riddled the driver's side of a faded green Jeep parked in front of the gas station.

Anxiety and dread swelled inside her. What happened in this town? She wanted to curse, but resisted in front of Benjie.

"Bathroom," Benjie repeated.

They made their way to the gas station, crunching over glass. Broken shards thrust from the frame of the broken front door. Inside, shadows crouched in every corner. She blinked to adjust to the dim light. The shelves were mostly picked clean. A rack of postcards was tipped on its side next to a rack still full of sunglasses.

"I guess cool shades and mail service aren't essential elements of the apocalypse." Finn grabbed a pair of sparkling purple sunglasses and slipped them on. "What d'ya think?"

Benjie made a face. "They're kinda ugly."

"Oh, yeah?" Finn grinned crookedly. "Well, Santa Claus isn't real."

Benjie's eyes widened.

Finn winked at him. "Just kidding. He totally is."

Willow glanced around the empty gas station, her nose wrinkling. "It stinks."

Finn sniffed his own armpits. "And all this time, I thought I smelled like roses."

Willow rolled her eyes, but Benjie giggled. She was glad Finn was distracting him. This place gave her the creeps.

The air smelled foul, like moldy prefab burgers and rancid milk and something else even more disgusting. A strange buzzing noise came from the back, almost like fluorescent lighting, but the electricity wasn't working.

She scanned the rest of the gas station. The back door was propped open. The floor near the freezers was sticky with pools of spilled pop. The coffee machine leaked all over the counter, brown stains dripping down the cabinets.

A dog stood in the middle of the center aisle.

Willow stared at it, startled. The dog just stood there, surrounded by empty shelves and crumpled candy bar wrappers. It wore a bright orange collar and looked like a pit bull, with short mottled brown fur and a narrow, angular head.

It was so strange to see a dog inside. The way it watched them unnerved her. Its ears flattened, tail down, the hairs along its spine rising. Alarm bells went off inside her head.

Before she could seize his hand, Benjie bounded toward the dog with a gasp of delight.

"No!" she cried.

The dog growled, spittle flying from its jowls. Its saliva was flecked with red. Blood stained its fangs.

Benjie skidded to a halt a few feet from the dog. He glanced back at

Willow, suddenly unsure. But he was still too close, and Willow too far. If she went for Benjie, she might scare the dog into attacking.

"Benjie." She forced her voice to remain calm, though she felt like screaming. "Don't move. Stand still as a tree. Don't look at the dog. Do you understand?"

Benjie whimpered.

Finn went stiff beside her. "He's scared like you, buddy. We don't want to make him more scared, okay?"

"O—okay," Benjie stuttered, his breath hitching. If he panicked, he would hyperventilate and trigger an asthma attack. She carried the inhaler the medical staff had provided at the base, but it wouldn't do any good unless she could reach him.

"Stay calm." She took a slow, small step forward, willing her body not to tremble, willing herself not to show her terror. Couldn't dogs smell fear?

The dog lowered its head, growling louder, hackles raised all the way now. Willow froze. It didn't back down. This was its territory, not theirs. They were the intruders. But they couldn't leave, not without Benjie.

Her gaze moved past the dog. A pair of legs poked out from behind the next aisle. Human legs. They weren't moving. She recognized the strange buzzing sound now. Flies. Hundreds, maybe thousands of flies.

Her veins turned to ice. She had to do something. That stupid animal wasn't just defending its territory; it was defending its meal. Or else it was stalking its next one.

It wasn't afraid of them. They needed to make it afraid. She searched the gas station, looking for something, anything that could help them. She didn't see anything that might be used as a weapon. A gun could be hidden beneath the register counter, but it was too far away to help them now.

Her gaze snagged on the rack of sunglasses. It was within reach. Carefully, she stretched, straining for the rack. "On my count, Finn, scream and yell as loud as you can. Benjie, you run like hell back to me, you understand?"

Benjie nodded, his breath ragged.

"One, two, three." Willow shrieked and jerked the rack of sunglasses, knocking it to the tile with a loud crash. Finn bellowed at the same time, flailing his arms and charging at the dog.

The creature yelped, startled by the crash and the suddenly crazy humans. It staggered back, its nails scrabbling on the slick floor, before turning and fleeing out the back door.

Benjie ran to Willow. She thrust the inhaler to his mouth, and he took in several deep, rasping gasps. "You're okay. You're okay," she repeated over and over, wrapping him in her arms. Tears stung her eyes. He was all she had left. She couldn't lose him. She would not lose him. "Don't ever do that again. Do you understand?"

"He's wearing a collar," Benjie gasped, trying not to cry. "He's a pet."

Willow squeezed him tighter. "No, he's not. Not anymore."

After a few minutes, she made Benjie sit by the rack of sunglasses until his breathing normalized. Finn moved to her side, his expression grim. "That dog was rabid."

"Something like that."

His eyes took on a distant look. "My dad had a Great Pyrenees, once. I named him Marshmallow—don't judge. He was huge but gentle as a lamb. When I was fifteen, a rabid raccoon attacked him. My dad paid for every experimental treatment available, but he still contracted rabies. We kept him in the backyard, hoping against hope.

"The vet-bot gave us an injection to put him to sleep. Dad wanted one of us to do it, but we kept putting it off and putting it off. One day, Marshmallow seemed like he was acting almost normal again. I went out in the yard to see if he'd gotten better. I brought one of my dad's golf clubs with me, you know, in case. To protect myself, if I needed to."

Willow felt a sinking feeling in the pit of her stomach. This story wasn't going to end well. "But he wasn't better."

Finn shook his head. "He wasn't better. And when he came at me, I froze. This is my Marshmallow—that was all I could think. I couldn't make myself hit him. I just couldn't."

Willow glanced back at Benjie, making sure he was safe. "What happened?"

"My dad ran out and grabbed the club from me. And my dad—he's not violent at all. He volunteered at animal shelters and nursing homes, and you know, literally wouldn't hurt a fly. I should've given Marshmallow the injection myself, to spare my dad. I should've been able to use the club when I had to. But I didn't. My dad's the one who had to kill Marshmallow, the dog he loved, in the most horrible way."

Willow didn't know what to say. She wasn't much good at this kind of thing. Finn was so good-natured and funny most of the time. It was easy to forget he'd suffered and lost things, too. "Your dad sounds like a good guy."

Finn trailed his finger in the dust on the top of one of the shelves. "He was. And Marshmallow was a good dog. Just like that pit bull."

"It's not them anymore." Willow shivered. "They turn into something else, you know?"

Finn blew the dust off his finger. "Yeah, I know."

They headed out of the gas station. "Well, at least we know one thing for sure." He reached down and tousled Benjie's hair, his typical crooked grin back on his face. "We're definitely finding a different bathroom."

8

AMELIA

Amelia rifled through another empty cardboard box. The shelves of every store they checked were almost completely cleaned out. It didn't make sense. "It's only been six weeks."

"The supply chain likely broke down a few weeks ago." Micah emptied a bag of rice into a plastic shopping bag. Less than a hundred grains spilled out. "They say stores only keep three days' worth of supplies on the shelves. And the last few years, with those antibiotic-resistant blights destroying crops around the world, most places had even less."

Amelia just stared at him.

"You didn't know how bad things were," he said without bitterness.

"I—your brother told me." Her face heated, fresh shame at her own arrogant ignorance flushing through her. "I've never—my family and friends never really talked about it."

He shrugged. "You elites practically lived in a different world. I wonder if it's still the same."

"What do you mean?"

"Are there still enclaves where everything—electricity, food production, the internet— works fine? Places where people don't know what's happening here?"

She hoped so, then felt a stab of guilt for thinking such a thing. "I don't know." She thought about all the hundreds of hungry people who might have come through here, kids and mothers with babies, all of them searching for something they wouldn't find. Her stomach rumbled. She ignored it. "We'll bring food back here, if there are any survivors."

Micah sighed. He smoothed the rice bag, folded it, and placed it back on the shelf.

She raised her eyebrows. "Really?"

"Old habits die hard." He shrugged with a grin, a messy curl falling into his eyes.

"Cleanliness is next to godliness?"

"Something like that."

She found herself smiling back. He was easy to like, with his polite, boyish charm. He was so different from his brother. Though they shared similar features—the same black hair, dark eyes, full lips and smooth, bronze skin—Micah was soft where Gabriel was sharp. Micah was steady, loyal, and sweet as a puppy, whereas Gabriel was all pent-up fury, passion, and coiled strength, his dark eyes alert and piercing as a falcon's.

She turned back to searching through a stack of boxes. Most were empty. There were a few flour sacks crawling with ants, another infested with a nest of mice. She would never be desperate enough to eat rodents.

Something grazed her shoulder.

Fear jolted through her. She flinched, her arm flying up to ward off a blow. She whirled, her heart slamming in her chest. "Don't touch me!"

Micah stared at her, mouth gaping.

Embarrassment flushed through her. Her heartbeat slowed, the fear draining from her veins. Ever since Kane, she was jumpy and nervous, like he might somehow creep up on her, a monster returned from the dead.

"I'm sorry," Micah said.

She rubbed her charm bracelet and licked her dry lips. "Look— never mind. You just startled me."

Concern flickered in his eyes, but he nodded. "Hey, before I forget, I found this in a drawer in the motel last night, underneath a Bible." He held out a long leather thong coiled in his palm. His cheeks reddened. "I thought you could put your charm bracelet on it and hang it beneath your shirt—you know, so nobody steals it."

For a moment, she didn't say anything. His thoughtfulness surprised her. But it shouldn't have. Micah was nothing if not kind-hearted. She looped one end of the leather thong through her bracelet, knotted it around her neck, and slipped it beneath her shirt. The cold metal settled against her chest. "Thank you," she said, her throat suddenly thick. "This—means a lot."

His grin widened.

He had the same dimple in his left cheek as Gabriel, she thought with a pang. "There's nothing here. Shall we hit the next place?"

A sudden noise outside the storage room stilled her. She met Micah's gaze. *Be careful*, his eyes warned. She nodded. Before she could speak or move, two people stepped into the doorway, blocking their only exit.

They were young, maybe college students. The girl was broad-shouldered but skinny, with stringy brown hair. The guy was taller, with a bristly beard and a backward faded baseball cap. It was hard to discern their facial features through their masks and protective eyewear. They both wore heavy-duty work gloves.

The guy held a gun. The girl raised a crowbar, pointing it at them.

His rifle was slung over his shoulder, but he didn't have time to reach it. He stepped in front of Amelia and raised his arms.

Amelia followed suit, her heart beating hard against her ribs. Had the world gone completely mad? "We were looking for some food, that's all."

"If this is your territory, we'll leave," Micah said.

The guy nodded to the girl, who took a hesitant step back. Amelia tried to read their intent, but couldn't see their eyes clearly behind their goggles. "Give us that gun," the guy said in a deep tenor voice.

Micah didn't move. "You've got a gun. We need to protect ourselves, too."

"You don't seem to be doing such a great job," the girl said. "You ain't even wearing gloves. You got a death wish or something?"

"Or are you immune?" The guy cocked his head, studying them. "You get exposed and not get sick?"

"We were quarantined at a naval base in Jacksonville for almost three weeks," Amelia said. "We got separated from our transport. We don't know what's going on."

The guy shook his head and eyed Amelia. "Lucky you."

Amelia remembered her mother's warning. She straightened her shoulders, immensely grateful her diamond bracelet was hidden from this guy's hungry stare. She forced herself not to flinch, not to show weakness. Maybe she could distract them, keep them talking. If they established a connection, the pair was less likely to try to hurt them. "What happened here?"

"The world went to hell, is what happened." The girl's voice came out high and reedy. She kept shifting from one foot to the other, her fingers trembling around the crowbar. She was jumpy. Maybe drugs. Or maybe she was just as scared as Amelia.

"Where are the closest functioning cities or bases?" Micah asked.

"Now that the net's down, nobody knows anything. All the channels play the same emergency alert drivel. Only thing I know is the cities still got food, but they're dangerous as hell."

"Why's that?" Amelia's stomach twisted. Sweat beaded her forehead. She didn't like that gun pointed in her face.

"'Cause that's where all the dead are," the girl said darkly.

"Come on, man." The guy jerked his head at Micah. "Give us that gun."

Outside, someone shouted. Probably Horne or Jericho. The pair jerked around, craning their heads, panic evident in the tension of their shoulders, the wild swing of their weapons.

"Those are the rest of our people," Micah said calmly. "They aren't bad, but they are armed and capable of defending themselves—and us. We don't want to hurt you, but I'm not giving you my gun."

The guy swore softly. He backed out of the doorway. "Come on!"

The girl paused, looking at Amelia. "I'd stay quiet if I were you."

Amelia raised her eyebrows. It wasn't a threat, but a warning. "Why?"

"This is Headhunter territory. They don't take kindly to those that steal from them. They'll hear you if you aren't more careful." She tugged two wrinkled respiratory masks from her pocket and tossed them at Amelia. "So be careful."

"Thanks," Amelia called after them as they disappeared from the doorway. Micah hurried out of the storage room after them. They slipped out the back door and were gone.

"They were scared," Amelia said.

Micah nodded. "I wonder what they would've done when I didn't give up our gun."

"Good thing we didn't have to find out." But what about next time? There wouldn't be a next time, she told herself. They'd be within a secure safe zone inside Fort Benning in a few days. All of this would just be another nightmare to add to all the others.

Outside, Horne shouted something again. He was gathering the group. Amelia and Micah joined Jericho, Silas, Finn and Willow, and everyone else milling in the parking lot outside the McDonald's next door. Willow and Finn carried backpacks. Willow handed out several pairs of plastic gloves.

"Keep your voice down," Amelia warned.

"What for, my dear? There's no one here." Horne flashed her an oily smile. His gaze flickered over her body. It only made her dislike him more.

Amelia ignored Horne. She turned to Jericho and explained about the couple and their warning. "We should be careful."

Horne grunted dismissively. "We've got our very own bodyguard and an arsenal of weapons. We're fine."

Amelia glared at him. He was a pompous fool, arrogant and conceited. She endured him at enough of her father's fundraising galas to form a solid impression. It wasn't improving.

"It's not noon yet." Jericho pointed at the sun.

Her stomach growled painfully. She tugged her SmartFlex out of her pocket to check the time. It was after eleven. Her battery blinked at less than three percent. Though few of the features functioned, she still liked knowing that it was working, that she'd have it when the world came back online.

"There's a big-box store about two miles to the east," Horne said. "I saw a road sign. That's our best chance to find the supplies we need —and food."

"I'm starving," Celeste moaned.

"We all are." Willow pulled Benjie closer to her. "What about what those people said? About that Headhunter gang?"

Horne shook his head. "Law and order breaks down for a few days and everybody thinks they're kings of their own castle. Don't worry so much, sweetheart."

Willow's eyes flashed. "I'm not your sweetheart."

Nadira turned to Amelia, her dark eyes wide. "You think it's dangerous?"

Amelia's mother moved to stand beside her. She worried her lower lip. "Everywhere is dangerous."

This time, Amelia didn't roll her eyes.

9

GABRIEL

The handcuffs bit painfully into Gabriel's wrists. The two-mile walk hadn't bothered him, though his throat burned with thirst, and he'd endured Celeste's moaning about blisters for the last thirty minutes.

They moved over the crest of the hill. The big-box store, Stuff 'N More, spread before them with its sprawling parking lot full of cars, half with their doors hanging open, their windows busted. A cart blew in the wind, rattled over the pavement, and smacked into a rust-red four-door sedan.

None of the store's windows were broken. The glass was covered with a dark reflective film.

Figures were sprawled on the ground, scattered mostly near the entrance, but a few more bunched in between some of the cars. They weren't moving. "Bodies," he murmured.

"In case you haven't noticed, there are bodies everywhere," Silas said with a flippant wave of his hand.

"I've noticed." They made their way down the steep slope and cleared the parking lot, walking single file through a row of several dozen cars. His heartbeat accelerated the closer they got. None of these people died from the Hydra Virus. "Entrance wounds. Bullets."

"I can see," Jericho said. "Look alive, people."

His gaze flickered between the cars, the bodies, and the ominously silent storefront. The hairs on his neck prickled. Something was off, something beyond the obvious.

"Give me a weapon." Gabriel balled his fists, straining against the cuffs. He was sick and tired of feeling helpless. There were predators here. They needed to protect themselves—and he could help them. He knew how to shoot, how to fight.

The rest of these people could go to hell, but he still cared about Micah and Amelia. He needed to know they were safe. "I can help."

"Shut up already," Silas said. "Your whining is making my ears bleed."

Jericho didn't respond. He raised his gun and crouched, carefully leading them between a couple of trucks, an SUV, and several sedans. Gabriel's pants snagged on a rusty bumper. Something with the cars. Something Jericho felt too, by the tenseness of his shoulders.

"Maybe we should find a shaded area for the women and children to rest while you guys appraise the situation." Horne licked his lips nervously.

"Let me guess, you're graciously volunteering your services?" Silas sneered.

"I'm merely making a suggestion in the best interests of all those involved," Horne continued in his irritating, simpering voice.

Gabriel twisted around to look back the way they'd come. His mouth went dry. The cars weren't randomly parked. The vehicle carcasses created a large, irregular funnel. The group was being funneled toward the entrance of the store.

It was a trap. "Micah, take them back—!" But he didn't get to finish his sentence.

A spray of bullets struck the pavement at their feet. Gabriel stumbled back. Jericho, Silas, and Micah leapt aside, raising their weapons wildly, searching for the threat.

Five armed men rose from the two-story roof, aiming rifles down at them. The glass front doors slid open with a soft hiss. Three more men strode out, cradling their own automatic weapons.

"Oh, crap," Micah whispered.

Gabriel clenched his jaw. He needed a *gun*, damn it. If they were going to force him to live, then at least he could do something useful. Micah stood only a few feet away, the brother he promised his mother he'd protect. *Just us. Always.* Behind him, he could sense Amelia's presence like a burning brand at his back.

The leader pulled off his respirator, but stopped a dozen paces away. "Here to shop?"

"Something like that," Jericho said.

Horne crossed his arms over his chest. "We need food and supplies."

"You and everyone else." The man chuckled like he'd told a particularly funny joke. But his eyes were vigilant as he scanned their group. He was muscular, with a lean, craggy face. He wore jeans and a leather vest, his black hair pulled back in a ponytail. He wore a brown animal fur draped across his shoulders.

This was a dangerous man. Gabriel had seen enough of them to know. The rest of his crew were just as rough: all brawny, heavily tattooed and pierced. The thugs in the parking lot wore masks, but the bastards up top didn't. One skinny guy boasted cropped blond hair. The other's eyes were slitted in an iron stare, his lips, nose, and ears studded with rings. They all wore pelts.

Gabriel gritted his teeth. He jerked at his handcuffs, but they held tight.

"We'll conduct our shopping and be on our way," Horne said, oblivious to the threat.

"Let me think about that," the guy next to the leader said. A silver chain linked his nose to his upper lip. "No."

"You have no right to deny access!" Horne puffed out his chest in an arrogant—and utterly useless—display of authority. "This store doesn't belong to you."

"Shut up!" Gabriel said.

"That's where you're wrong," Ponytail said. "It all belongs to us. We're the law, the gov'ment, everything you can think of. We're it." His eyes slid past Gabriel, resting on Amelia and her mother. His grin widened. "Unless you got something worth trading for."

Heat flushed through Gabriel, that old familiar rage awakening inside him. If these thugs hurt Amelia, he'd kill them. He'd saw off their heads with a dull, rusted knife. He yanked on his handcuffs until he felt the skin tear. Droplets of blood ran down his fingers.

"We don't have anything to trade," Jericho said.

"They don't got nothing," Sidekick said. "Not even masks. No idea how they're alive and kickin'. They can't all be immune."

"Oh, I think they have something." Ponytail's gaze flickered to Elise, then Celeste, then came to rest again on Amelia. "Everyone has something."

"We have a few high-end SmartFlexes," Horne said. "I own a particularly expensive one with rubies. Latest generation. Top of the line. We're willing to trade. We've got a girl with a diamond bracelet."

Amelia hissed out an outraged breath. Ponytail noticed, his eyes narrowing as his mouth widened in a sharp, toothy smile. "How about we take the diamonds—and the girl."

"Go to hell, you asshole," Gabriel growled.

The smile didn't leave Ponytail's lips. "This is a new economy, see. A new world order. We trade in resources. That's all that's left, at least out here where the gov'ment left us long ago to fend for ourselves. Humans are resources. Some understand that. Some don't."

"Whatever you're insinuating, we'll pass." Nerves trembled Micah's voice. "We're leaving now."

"Nah, I don't think so." Ponytail stepped forward. The men on either side of him raised their weapons.

Jericho leveled his rifle at the same time. "I've got you in my sights. You sure you can take me out before I get your leader?"

Sidekick snorted. "He ain't our leader."

"He'll be dead all the same." Silas trained his gun on Sidekick. "And so will you."

Micah's gun pointed at the guy to Ponytail's right. Horne pulled out his pistol but kept it hanging loosely at his side, his arm shaking. Gabriel wasn't surprised. The big-talkers were always the biggest cowards. He stood helpless in his cuffs, filled with impotent rage.

For a long moment, no one spoke. Tension sizzled the air.

He could charge Ponytail and head butt him in the belly. He'd likely get shot, but it could be enough of a distraction for Silas, Micah, and Jericho to take out the sidekicks. But those damn assholes on the roof could pick off everyone else in a matter of seconds. It was too dangerous.

He glanced around. A silver Ford truck parked in front of the store, one door open. To his left was a minivan, an SUV, and a burnt-orange sports car leaking fluid. There were several more cars to his right. If they could get behind the vehicles, use them for cover, maybe they'd have a chance.

Ponytail rubbed his stubbled jaw. "Who do you think is gonna win this game of chicken?"

"It doesn't have to be this way," Micah said. "We can all walk away, no harm done." Micah the negotiator, the peacemaker. But Micah didn't recognize the greedy gleam in Ponytail's eyes the way Gabriel did. Things wouldn't end peacefully this time.

Something erupted from the silver truck's opened door. Gabriel caught only a glimpse of color, a large shape careening straight toward Amelia.

"No!" he cried hoarsely.

But it was too late.

10

AMELIA

Amelia stood, her muscles tensed to flee, her gaze glued on the thug in the leather vest. His viper eyes reminded her of Kane. Her heart was a frenzy inside her chest, beating so hard she could hardly breathe, hardly think. She would die before she let them take her. She would die before anyone hurt her like that again.

"Amelia," her mother said in warning.

But Amelia wasn't listening. Her pulse thundered in her head. She would run. If they shot her, at least she'd die free.

Someone—Gabriel—shouted.

She didn't even see the thing until it grabbed her by the hair, yanking her head back and spinning her sideways. She stumbled, confused and terrified. Something gripped her shoulders and jerked her to her feet.

A man lunged out of nowhere and grabbed her. She shrank back. There was something very, very wrong with him.

"Help me!" He screamed into her face, blood-flecked spittle striking her cheeks and forehead.

His eyes bulged. They were bloodshot, the veins bursting until his whole eye looked red. Blood smeared below both of his eyes and around his gaping mouth. His skin was gray, his face both bloated and gaunt at the same time. Red-specked foam glistened at the corners of his mouth. A fetid stench emanated from him, of something rotting.

His hands gripping her arms were burning hot, his whole body radiating heat like a live ember. "Save me!" he shrieked.

The people who'd been near her scattered.

"Amelia!" her mother screamed. Amelia twisted, desperate to break free. But the man gripped her with iron strength. How could he be so sick and still this strong?

Her mother tried to reach her, but Finn was there, holding her back. "Stay clear!"

"Let me go!" Amelia gasped.

The man coughed again, spraying her chest and hair. She closed her eyes and lunged back. He stumbled with her, knocking them both to their knees.

A bullet whistled past her ear and struck the man in the head with a soft pop. He went limp and slumped to the ground.

Amelia knelt there, frozen, her arms stretched out, staring in horror at the blood splattered over her clothes, her hands, her chest and face.

"Amelia!" Gabriel said.

She dimly heard other voices calling her name. The roaring in her ears drowned everything out. A sick man attacked her. Then he died, right in front of her, inches away. Blood drenched her clothes and skin. Infected blood.

She sucked in her breath, a wave of dizziness rushing over her.

"Damn, that Hydra virus is nasty," Ponytail cackled. "Good thing Jinx up there is such a great shot. You can thank her later. Except you won't live that long. What a pity, too. You were a real stunner."

Her head roared. She swayed on her feet. The body was splattered with red, blood dripping down the hollowed, veiny cheeks. She'd been exposed. She'd get sick. Then she'd die, just like everyone else. She began to tremble.

"I wouldn't let her mom get too close," Ponytail said. "Ten feet is what the CDC advised, right? That was before they went offline." He clucked his tongue. "No use killing off more of you than necessary. Though that kid is probably a goner, too."

Amelia turned slowly, fresh dread overtaking her. Benjie stood only a few feet behind her, his mouth gaping, his eyes wide and glassy with shock.

"No!" Willow said. "No, no, no!"

"Y'all are in luck," Ponytail said. "I'm feeling generous today. So get yourselves the hell out of our town before I change my mind."

Amelia didn't move. No one moved.

"Did you not hear me? Let me make myself clear."

A spray of bullets struck the pavement in front of Jericho and Silas, inches from their feet.

Ponytail smiled. "Now run."

They ran.

11

WILLOW

Willow fled with the others, her feet pounding the pavement, terror carving a hole in her chest. Every hair on her arms and the back of her neck stood on end.

She kept expecting the bullets to start flying, for a stray fragment to puncture her exposed back, for Micah or Finn or Nadira to pitch forward, blood spurting from fatal wounds.

But there were no shots. Just their own frantic breathing as they dashed up the hill and raced across the meridian. Her side ached, her mind screaming with a riot of competing thoughts—Run—Get safe—Those assholes—Benjie—How dare they—Benjie—No, no, no!

Jericho swerved off the road, dashed behind an abandoned pharmacy, and came to a stop, hardly winded. The rest of the group staggered after him and formed a ragged, exhausted circle.

The long grass tangled around her ankles, and she nearly tripped. Her body screamed at her to rest, to collapse, but she couldn't. Not until Benjie was safe.

"Get away from me!" Horne whirled on Amelia.

She stood a good fifteen feet from the rest of the group, one hand pressed to her ribs, her other stretched out, palm up, as if warding everyone away. Her skin was pale, her face and hair speckled with the dead man's red-tinged phlegm and blood.

"That man . . ." she gasped, shivering in shock.

Willow searched for Benjie. He slumped a few feet behind Finn and Nadira, who both stood across the circle from her. She met Finn's gaze. He nodded. "He's okay, Willow. Just don't come closer."

Next to Willow, Silas stood frozen. A pang of sympathy struck her. Amelia was another rich elite, a spoiled rotten princess, cold and aloof. But she wouldn't wish this horror on anyone.

"She's infected!" Horne pointed his pistol wildly at Amelia.

Amelia took a step back, both arms out as if in supplication. Her jaw worked, but no words came out. The sun burned too brightly. Everything seemed too harsh, too detailed, too colorful, like nature itself mocked them.

"No, she's not!" Elise lunged for her daughter in desperation.

Jericho seized her by the waist with one arm. "Stay back," he warned.

"Look at her." Celeste grimaced. "I'm sorry to be the one to say it, but of course she is."

Elise slumped in Jericho's arms, tears streaming down her face. "She needs me! Silas, help her!"

Silas took a hesitant step forward, his features locked in an expressionless mask.

"Don't!" Jericho turned to Horne. He still held Elise with one arm. With his free hand, he pointed his own gun at Horne. "Put down that damn pistol."

Horne's hands trembled. A lock of blonde hair fell into his eyes. "Not until she's no longer a threat."

Nadira folded her right hand over her left and pressed them against her belly, her mouth moving silently. Her eyes shone with unshed tears. "We should all calm down," she said in a halting voice. "I'm sure it's not as bad as it looks."

Benjie lifted his arm and coughed into the crook of his elbow, the way their mother taught him. It didn't matter. The sound struck them loud as a gunshot.

Willow froze. Everyone near her brother backed frantically away, even Finn, until a ten-foot radius surrounded both Amelia and Benjie.

Horne turned his gun on Benjie. "You, too!"

Willow didn't think. She launched herself at her brother, desperation rising within her. "Leave him alone! He's fine. He has asthma. It's just asthma, that's all!"

Finn leapt in front of her. He was impossibly fast for such a big guy. He stood between her and her brother like an immovable mountain. She tried to dive around him, but he moved and blocked her. No one else spoke or moved.

Fear gripped her. All she could see was that bastard Horne pointing a gun at her baby brother. If he hurt Benjie, she'd kill him. She shoved helplessly against Finn's broad chest. He wouldn't let her through. "Let me go!" She beat at him with her fists. "Let me go!"

Finn's kind face contorted as he looked down at her. "I'm sorry, Willow. I can't."

"Everyone needs to calm down." Micah raised his hands and stepped into the center of the circle. "Benjie, Amelia, do you promise to stay where you are and not move until we figure this out?"

They both nodded. Amelia balled her hands at her sides. Benjie crossed his skinny arms over his rib cage as if that could keep him from shaking. He stared at Willow like he was drowning.

She felt her heart breaking into pieces. He was so small and frightened. And she could do nothing to save him.

Horne kept his gun on Benjie.

"Leave him alone!" Willow shrieked. "He's a kid!"

"Lower your weapon, Horne," Jericho said, "before I make you."

Horne holstered his gun with a scowl. "I'm just doing my part to keep everyone safe."

Everyone stared at each other in shock, fear, and confusion.

"What's the play here?" Gabriel glanced between Amelia and Jericho.

"It's simple," Horne said. "We leave them."

"You bastard!" Willow surged with anger. She would have lunged at Horne and scratched the self-satisfied smirk off his perfect face if Finn hadn't enveloped her in his bearish arms.

"Jericho." Elise turned to him, her eyes pleading. "You can't do that. You know we can't do that. Your allegiance is to the Black family. You have to take care of her!"

"We aren't leaving anyone," Micah said. "We'll find a way to quarantine Amelia and Benjie. They can stay ten or twenty feet behind us for fourteen days, or until we reach Fort Benning."

"Look, no one wants to make the hard decision." Horne patted his hair, smoothing the stray strands that remained stubbornly out of place. "No one *wants* to leave them; of course not. But you've all seen what the Hydra Virus does." He gestured with his arms. "Look around you. It's devastated our country. It's simply too dangerous to have two infected people in close proximity."

Celeste stared at Horne with her mouth open, as if even she felt surprise at the harshness of the man's words.

"There must be another way." Nadira tucked a stray strand of hair beneath her hijab. "We can't leave our own people behind. It's not right."

Horne huffed. "Our goal must be survival now. Isn't that what you said, Jericho?"

Jericho's face darkened. He didn't seem to appreciate having his own words hurled back at him, not by the likes of a self-serving asshat like Horne.

Willow shoved at Finn's arms, but he held her tight. "Not at the expense of a little kid! What's wrong with you people?"

Horne looked at Willow, his lips pursed almost primly. "It's nothing personal, dear. As a CEO of a major company, I've often made tough decisions for the betterment of all—"

"You're not the CEO of horse crap. Not anymore." Silas glared at him. "So stop talking. The sound of your voice is making my ears bleed."

Horne shot Silas a baleful look. "Just who do you think—"

"Enough!" Jericho released Elise and strode up to Horne, not even flinching as Horne's gun wavered in his direction. Jericho forcibly ripped the pistol from his grasp.

"How dare you—"

Jericho shot him a look so menacing that Horne shut his mouth. He turned to the rest of the group. "We're implementing Micah's plan. We quarantine the two exposed individuals by maintaining a safe distance and using gloves and masks at all times. We hoof it to Fort Benning double-time, so they can receive treatment if they're infected."

Elise glanced at Amelia. "We can live with that arrangement."

Willow sagged against Finn in relief, the adrenaline draining out of her. They weren't going to abandon Benjie, which would force Willow to leave the group. Now she had to convince them to let her go to him. "Benjie's just a kid. He needs me. Look, I don't see any blood on him. I'm sure he's fine—"

Nadira touched her shoulder, her dark eyes wide with compassion. "I will pray for Allah's protection over all of you. I believe he'll be okay. But we need to follow safety guidelines, for everyone's sake."

Willow nodded numbly. She knew Nadira was right. But she hated the thought of Benjie left frightened and alone. "Who's going to tuck him in the way he likes? Who's gonna make sure he has his inhaler and help him through his nightmares? Who's gonna keep him safe?"

Finn wrapped his arms around her. She buried her face into the soft warmth of his chest. It felt natural, like she belonged there.

"Listen to me," Finn said in a low baritone, the sound rumbling against her cheek. "Benjie's a brave kid. He's the strongest kid I know. He's strong like his sister, you hear me?"

She managed to nod, fighting back the tears.

"So this isn't gonna be a walk in the park for anybody, but we're all gonna make it through. You and me, we'll still be here for Benjie, okay? We'll keep him safe. I promise you."

She let herself sink into Finn's comforting embrace. She wanted to believe his words with every fiber of her being. Benjie would be safe. He'd be okay. He had to be.

12

AMELIA

Amelia stared in horror at the blood on her arms, waves of dizziness washing over her. Her skin crawled. So much blood. Infected, diseased blood. All over her clothes, her skin, her face, on her lips. She could almost feel the virus replicating, sinking into her skin, poisoning her from the inside out.

Revulsion clawed at her throat, mingled with rising panic. She wiped furiously at her face. "Get it off! How do I get it off?"

"It's okay." Nadira tried to console her. "It's okay. We'll help you. We'll find a way to clean you off. You'll be okay."

But it was a lie. Everyone knew it. They stared at her in shocked pity, like she was already infected, like she was already dying. Her throat closed, cutting off her air.

Several feet away, Benjie started to cry. He was just a kid. He must be terrified.

Willow pulled away from Finn. "Benjie, breathe. Just breathe, okay?"

"Lo Lo!" Benjie reached for his sister.

"I'm sorry. I can't—I have to stay away from you for a while. I'm so sorry." Amelia felt the pain in Willow's voice like a punch in the gut.

Benjie whimpered, tears leaking down his cheeks. "I want Zia. I want Mama."

"She's not here, you know that." Willow's voice cracked.

Amelia closed her eyes, forcing herself to stop scrubbing the diseased filth from her body. She gripped her charm bracelet through her shirt and took a deep breath. She needed to get it together. Panic was not an option. "He won't be alone."

Willow stared at her with glassy eyes. "What?"

It felt like she was speaking from a great distance, like her words were coming from someone else. "He's not alone. I'll take care of him."

"You promise?" Willow asked, hope in her voice. In that moment, she sounded like a little kid.

"I promise." Amelia looked over at Benjie. She knew nothing about kids. Declan Black never had much use for children, including his own. She pasted a smile on her face, even though she was on the verge of fracturing into pieces. She could keep it together for this kid. She could do that much. "We'll figure it out. Okay?"

Benjie swiped at his eyes with his fists. Slowly, he nodded.

"Now that we're situated," Jericho said, shooting Horne another look, "we need to head for Fort Benning ASAP." He didn't say, *before you start showing symptoms.* "We can search for some old-model jeeps and trucks we can hotwire, but staying off the major roads will set us back. For now, we hike parallel, steering clear of people as much as we can, for their sake and ours."

"Wait!" Willow pulled a crumpled green paper from her pocket and uncreased it with shaking fingers. "We found this earlier. FEMA has regional medical centers. South of Macon is the closest one. That's where we need to go. They say they can treat it. Maybe they have a cure."

"They're claiming they've developed a cure in less than six weeks?" Silas scoffed. "That's impossible."

"We're going," her mother insisted, turning to Jericho. She pointed at the paper in Willow's hands. "We're getting help."

"But they don't have a cure—" Silas started.

"You don't know that!" her mother cried, hysterical.

"The government says they have a treatment, if not a cure," Willow said. "Why would they lie?"

Amelia remembered the earnest look on President Sloane's face when she'd announced a state of emergency and martial law. She seemed so honest, sober, passionate, and determined. Nothing like the corrupt, slimy president before her. Was she lying?

Maybe the CDC or WHO had stumbled upon a treatment. It was possible, wasn't it? But the logical part of her brain told her it wasn't.

"Change of plans. We'll head for the FEMA center outside of Macon." Jericho took the flyer from Willow and entered the coordinates into his SmartFlex's GPS. It beeped. "Warning, low battery. Please charge me within the next two hours," a smooth female voice droned far too pleasantly.

"Amelia needs to clean herself of contaminants," Nadira said. "Benjie, too."

Jericho nodded. "We still have seven hours of daylight. There's a single lane road between the gas station and the barber shop. It leads to a small cluster of homes. We'll look for a house with solar panels and working water. And if we're lucky, some food."

"What if the owners won't let us in?" Micah asked.

"We'll worry about that when it happens." Jericho adjusted his rifle so it pointed down toward the ground. "We need to bug out before those Headhunter assholes decide we're worth the hassle."

"Listen to Amelia," Willow said to Benjie in a choked voice. "Everything will be okay. I promise." She turned and locked gazes with Amelia. Amelia felt the weight of the responsibility placed on her shoulders. Benjie was all Willow had in the world. She'd do everything in her power to protect this kid.

Willow placed something gingerly on the ground and stepped back. "Here's his inhaler. If he's wheezing, has shortness of breath, or can't stop coughing, or his face gets all sweaty—ask him if his chest feels tight—"

"I will, I promise," Amelia said.

Willow gave a sharp nod and spun to join the rest of the group. Amelia watched them move ahead of her, then counted twenty paces under her breath. She picked up the inhaler and tucked it inside her pocket. "Our turn, Benjie."

"Okay, Miss Amelia." Benjie moved toward her, reaching out his hand.

Amelia shook her head. "I'm sorry, but we can't touch. And you should stay at least five feet away from me, just to make sure. I don't see any blood on you. You might not be infected."

Benjie's face fell, but then he brightened. "Maybe you're not sick, either."

"Maybe." Acid stung the back of her throat. Even though he was terrified, the kid still tried to comfort *her*. She hadn't been around children much, but she liked this one. Even so, she knew deep in her heart that his words weren't true. Couldn't be true. She was infected. But Benjie still had a chance.

They trudged along the grass shoulder, following the group back through the abandoned town. The irony of the situation wasn't lost on her. Her whole life, she'd lived in fear of her deadly form of epilepsy, always careful to hide the secret, illegal medication her father developed for her.

Every seizure was potentially devastating, resulting in brain damage, memory loss, reduced functions like balance and coordination, and even death. Very few people with her prognosis saw the age of twenty.

By now, she should be severely brain-damaged. Or dead.

All this time, she'd worried about her medication running out. On the half dosage, she was twice as likely to have a seizure. And in less than two weeks, she'd be out completely.

But she was still alive. Against all odds, she had survived. She survived epilepsy and her migraines. She survived her father's rages. And then she'd survived the hijacking of the *Grand Voyager*, Gabriel's betrayal, and Kane's assault.

She had survived it all, only to be taken down by this—the disease-infested droplets from a simple cough. She would laugh if the tears wouldn't come soon after. She couldn't cry. Not yet. She had Willow's brother to think about now.

After an hour of walking, they crested a small hill and glimpsed a cluster of houses. A sound came from behind them, like something scuffing against the pavement. Amelia twisted around, scanning the empty street.

"Miss Amelia?" Benjie asked.

She raised her finger to her lips, her instincts on high alert. But there was nothing. There were no people. The sun shone on the metal roof of the gas station, glittering glass strewn across the parking lot. A faded yellow sedan slumped on the side of the road like a dead thing. No breeze stirred the grass or scuttled the leaves on the ground.

Still, the back of her neck prickled. The hairs on her arms stood on end. They were being watched by something; she was sure of it.

She turned around slowly and gestured for Benjie to keep walking. They were falling further behind the group. She tried to walk softly, stepping over scattered leaves and crumpled trash, straining her ears for anything unusual.

It came again. That scuffling, scratching sound.

She whipped around.

Something darted behind the sedan, a shape slinking low to the ground. Some kind of animal. A wide snout poked out from behind the car's bumper, then a black, furred face. A pair of brown eyes stared unblinking back at her.

"It's a Rottweiler," she said. "Someone's pet."

"There was a dog in the gas station," Benjie said in a trembling voice. "It was mean. Lo Lo said they aren't pets anymore."

The way the Rottweiler stared at her, silent and unmoving, unnerved her. Her fingers found her charm bracelet through her shirt. "Maybe you're right."

She picked up her pace to catch up with the others. Benjie hurried beside her. When she turned back around to check again, the dog wasn't there. Still, she felt its presence. For a long time, the hairs on the back of her neck remained raised.

She didn't want to let her brain formulate the thought her gut already knew. The dog was stalking them.

13

MICAH

M icah sensed movement out of the corner of his eye. But when he looked, nothing was there. He shook his head and scanned the neighborhood again.

Still nothing. Everything was quiet and still. Eerily quiet.

No electric hum of cars driving to and from work. No dogs barking. No children shrieking and playing in the yards. And no surveillance drones buzzing about.

They were in a small subdivision of older homes. The abandoned houses were ransacked, their windows broken, their front doors smashed to pieces. Graffiti sprayed the walls of some.

But other houses were left alone, the ones that entombed the dead. Not even the Headhunters wanted to risk infection that badly, it seemed. But they didn't need to. There were plenty of other places to scavenge.

But Micah's group *was* that desperate. The two bug-out backpacks Finn and Willow carried would only feed their large group for a couple of meals, if that. They needed supplies to make the trek to Macon's FEMA center.

If they didn't find vehicles, Jericho estimated it would take a week on foot, since they weren't conditioned and would have to travel at the pace of the slowest in the group, an eight-year-old boy.

"Keep your gloves on at all times and don't touch your face for anything," Nadira instructed. Her mother had been a midwife back in Syria, which was the closest thing to a doctor they were going to get. "We need N95 masks to protect our noses and mouths. And goggles, glasses, protective eyewear, whatever you can find."

"And guns and ammo," Jericho said.

"Try garages and sheds, first," Micah said. "We should stay out of the houses as much as possible."

"I'll keep watch on the prisoner and guard this end of the street." Jericho pointed. "Silas, you take the other end. Whistle if there's trouble."

Silas nodded and took off down the tree-lined road at a jog. Benjie and Amelia sank down beneath a maple tree in someone's yard. Amelia leaned her head back and closed her eyes, her fingers twitching reflexively. She was playing the violin in her head, Micah realized.

He forced himself to tear his gaze from her as the rest of the group broke into threes and fours. Micah joined Willow and Finn. Nadira joined up with Elise.

"Why don't you come with me, Celeste?" Horne demanded more than asked, his hand on the butt of the pistol Jericho had reluctantly lent him. "You never know what might be out there."

"I'm perfectly fine, thank you." She tugged on one of her coppery coils, looking a bit lost.

Nadira tapped her arm with a friendly smile. "Would you like to come with us?"

"I suppose," Celeste said airily, though she looked relieved.

"I'm willing to stay put and keep an eye on the kids." Horne gestured at Amelia and Benjie with an oily smile. "Wouldn't want anything untoward to happen with no one to guard them."

Micah met Amelia's gaze. She rolled her eyes. He grinned back. Horne was as transparent as a glass jar.

"Fine." Jericho frowned as he gave last-minute instructions. "Touch only what you have to. Any infected have likely been dead for a while, just like at the hotel. But stay on your toes."

Micah didn't want to imagine the dead. He stared at the rows of silent, empty houses, trying not to shiver. A tricycle lay on its side in a winding driveway. On a white peeling porch, overgrown yellow and purple flowers tumbled out of several ceramic planters.

The houses were old and dated, built sometime near the turn of the century. But still, you needed money to live anywhere outside the cramped, overcrowded cities. This place looked . . . safe. That was the word he needed. Or at least, it had been.

"How is Benjie?" he asked Willow as they walked.

Her lips tightened. "No coughing other than the usual. And Amelia?"

"The same." It was still the first day of exposure. They wouldn't know whether Amelia and Benjie were infected for a while yet. He knew he shouldn't hope, but he couldn't help it. It was in his nature. "We'll make it to the FEMA treatment center in time. Don't worry."

Her eyes told him she never stopped worrying. Benjie was her little brother. Gabriel felt that way about Micah, once upon a time. He bit the insides of his cheeks and forced himself to think about something else. Thoughts of Gabriel were too painful. "Let's get this over with."

Micah, Willow, and Finn spent the next several hours searching a half-dozen garages. They filled trash bags with tarps, a couple of tents, a solar stove, a few bent pots and pans, a bunch of canned and packaged prefab food, and several pairs of work gloves. They didn't find any masks.

They searched a small garden shed behind a brick house, the ceiling so low Micah had to stoop. Finn bent nearly sideways. Only Willow could stand straight.

Micah pushed behind a metal shelving unit heavy with drills, hammers, and other tools, grunting and coughing in the swirl of dust. "We should take a few of these hammers."

"For what?" Finn stared at him.

"For protection," Willow said. "We don't all have guns."

"Hammers wouldn't have protected us against the Headhunters," Finn said quietly.

"True, but we don't know who we'll meet and what they'll want." Micah hated saying the words, hated the thought of using a weapon against another human, whether a gun or something else. But they also needed to protect themselves. He hated that he was being forced to become something he didn't want to be. "Hopefully, a show of force will scare most people off."

He handed a hammer to Willow, who tucked the handle into her belt. When he handed one to Finn, he shook his head. "No thanks, man."

Willow frowned. "Are you sure?"

"I really don't need it."

Micah shrugged and shoved it into his own belt instead. He adjusted the rifle slung over his shoulder. He was about to shove the shelf back into place when he noticed an old, cob-webbed cardboard box tucked into a dark corner next to a couple of rusted shovels.

"Can you give me a hand, Finn?" Together, they lifted the shelf and moved it out of the way. Micah opened the box gingerly. A thick, brown-furred spider scurried over the lid. He bit back a squeal and swatted it away. He despised spiders. Loathed them.

The box was full of painter's supplies—brushes, a canvas tarp, blue tape, and buried at the bottom, several packages of masks. More spiders scuttled across the supplies, crawling over everything. "Ugh!" Micah backed away, fighting down his revulsion.

Finn laughed good-naturedly. "No worries. We're all scared of something." He leaned in and brushed off the spiders. "I will remember this little nugget of information for later, however."

There were six masks in the box. They each put one on, stashed the other three in Willow's trash bag, and kept moving.

The late afternoon sun had lengthened their shadows by the time they found the first house with solar tiles. In some cities, thirty to forty percent of buildings were solar-powered. In desert states like Arizona, he'd heard it was more like eighty percent.

Out here in the boonies, things were different. People were too poor for much but surviving.

The house was nestled among pine trees at the end of a long drive-way. It was a two-story colonial with white siding and crisp red shutters. Overgrown grass bristled in the yard, but it was weeded not that long ago. Someone had bothered to paint the entire house. None of the windows were broken. The front door hung half-open, squeaking in the slight breeze.

Micah pushed down his dread and strode up the front steps. They'd avoided going inside an actual house yet. But Amelia needed to get the blood and infectious fluids off her. If the water worked, they all needed to drink and wash up.

"Go in quiet," Willow whispered behind her mask.

Micah nodded. He pushed the creaking door all the way open with the muzzle of his rifle. They paused for a few moments in the doorway, blinking and waiting for their eyes to adjust to the dim light.

At first glance, the living room looked normal—couches, coffee table, a huge holoscreen on the far wall. The other walls were covered with digital photos of a Chinese family with shiny white smiles, two little girls in pigtails grinning in every picture.

Willow tapped his shoulder and pointed at the coffee table. An old-fashioned picture frame was knocked over, the cracked glass spidering over the picture of the girls on swings. He nodded, his gut tight, and moved quietly into the house.

In the kitchen, bowls of oatmeal were still on the table, the food shriveled, crusted, and covered with ants. An electric candle set glowed in the center of the table. So the electricity worked, at least.

Willow picked up one of the candles. "Whoever lived here left in a hurry."

Micah moved carefully down the hallway. A cramped bathroom, no toilet paper. The first bedroom frilly and pink, drawers opened, clothes and faded stuffed animals strewn everywhere, graffiti spray-painted on the walls. The second bedroom, the master, large enough for a bed, the mattress half-yanked off, a scarred dresser with broken drawers, and a bookcase.

Micah let out his breath, his heart leaping in his chest. Real, physical books filled the bookcase. Half of them were knocked from the shelves, the pages torn from their bindings, but the lower shelves were untouched, as if the thieves hadn't bothered to bend down. A surge of anger swept through him at the destruction.

He squatted on his haunches, running his finger along the aged spines, and picked out a dog-eared copy of *The Old Man and the Sea*. His mother had read this book to him before she died. It'd been one of her favorites. His throat tightened at the bittersweet memory. *Be good,* she always said to him. *Be brave.*

"Whatcha got there?" Finn stuck his head in the doorway. He carried a rectangular box under his arm.

Micah held up the book. "'Man is not made for defeat,'" he quoted his favorite line.

Finn flashed a crooked smile. "And here I thought it was about a fish. Look what I scored." He carried an old board game, 'The Original Game of Sorry', scrawled in faded red letters across the bent cardboard cover. "I thought Benjie'd get a kick out of it."

Willow appeared in the doorway, her hands fisted on her hips. "And *I* thought we were scavenging for important things, like food."

"This is important," Micah and Finn said at the same time.

Willow rolled her eyes. "That's it. We're all gonna die." Her face was still tense, but her snarky attitude was back. Micah marked it as a good sign.

He tucked the book in his back pocket. He was about to turn from the bookshelf when something caught his eye. Something metallic glinted in *The Old Man and the Sea*'s empty slot. He reached in and pulled out a tin of prefab tuna. Two dozen more were wedged between the narrow hollow between the books and the back of the shelf.

He raised one in triumph, unable to keep the grin off his face. "See? Literature can feed the soul. Who feels like fish?"

14

GABRIEL

G abriel sat on the floor, leaning against the cabinets, his handcuffed hands resting on his knees. The fishy, chemical smell of faux tuna filled the room, making his stomach growl. He hadn't eaten in two days.

No one turned the lights on to keep any inquisitive souls from noticing them, but they did use the water, filling empty water bottles and wiping themselves down with washcloths. Only Amelia took a full shower. Nadira rummaged in the closets and brought her a fresh change of clothes. Amelia and Benjie were sealed in the kids' room for the night.

Jericho found a wheel of wire and strung it around the perimeter of the house, setting up a trip wire. He stationed Silas at the kitchen's back door and took the front entrance himself. "Micah and Finn will switch after four-hour shifts," he instructed.

"You need me," Gabriel said again. "You don't have enough people to take shifts. None of you will get enough sleep. You need to be alert."

Silas snorted. "Right. Like we're gonna let you take watch so you can sneak off in the middle of the night and escape. Or, you know, slaughter us all in our sleep."

"I won't," Gabriel lied. He would in a heartbeat—not the killing, but the running. But not to escape. Remaining here, so close to Micah and Amelia and yet so far away was its own sort of torture. He couldn't stand the wounded look in his brother's eyes, the grief and betrayal in Amelia's.

He needed a gun and a clearing in the woods where he could put an end to the guilt and loathing eating away at him.

But he wouldn't be running as long as people surrounded him. Nadira stood at the stove, humming to herself. Jericho, Elise, and Horne murmured in the living room, while Willow, Finn, Micah and Celeste squeezed around the scarred kitchen table.

Celeste stared at the pinkish meat substance with a look of horror on her face. She poked listlessly at her opened tin. "This tastes like dead worms. And looks like it, too."

"Something you have experience with, then?" Willow asked sweetly.

"Of course not. It's a phrase." Celeste's mouth twisted in distaste. She pushed the tin away. "I'm not hungry enough to eat like an animal."

"Suit yourself." Finn reached out, grabbed her meal, and shoveled it down in several gulps.

Celeste slitted her eyes in disgust. "Your manners are atrocious."

"Thank you." Finn let out an enormous burp. "I maintain the firm belief that it's rude to waste food."

"If you call that food," Celeste said. "You know what we really need?"

Willow slouched in her seat. "Safety? Freedom?" She slanted her eyes at Gabriel. "Justice?"

"A toothbrush."

"Well, that was a bit of a letdown." Finn lifted the tin and licked it clean. "Here I was, all prepared for a mind-blowing revelation."

"How are you not revolted by the state of your hygiene?" Celeste's delicate face scrunched into an un-delicate frown. She tugged on one limp, straggly coil. "I'm dirty and sweaty and disgusting. My scalp itches from who-knows-what. And my teeth are all furry."

Nadira turned from the stove and ran her tongue over her teeth. "It is pretty disgusting."

Celeste raised her hands. "See? At my mom's penthouse, I showered twice a day. Three when I was at my dad's."

"We're a long way from your penthouse, Dorothy," Finn said.

"What was your first clue, Sherlock?" Willow shot back.

"Everybody just shut up already," Silas muttered, glowering at them all.

Gabriel leaned his head back against the cabinet door, tuning out their meaningless prattle. He was more exhausted than he thought. Every muscle ached. A soul-deep weariness dragged at him. His eyes closed. He almost drifted off when he sensed movement. He forced his eyes open.

Nadira crouched next to him. "Here." She held out a spoonful of the foul-smelling prefab meat.

He turned his head away. He refused to accept their pity. They'd made it clear how much they loathed him. *Not Nadira*, his mind whispered. She'd been kind to him from the beginning, which only worsened his shame.

"You need to eat," Nadira said softly.

Willow narrowed her eyes. She tugged the same pair of gloves on and off, over and over. "What are you doing?"

"Feeding him."

"He doesn't deserve to eat." Silas stood at the counter near the back door, systematically dismantling and cleaning the rifles.

"We can't let him starve," Micah said.

"Everyone knows you'll let him go the first chance you get," Silas said to Micah. "You're soft because he's your brother."

"That has nothing to do with it."

"That has everything to do with it." Silas smirked. "Family first, right?"

Every word they spoke struck Gabriel like a lash. He bowed his head, fighting off his anger. He deserved this. But Micah didn't. But because of him, Micah's every move was suspect. He endured the contempt meant for Gabriel.

"We're giving him food that should be used for the rest of us." Willow slapped her gloves against the table. "It's a waste of resources."

Micah glanced at Willow with a frown. "You don't mean that."

Her lips pressed into a thin line. "Don't tell me what I think, Micah! You know what he did. Everyone here *knows* what he did."

"I know what he did," Nadira said very quietly. "He and his people killed hundreds and sank the *Grand Voyager*. They unleashed a bioterrorism weapon on American soil."

Gabriel winced. The girl in the yellow bathrobe hovered in front of his vision, so young and innocent, her face accusing. *You did this. You killed me.* Pain slashed through him, making him wish he could claw his own traitorous heart out.

"He murdered my sister and my mother!" Willow hissed, unable to contain her anger.

Nadira blinked. She tucked a strand of dark hair into her headscarf. "Yes. And he killed my best friend. Everyone in this room lost someone. He is a prisoner. He will be held accountable for his crimes. But that doesn't give us the right to starve him or treat him like an animal."

"He *is* an animal. And no one should ever forget it, not for one second." Willow shoved out of her seat and stormed out of the kitchen into the backyard, slamming the back door behind her. Micah and Finn scraped back their chairs and went after her.

Silas slouched in his seat and stared at Gabriel with hard eyes. "She's right. You're a waste of resources. Someone should take you out back and put you out of your misery."

Gabriel jerked his chin. "Then do it!"

"Maybe I will."

If he couldn't do it himself, maybe someone like Silas would do it for him. If he could provoke Silas into the anger he recognized boiling just beneath the surface. Silas was angry—at what, Gabriel didn't know or care. What did an elite have to brood about? But maybe he could use that anger to serve his own agenda. "What are you waiting for? You all talk, then? Just as I thought. You're nothing but a spineless worm."

Silas slammed his fist into the table. He leapt to his feet and lunged at Gabriel. Before anyone could stop him, he punched Gabriel in the face.

Pain exploded behind his eyes. But he didn't flinch. In a terrible, twisted way, it felt good. That was easier than he'd thought. He leaned forward, goading Silas with a twisted smile. "You don't have the guts."

Silas punched him again. Gabriel's head snapped back against the wall.

"Stop it!" Nadira tried to grab Silas's arm, but Silas pushed her aside. The plate fell from her hands, shattering against the kitchen floor.

"That's for Amelia, you gutter rat!" Silas spat.

Gabriel flinched. The pain splintering his face wasn't enough to prevent the stab of guilt in his gut or the wretched ache of his heart. Amelia was in one of the back bedrooms, scrubbing herself clean. Only she wouldn't be able to get clean.

Gabriel had seen how that diseased man coughed directly into her opened mouth. Any hope the others held out was futile. She would get sick and then she would die. Nothing and no one could stop it.

A memory pierced him—her lips on his, her hands tangled in his hair, her hesitant, trusting smile. How she looked at him like he alone could save her.

Shame burned hot in his chest. He needed to hurt. He needed to hurt badly, until the pain stole every agonizing thought away. "Just do it, you bastard!"

"I—should—kill—you!" Silas smashed his fists into Gabriel's nose, his right cheek, his jaw, over and over.

"Silas Hunter Black!" Elise sprinted in from the living room. "Stop that right now!"

Then Jericho and Micah were suddenly in the room, dragging Silas off him. Silas sat back on his haunches, breathing hard, his knuckles bloody. He stared at Gabriel in sullen fury.

Gabriel grinned at him with red-stained teeth, blood bubbling over his lips from a cut in his tongue. His lip split, pain lacerating his face. He spat a globule of blood on the floor. "That your best shot?"

"That was just practice. You wanna go another round?"

"Get out!" Micah turned on Silas, his voice rising. "I'll take your shift. Go!"

Silas gave an insolent shrug and climbed to his feet. "I don't know why someone hasn't killed you already." He wiped his fists on his pants, grabbed one of the cleaned rifles, and sauntered into the living room.

Micah looked at Gabriel, his mouth working like he wanted to give him a piece of his mind, but couldn't think of what to say. His expression was pained, his mouth taut.

Gabriel couldn't bear to see the condemnation in his brother's eyes. Dark rage filled him. To Gabriel, anger always tasted better than the bitterness of despair. He lifted his cuffed hands and gestured at his wounded face. "You want a go, too? Have at it."

A shadow crossed Micah's face, anger mixed with something else. Not hatred, but sadness. *Just us, always.* Not anymore. Never again. It struck Gabriel like a blow worse than any Silas landed.

Micah turned away from him and spoke to Nadira instead. "Do you need help?"

Nadira squatted on the floor. She wiped the spilled meat and shards of ceramic with a hand towel. She smiled demurely up at Micah. "I've got it. Don't worry."

Micah strode out of the room without speaking a word to Gabriel. What did he expect? He deserved it. He deserved his brother's hatred, Amelia's, everyone's. He deserved pain, despair, and death. He deserved all of it.

For several moments, Nadira worked silently. Then she tossed the towel in the sink and brought him another plate of food.

"Thanks, but no thanks," he said even as his stomach knotted at the heady aroma. Even prefabbed chunks of tasteless protein sounded good if you were hungry enough. He rattled his handcuffs. "As you can see, my hands are tied."

Nadira knelt beside him. "You have two choices. I can spoon-feed you, or you can hold the plate with your hands and slurp it up."

He wanted to refuse it, to willfully choose starvation as his punishment, but he was too weak. His body's hunger and need overwhelmed him.

He grabbed the plate roughly from her hands and brought it to his lips. The food tasted delicious. He didn't care that it was prefab. He gulped it down as fast as he could, ignoring the stinging in his lips.

Nadira stared at him. Her eyes were huge, dark as the girl's with the yellow bathrobe.

"What are you looking at?" he snarled. He closed his eyes, and still he couldn't un-see that little girl's glassy, haunting eyes.

"You need to find peace in your soul."

He wanted to stew in his own misery, to succumb to the howling darkness inside his own soul. "Go away."

"You can have forgiveness, if you want it."

Forgiveness didn't exist for the likes of him. He knew that. He wouldn't be deceived, not anymore. "Thanks for the meal, but I don't need a damn pep talk."

She dabbed a napkin against his bloody lip. He jerked his head back.

"My parents are Muslim. Before all this happened, I wasn't sure what I believed." Her voice was soft, almost shy, but there was no hesitation in her words. "But I know this much is true. Allah forgives all sins."

"I doubt it."

"It's true. And I'm praying for you."

He snorted. "Don't pray for me. There are plenty of better things to waste prayers on."

She touched her hijab reverently. "My mother taught me no prayer is ever wasted. And no soul is beyond hope. Anyone can seek and find redemption. It takes time and effort and sincerity, but it's waiting for you."

He clenched his jaw. "The only thing waiting for me is punishment, and death."

She sat back and wiped her brow with the back of her arm. "Punishment and redemption are two different things. You can have peace even in prison, even in front of a firing squad."

"Who says I want redemption?" Almost against his will, he glanced at her. Her gaze was like Amelia's—it stabbed straight through to his ugly, blackened heart. She was sincere, her goodness obvious in every line of her delicate face—but she was wrong.

There was no redemption for him, and there never would be.

15

MICAH

"Did you hear that?" Micah asked.

Next to him, Finn and Willow paused to listen over the buzzing insects and birdsong. "An engine," Willow said. "Loud. Not electric."

"More than one," Silas said from behind them.

Micah glanced at the bruises and cuts marring Silas's knuckles and looked away. Gabriel's face looked worse, his left eye swollen shut, his lip busted, and several purple bruises darkening his bronze skin. Silas was a cocky jerk, but Micah couldn't fault him for punching his brother. Micah had fantasized about doing it himself more than once.

"Motorcycles," Horne said. "We should talk to them."

That didn't sound like a great idea, but he said nothing. He wasn't in charge. Jericho knew what he was doing, even if Horne was an impulsive hothead.

"If it's another military transport, maybe they'll stop this time." Elise adjusted her backpack. They found one for each person in their scavenging, although most were the size of school packs and weren't even full. They found enough food and water for two days, maybe three.

They'd hiked parallel to the highway for four hours since

departing the town of Mayfield at dawn. No one bothered them in the night, though Micah doubted anyone slept well.

He spent his watch hunched on the couch next to the window, peering anxiously into the darkness, trying to discern movement amongst the shadows. He saw something move a few times, his heart bucking in his chest, but it was just stray dogs skulking behind cars and around the corners of several houses.

Amelia and Benjie stayed a safe distance behind the group. Neither showed any symptoms yet. The virus was supposed to be fast-acting, wasn't it? Virulent and deadly. Maybe they'd still make it.

The engines roared closer. It sounded like they were coming from two different directions.

"We don't know whether they're hostiles or friendlies," Jericho said. "Based on previous experience, my best guess is hostile."

"We're shooting blind here," Horne argued. "Maybe they can tell us about the state of the FEMA camp and how Macon is holding up. And where we can get some damn transportation. The more information we can gather, the better. I'm going—you can join in if you feel like it."

Jericho sighed. "Silas, Micah, and Finn, come with me. I'm tying the prisoner to a tree. Elise, keep an eye on him."

"I want to come." Willow stepped forward.

Jericho shook his head. "You have no weapon and no training."

Willow pointed at Finn. "Neither does he."

"His size is his weapon." Silas thrust his bruised fists into his pocket and smirked at her. "You're the size of a housefly."

"Screw you."

Micah gave Willow a sympathetic shrug. It was safer for her—for all of them—if she stayed behind. He shoved his glasses up the bridge of his nose with his thumb, adjusted the rifle sling digging into his shoulder, and joined Silas and Finn. Horne tried to take the lead, but Jericho moved swiftly ahead of him.

They crept through the trees and scrub brush. They were on a small hill, above the highway. Jericho gestured for them to sneak the last dozen yards on their hands and knees, and then their bellies.

Micah pushed aside a thorny bush and looked through two slim birch trees.

A dozen motorcycles were parked in the center of the westbound lane. None of the bikes were autodrive. Bikers were the type who believed they controlled their own fate. Two of the motorcycles swerved in front of a white pickup and forced it off the road.

The bikers were hulking, even from a distance. A few wore face masks and gloves, but several didn't. They wore furs across their shoulders—like the thugs at the Stuff 'N More store.

These bikers wore mostly dog pelts: a couple German shepherds, a Doberman, a bull mastiff, one that looked distinctly wolfish, and another that had to be a leopard pelt. He didn't have time to wonder where they'd found a leopard—the zoo?—before the men were on the move.

Several of them sprinted to the truck, forcing open both doors. They dragged out two men, a woman, and a girl who couldn't have been older than twelve, all wearing masks.

One biker—the one with the leopard skin—shoved the people to their knees in a line in front of the truck's front fender. Micah sucked in his breath, his grip tightening on his gun.

The bikers tore open the tarp covering the back of the truck and dumped out backpacks, blankets, and a solar stove. They took it all, laughing and shoving each other.

The shepherd and Doberman came around the front, gesturing at the woman and girl and grabbing at their hair. Hatred welled in Micah. These guys were thieves and bullies. Predators.

Micah stiffened. On his left, Finn let out a gasp. Micah watched in horror as German Shepherd dragged the girl to her feet and yanked her toward the waiting bikes.

The woman wailed. The man rose to his feet as if to protect the girl. Doberman, Wolf, and Leopard leveled their guns, shouting for him to stand down.

But he didn't. He lunged for German Shepherd. Leopard's gun bucked. The man crumpled.

Micah jumped to his feet almost without thinking, rage blinding him. How dare they attack innocent people? It wasn't enough to steal from them—the monsters had to kill them, too? Those people needed help, they needed—

Jericho swore and grabbed him from behind, yanking him down hard. Micah's breath was knocked from his lungs as Jericho shoved him against a tree trunk and covered his mouth with one hand. "What the hell are you doing?"

"They need help!" Micah forced out.

"You can't save them."

Horne's face went white. "Don't be stupid. You'll get us all killed."

Micah tried to wriggle from Jericho's grasp, but the man was too strong. Jericho released his hand from Micah's mouth. "Are you good?"

Micah nodded bitterly. There was nothing good about this situation. Nothing at all. In that moment, he hated Jericho with all his heart.

Jericho let him go but kept his hand on Micah's backpack. Micah rolled back onto his belly, gasping for breath, his shoulder aching. He peered down at the road.

Most of the men were on their bikes, their engines idling, waiting for German Shepherd and Doberman. They put the woman on Leopard's bike, in front of him. Her hands were zip-tied behind her back, a black sack tugged over her head. Her shoulders quaked—she was weeping.

German Shepherd and Doberman wrestled with the girl. She was small, but she kicked and flailed and shrieked like a banshee. She was brave, braver than Micah's own group lying here, watching and doing nothing, like pathetic cowards.

Outrage burned in his veins. His finger twitched on the trigger. He could kill them. He wasn't a good shot yet, but surely his rage alone would guide his bullets to pierce straight through the center of their black hearts.

The girl shrieked and gave a wild kick, striking German Shepherd in the face. He stumbled back, losing his grip on her waist.

She landed hard on her side but was up in a heartbeat, sunlight glinting on a blade in her right hand. She lunged headfirst at Doberman, stabbing at his side.

Micah couldn't tell how deeply she'd wounded him. Doberman whirled with a roar of pain, seized the girl by the neck, and shot her point-blank in the chest.

Micah reared back, stunned, his mind reeling. *No! No, no, no!* That didn't happen. It didn't, it couldn't have. But it did. One second she was there, on her feet, kicking and screaming.

The next second, she was on the ground, not moving. The bikers sprinted to their motorcycles, gunning their engines as they took off in the opposite direction, tires squealing.

Be good, be brave. His mother's dying words echoed in his head. Micah bucked out of Jericho's grasp.

He leapt to his feet and plunged down the hill, dodging trees, tripping on roots, scrambling up again, his heart raging in his chest, a desperate prayer on his lips that the girl was okay, that the bikers wouldn't bother to look back as they roared westward, already dim specks on the horizon.

He ran across the highway and knelt over the girl. Her dirty blonde hair fanned out beneath her head, only a small red dot marring the lime-green T-shirt covered with those glowing phosphorescent flowers. She stared up at the sky, gasping, her lips tinged purple.

Maybe she would be okay. *Please, God, make her be okay—*

Something wet touched his knees. The blood came from the exit wound, leaking out from beneath her left side. He grabbed her hand. "Hold on, okay? We'll get help."

She turned her head to look at him, her eyes filled with desperation and fear.

Micah lowered his mask so she could see his face, so she would know that someone was here, someone kind and good who would mourn her loss. "You're not alone."

Her body shuddered. After an agonizing minute, her chest stilled. Her eyes went dim.

Micah didn't release her hand. Acid burned the back of his throat, his stomach roiling. Sorrow and anger formed a toxic knot inside him. He didn't know her, but he grieved for her all the same.

Jericho and the others strode down the hill. Horne shook his finger in Micah's face. "You nearly got us killed!"

"You put us all in danger." Jericho's expression was stony, his voice even but edged with a restrained fury Micah hadn't heard before.

He didn't care. His own anger choked his throat. He blinked back stinging tears. "We could have saved her!"

"No, we couldn't have."

He gently closed her eyelids, crossed her arms over her chest, and staggered to his feet to face Jericho. "Why? Was she not one of your people? Not valuable enough to save? Not an elite?"

Jericho seized Micah by the throat. "Never do that again! Do you understand?"

"I'm not getting killed just so you can appease your conscience," Horne huffed.

Silas gave him a withering stare. "We should leave your ass."

"Shut up for once, Silas!" Jericho said.

Silas flinched, his face contorting, but he said nothing.

A sob clogged Micah's throat. "We're not like them. We can't be like them. We're the good ones!"

Jericho's black eyes flashed. "And you'll take your good heart to the grave with you, along with everyone else."

"You don't get to decide who lives or dies!"

"Yes, I do! There were twelve men with twelve fully automated assault rifles to our three. How good a shot are you at fifty yards under stress? Huh? We would've been lucky to take two or three down before the rest of them stormed us and killed every single person you care about." He released Micah's neck and shoved him. "*Think*, Micah!"

Micah stumbled back, rubbing his throat. Jericho was right, and Micah hated that he was right. But he would not give up. They were better than this. They had to be better than this. "If we can help people, we need to help them."

"We will." Jericho spat on the ground. He glanced at the girl, his face darkening. "Do you think I wanted this? I did not. But I will not put our own people at risk. Are we clear?"

Micah nodded, though he still disagreed. Life was all about risk. You just made sure you risked for the right things, the things that mattered.

"All acts of bravery and sacrifice come at a cost. You better be damn sure you weigh that cost before you act. Sometimes the price is simply too high." Jericho gripped his shoulder, his face softening almost imperceptibly. "This world isn't the world you knew, son. Not anymore."

Micah stared at the dead girl. The world he'd known wasn't so great, either. Life had been harsh and terrible for a long time. For too long. "Maybe we're the ones who need to make it better."

16

AMELIA

Amelia counted the hours since her exposure to the Hydra Virus in her head. Seventy-eight hours. Over three days. And five days since the attackers ambushed their transport.

Since the highway attack on the little girl and her family the afternoon before, the group was quiet, focusing on traveling as far as they could, as quickly as they could. Even Celeste managed not to complain.

After another long, exhausting day of walking, they found shelter in a small-town dentist's office. Amelia and Benjie were quarantined in an exam room.

Shadows filled the room as the sun began to set outside. Amelia leaned against the cushioned dental chair, the silent machines arrayed around it eerie in their stillness. A service-bot slumped in the far corner next to its charging station, its power long since run out.

"Wanna see a magic trick?" Benjie sat cross-legged beneath a desk about ten feet from her, playing cards spread in a circle around him. The colored pieces of the board game Finn found for him were lined up on an office chair like little soldiers. They played *Sorry* together four times, Benjie taking Amelia's turns for her.

"Sure." She forced a grin.

Benjie sneezed and wiped his nose on his shirt-sleeve. She couldn't tell if his symptoms were worsening or if his asthma and allergies were acting up.

He shuffled the deck, told her to pick a card—"Tell me when, okay? Make sure you tell me. I'm not looking, see?"—then reshuffled and managed to pick her exact card five times in a row.

"How did you do that?" she asked, genuinely impressed.

He grinned. "A magician never reveals his secrets."

"I guess that's true." Amelia leaned back against the chair. She ignored the grumbling in her belly, focusing on the permanent indents on the pads of her fingers instead. She missed playing. She missed the focus and discipline. She missed the soaring joy of the music, how it thrummed inside her like a living thing.

The violin was so much of her life back home—four hours every day practicing Bach and Dvorak and Tchaikovsky again and again, until she was good enough, until she was perfect; the concerts and competitions; her dream of attending Julliard and becoming a violin virtuoso. It was her way to chart her own path, to escape from her father's control.

Now it was all ashes and dust.

"Knock, knock." Nadira stood in the doorway. She wore gloves and a mask pulled over her face and nose. She took turns with Willow and Micah, bringing them their meals every day. Today, Nadira brought them a can of cold beans and a foil pack of some horrible-tasting prefab protein smoothie. It went down like pink slime.

Nadira put the food down and took several steps back.

"Thank you." Amelia retrieved her can, spoon, and foil pack and sat back down so Benjie could get up and take his share.

When they were both seated, Nadira returned to the doorway. She wore a baseball cap with her hair bound in a braid and tucked into the back of her shirt. "How are you feeling?"

"Okay, so far." Other than a few coughs, Amelia felt fine. But she knew better. In between seizures and migraines, she always felt fine. But her body still betrayed her. She knew better than to trust it.

The Hydra Virus lived inside her. It warred against her body's defenses. First would come the coughing and sneezing. Then the boiling fever. Then the bleeding, and whatever horrors came next, whatever it was that made the corpses twist and writhe in agony.

She would fight it as best she could, but the war was coming. And judging by the wasteland around them, most people had lost.

"I'm fine, too," Benjie chimed in.

Nadira nodded, the skin around her eyes crinkling. "That's so good. I've been praying three times a day for you."

Amelia wasn't too keen on prayers. They didn't do anything for her mother. Prayers hadn't saved her from the horrors of the *Grand Voyager*. But it couldn't hurt. And Nadira was always kind. "Thanks." She took a bite of the cold beans and swallowed the tasteless lumps without chewing. "How much is left?"

Nadira hesitated. Her cargo pants hung around her hips. She was too thin.

"How much?"

"A day's worth. No more."

"Do you want my beans?" Benjie asked, wrinkling his nose.

"Your body needs energy to fight the infection." Nadira's voice filled with compassion. She winked at him. "And to grow big and strong."

Amelia sighed. It felt like they'd been traveling for weeks. Hunger gnawed at her stomach, exhaustion burned her eyes, and her feet ached. But she wouldn't complain. It wasn't like they had any other options. "How far away are we?"

"Still three or four more days by foot."

"I wish we could just drive there." Benjie sighed. "Or fly on a hover craft."

Nadira shrugged. "Horne found an old manual drive sedan with some gas in it, but Jericho says the noise will attract hostiles. We wouldn't all fit, anyway."

"I guess."

"It's almost dark. We'll bunk here for the night. Silas and Micah are setting up a perimeter. I'll bring you some blankets."

Less than fifteen minutes later, Amelia wrapped herself in a fleece auto-warming blanket Nadira scrounged up from somewhere. Sleep was the last thing on her mind. The beginnings of a headache pulsed behind her eyes. She hoped it wasn't a migraine.

Benjie made a nest of his blanket and curled up like a puppy. He clasped his backpack to his chest as if it were a favorite stuffed animal. "Are we still going to get sick?"

Most people would probably make something up to help him feel better. But for some reason, she couldn't lie to him. She held no hope that the FEMA center would help them. The CDC couldn't have developed a vaccine so quickly. Their only chance was if they weren't infected at all. "I don't know."

"I miss Lo Lo," he said pensively, staring up at the darkening ceiling.

"I know." She wasn't good with kids. She didn't know how to be or what to say. She felt awkward and uncomfortable, like anything she tried would be the wrong thing.

Benjie sniffled. "I miss Zia—" His voice cracked as he started to cry. "And my mom."

She felt a hollowness in her chest. In an instant, she was back in the bridge, re-experiencing the terror, the gut-wrenching fear for her mother's life, for Silas, even for her father. How much worse must it have been for a kid? "I'm sorry."

Benjie cried softly. She could do nothing to comfort him. She couldn't even hug him or hold his hand. She lay there for several minutes, listening helplessly to Benjie's grief.

She had to do something. She pressed her thumb into the indentations on the pads of her fingers, permanent reminders of the hours, days, weeks, and years she spent practicing. All she knew was music, and she didn't have a violin.

"I can't sing worth a damn," she said haltingly, "but I could try to hum something, if you want."

"Yes please, Miss Amelia," Benjie choked out.

She didn't know any kids' songs or even the popular stuff everybody streamed on their SmartFlexes. She pretty much only knew classical songs. She hummed the first song that came into her head: *Brahm's Lullaby*.

As she hummed, she stared up at the pocked ceiling, her eyes gritty and burning. Gradually his sobs lessened to sniffles and the occasional hitching breathes. Finally, after she'd hummed most of Prokofiev's *Peter and the Wolf* and Tchaikovsky's *Nutcracker Suite*, Benjie drifted into a restless, fitful sleep.

Amelia both longed for sleep and dreaded it. Kane came for her in her dreams, when terror lunged out of the dark, clawed and fanged. When sleep finally descended, the nightmare came, like it always did.

She was back in the captain's suite on the ship, fighting for her life. Kane's meaty hands closed around her neck, cutting off her breath. Terror pulsed through every cell of her body, as darkness blurred her vision.

His beady eyes and that wide, gleaming crocodile smile leering at her, his hands ripping at her clothes. Fear pounded inside her head, the migraine splitting her skull open. She was dying, and she was helpless to do anything to stop it.

She awoke gasping, trembling, drenched in sweat. A headache pulsed against her skull. The terror didn't fade. She searched the room frantically, half-expecting the shadows to lunge at her with dripping fangs and Kane's crazed, violent eyes.

She shuddered, her fingers grasping for the comfort of her charm bracelet beneath her shirt. She'd never escape him. She'd never escape that soul-swallowing terror and despair. He was dead—she'd killed him—but his ghost still haunted her.

Gabriel's face flashed through her mind. She pushed it out. Surrounded by the chaos of the terrorist attack, she'd felt safe with him. He promised to protect her. She'd been dumb and naïve enough to believe him. Every time she looked at Gabriel, she saw the look in his eyes when he betrayed her.

She lay back on the sweat-drenched carpet. Sleep wouldn't return, not tonight. That's when she felt it. The first wave of heat flushing through her, from her toes to the top of her head.

It was too early. But it was here.

The fever.

17

WILLOW

For the first time in a week, Willow wasn't hungry. A few hours after leaving the dentist's office that morning, they found a gas station with several bags of expired chips stored behind a box of bleach in a janitor's closet. They ate chemical-infused junk food until they were stuffed.

"Each of you should be armed," Jericho said. "I will train a core group with the basics of fighting and shooting a gun. We must protect ourselves."

Willow and the rest of their group stood in a loose circle in the overgrown yard in front of a small, dilapidated house they'd commandeered for the night. Jericho decided to stop early so they could rest and, apparently, learn to fight.

He stood in front of the small pile of rifles, handguns, knives, and boxes of ammo they'd scavenged over the last few days.

"There's no law anymore, no justice except what we make ourselves," Jericho continued.

Horne frowned at the weapons. "This is a bit . . . extreme, don't you think? Most people are still civilized. I don't see why we need to traipse around armed to the teeth like some sort of deranged gang."

Jericho picked up a few of the knives. "I served as private security after the Springfield bombing and in Arizona during the drought riots. I was fourteen when the government fell in Nigeria. I lived through—" His mouth hardened. He gave a quick jerk of his head, as if reliving some terrible memory. "It's not a lack of structure that turns people dangerous. It's a lack of food, of resources, combined with an ability to act with impunity, in any manner one sees fit. Some will revert to their bestial natures; others will do anything to protect their own. Bottom line, if you're not willing to do the same, you won't survive. In this world, the only rule in any fight is to win."

He handed Willow, Elise, and Celeste a knife and sheath to strap to their belts. He gave another knife and a small switchblade to Nadira. "Give these to Amelia and Benjie. Benjie can have the switchblade. Even a kid can learn how to use it."

Celeste held hers with the tips of her fingers, frowning in distaste. "What am I supposed to do with this?"

"It's not gonna bite you, that's for sure," Willow said.

Celeste smiled sweetly, but her eyes were spitting venom. "Cut the sarcasm, would you?"

Willow smiled just as sweetly. "If you don't want a sarcastic answer, don't ask a stupid question."

"Guys, we're on the same side here," Micah said.

"Tell *her* that." Celeste pouted. "She's the mean one."

Willow had no response that didn't involve a black eye on Celeste's part, so she turned away with gritted teeth and focused on the weapons at their feet. "How about that one?" She pointed at a slim knife with a leg strap. "That goes in your boot, right?"

Jericho handed it to her. "Be careful."

She grinned. Micah's hope had rubbed off on her. Benjie wasn't coughing yet, and she'd started to believe he might be okay. She felt better than she had in days. "Let's get this party started."

Nadira and Elise went back inside the house to prepare what little they had for dinner. Celeste followed them since she had nothing else to do, flipping her curls and slanting her eyes at Willow as she went.

Willow didn't care. She strapped the knives to her belt and lower calf. She wasn't going to cook just because she was a girl. She knew how—her *lola* taught her—but to hell with that. She wanted one of those guns.

Gabriel leaned against a tree, his arms cuffed in front of him, watching with narrowed eyes. The right side of his face was still puffy, his lip purple and swollen. "Give me a weapon. I know how to shoot. I'm better than Silas."

Silas shoved his hands into his pockets and glowered at him. "Not on my worst day."

Gabriel ignored him and turned to Jericho. "Release me and let me have a gun. You need me."

"We don't," Jericho said curtly. "End of discussion."

Unease twisted Willow's gut. She was glad Jericho wouldn't release Gabriel Rivera. That was a good thing. He couldn't be trusted. He was a terrorist, a traitor, and a killer. She hated the fact that he was allowed anywhere near them, near Benjie.

She glanced at Micah, whose mouth pressed into a thin line. Micah had it worse. And Amelia. She could bear it if they could.

Still, she'd be happier with a better weapon than a knife to defend herself. Just in case.

Jericho grabbed two assault rifles and handed them to Micah, Horne, and Finn.

Finn dropped his hands and shook his head. "No thanks."

Jericho paused. "Come again?"

Finn shifted uncomfortably. "I'd prefer not to carry a gun."

Willow stared at him, lifting her brows in surprise.

"You'll have to elaborate," Silas drawled, all smirking and superior. "I don't believe I heard you correctly."

Finn shrugged his massive shoulders and flashed an apologetic grin. "I . . . don't want to kill."

"You must be jesting." Horne scratched the stubble on his chin. "You're built like a tank."

Finn looked from Horne to Jericho, the grin fading from his face.

"It's how I was raised. My dad—I mean, he's dead now, but he was Buddhist, and I—it feels wrong, you know? I just can't. I'm sorry."

"Nobody wants to fight, to kill," Willow said. "Sometimes we have to."

"I'm sorry. Even if you gave me a gun, I know myself. I wouldn't be able to pull the trigger."

"We need you." Jericho stared up at Finn, who towered a full half-foot above him. "You understand that?"

"Will you fight, at least?" If she were Finn's size, she'd have found a way to save Zia and her mother. She'd have mowed down any terror-ists stupid enough to get in her way. "You could slam two of those Headhunters' heads together and crack their skulls open like eggs."

Finn shook his head. "I guess I'm a delicate flower," he joked, but it fell flat.

Horne and Jericho stared at him like he'd transformed into some bizarre creature they didn't recognize. Silas sneered in contempt. "More like a pansy-ass coward."

"Silas!" Micah said. "Stop it."

Finn only looked down at the rifle in Jericho's hand. "He's right."

Willow touched his arm. She didn't agree with his resistance, but she understood it. Finn was gentle, a giant teddy bear. He didn't have a violent bone in his body. He was simply goofy, soft-hearted Finn. *Her* Finn. Her friend. "You're no coward."

"He's right," Finn said sheepishly, his shoulders slumping. "I would freeze, failing when you needed me most."

"We aren't going to escape the next gunfight unscathed," Jericho said. "Do you understand that? We need to win. And to win, we need manpower."

Willow stepped forward. "I'll do it."

Silas made a contemptuous, disbelieving noise in the back of his throat.

She ignored him. "Teach me to fight."

"Right," Silas scoffed. "You're just a pathetic little girl."

She raised her chin. "Exactly. You not only underestimate me, you barely even see me." She had no skills. She had no clue how to fight. But she was stronger than they expected from her years of hefting fifty-pound bags of fertilizer. And she was stubborn and determined as hell. She would do anything to protect Benjie. Anything. *They're your responsibility. Take care of them.*

Her desperate resolve had to be worth something. She turned to Jericho, her gaze fierce. "You can use that, can't you? The element of surprise?"

"We're not playing, here," Horne said sternly, like she was actually a little kid. "These are real guns, with real consequences."

Willow scowled. "You don't see me as a threat. I get that. But no one else will, either. So use that. Teach me to be a threat."

"Maybe you should give her a shot," Micah said. Willow gave him a grateful look.

"Maybe you shouldn't," Silas said, his voice dripping with disdain.

Micah cocked his head. "It's not the size of the dog in the fight, it's the size of the fight in the dog."

"Didn't Mark Twain say that?" Finn asked.

"Who cares," Silas said.

Jericho said nothing. He stared at her with a hard, appraising gaze.

"You aren't seriously considering—" Horne started.

Jericho raised his hand to silence him. "Show me what you can do."

Relief flooded through her, strengthening her resolve. She could do this. She *would* do this.

"Hit Silas."

"I'd be happy to." Her pulse jumped, her mouth instantly dry. She entered the circle of trampled grass and faced Silas.

He put up both hands, palms out, as targets for her to aim for. He widened his stance, a mocking smile on his lips.

She tensed, gathering her strength, and punched his left palm. His hand didn't even move. Silas smiled wider.

"Try again," Micah encouraged.

She gritted her teeth and struck Silas's right palm. It landed weak and pathetic as a slap.

Silas sneered. "Done yet, little girl?"

Horne whispered something in Jericho's ear, a self-satisfied smirk plastered on his face. Jericho started to turn away, glancing back toward the house. They were already dismissing her. She was losing her chance.

Willow huffed a breath and shoved her hair behind her ears. *Come on. Focus!* She could do this. She was tired of feeling helpless, tired of being a victim. She needed to be a fighter, a warrior. And this was how she was going to do it. "One more."

Silas shrugged and lifted his palms.

She made to strike Silas's other palm, but instead, she lunged forward, swinging high to draw his attention. At the last second, she raised her knee and slammed it into his groin.

Silas bent over, gasping. He clutched at his crotch and crumpled to his knees, swearing a blue streak.

Jericho turned back around. Horne and Micah stared at her, mouths gaping.

Finn clapped. "Well played, my fierce friend. Well played."

"You—broke the rules!" Silas croaked.

She fisted her hands on her hips, the heat of victory flushing her cheeks. "The only rule of fighting is to win."

Silas's face turned an angry red. She tensed, waiting for him to swear at her, snarl ugly insults, or even punch her, like he'd beaten Gabriel. She didn't put anything past a bloodthirsty sociopath like him. Instead, he did something so startling her mouth fell open.

He laughed.

She stared stupidly at him.

He still bent double, clutching his groin and sucking in ragged breaths. Tears leaked down his cheeks. "I will. I'll—teach you."

Instead of spouting something clever, all she managed to sputter was a lame, "What?"

For once, his mouth twisted in pain, not a sneer. Yet his eyes sparked with something she couldn't read—bemusement? The faintest glimmer of admiration?

He straightened with a wince. "Jericho trained me since I was twelve years old. You want to know how to take out an opponent twice your size, how to shoot worth a damn? I can teach you. I won't offer twice."

Silas was the last person she would've chosen, but she'd seen him kill on the *Grand Voyager*, and she'd watched him spar with Jericho. He could fight. Desperate times called for desperate measures, didn't they? "I accept."

Jericho nodded in approval. He handed her a handgun and a holster. "You start now."

She liked the heft of the gun in her hand, the cold, hard feel of it. She attached the holster and slid the gun inside it. She liked the comforting weight against her hip. She could get used to this.

For the next two hours, they trained. Jericho worked with Micah and Horne while Silas showed her how to fight dirty as hell. There were no rules now except staying alive.

He showed her the proper fighting stance—legs shoulder-width apart, knees bent, hands up to protect the face.

She crouched, studying his movements. "Okay."

"On the count of three. Ready? One. Two—"

He made to punch her in the face. Startled, she jerked back, but not fast enough. As his right fist grazed her cheek, he seized her hair with his left hand and yanked so hard, several strands ripped from her scalp.

"Ouch! You didn't wait until the count of three!"

He flashed her a mocking smile. "And your hair didn't spontaneously combust. The world is full of disappointments."

"What the hell does that mean?"

"There's no honor in survival, cupcake." Silas opened his fist and let her black hair swirl to the grass. The smirk slipped from his face. "There's you or him. That's all. You think you can do whatever it takes? You think you can bite, rip, kick, and claw? Kill?"

She touched her scalp gingerly, blinking back traitorous tears. Her sister's face flashed in her mind—her dull, unseeing eyes. "Yeah, I do."

"If your attacker's hands or arms are close to your face, bite him. Sink your teeth into muscle. When you kick, aim at the kneecap. Try to shatter the bone. Bite his face. Gouge his eyes. Dig your thumb deep into his eye sockets. But those things won't take him out. They'll buy a few seconds, if you're lucky. You need to know your next move, and your next."

His gaze traveled over her body, studying her. "Your smallness is your weakness. But you can make it your strength. You need to concentrate on low blows, literally." He smirked at his own joke.

She didn't. "How?"

He showed her the sensitive parts of the body: how to do the most damage to the throat, the groin, the nerve clusters in the upper thighs, where to slice the femoral artery. Silas lost his sardonic tone as he worked with her, his expression focused as he demonstrated several strike moves.

He moved with a supple grace, with a coiled, deadly instinct, like a cobra or a panther. No wonder Jericho had agreed to train him to fight —he was born to it.

In contrast, Willow felt like a lump of inert clay. But she would learn. She had to.

Silas flicked his wrist near his waist and slipped his knife into his right hand. "Your blade should be felt, not seen. Hide it until you're ready to use it."

He juked to the right. She tensed, focusing on his knife hand, expecting him to swipe at her. He'd get a thrill out of scaring her. She'd make sure he failed. She wasn't going to fall for any more of his nasty tricks.

She barely glimpsed the left hook arcing toward her head. She managed to raise her arm in a block, but he struck her with such force that her arm bent like paper, the blow sending pain spiking into the side of her skull. She staggered, her vision going blurry.

"Ready to give up yet?"

Nausea swirled in her stomach, but she forced herself to stand and face him. "No way."

"Okay, then." A faint, satisfied smile ghosting his lips. "Don't block a strike from a bigger, more powerful opponent. It'll knock you out. Dodge it. Cover your head with both arms, duck, and move in swift and sudden, like this. Your guy's not even done swinging, and you've got access to all his vulnerable spots. A punch or a knife blade to the liver, here—" He demonstrated, punching her lightly beneath the ribs.

She gasped from the pain. "You bloody bastard."

"You wound me." Silas bowed theatrically.

"One can only hope."

"You'll have to try harder than that." He crouched, gesturing for her to attack him. "Don't hold back. Come at me with everything you've got."

She wiped sweat out of her eyes and steadied her breathing. The pain fed her anger. She wanted to wipe that smug look right off his face. She wanted to hurt him. "Oh, I'm going to."

He grinned, his cunning gray eyes as close to sparkling as she'd ever seen them. "Good."

18

MICAH

The next morning, they set out at dawn. Micah took the lead with Silas, Horne, and Jericho. Gabriel glowered behind them, while Finn, Willow, and the others took up the rear. Amelia and Benjie still trailing the group by five to ten yards.

He could hear Amelia coughing, though she claimed she felt fine. She was too quiet, her eyes slightly glassy. "Headache," she'd mumbled when he asked her.

Micah bit the inside of his cheeks. If she was infected, they needed to get to the FEMA treatment center as fast as possible.

They spent the morning walking alongside a road lined with empty houses, most of their cars still in their driveways. A few of their windows were broken, and the stench of dead and rotting corpses wafted in the cool breeze. The masks did nothing to filter the fetid stink.

By early afternoon, the wind had picked up, ripping gold-tinged leaves from the trees and sending them skittering across the road. The sky thickened with roiling, rapidly moving clouds.

He shivered in the chilly air. They needed to find sweaters and jackets. Winter still came eventually, even though global warming delayed it more and more.

"Storm's heading our way." A wind gust raked his wavy hair across his face. "It looks like it could be bad."

Willow rolled her eyes. "Thanks for the update, Captain Obvious."

"We'll find shelter soon," Jericho said. "It'll hold off for a while."

They turned a corner and passed yet another row of abandoned cars, though most of them were pushed to the shoulder, making a single-lane path.

"Someone's come through here recently," Gabriel said.

Jericho nodded grimly. "Look alive, people. Stay on your toes."

Something orange and black flashed in the corner of Micah's eye. He stopped dead in his tracks and stared into the bed of the gray, mud-splattered truck directly to his left.

Gabriel bumped into him. Micah flinched but didn't move. "A tiger," he whispered. Then louder, half-disbelieving his own eyes, "There's a tiger in that truck."

"Stuffed, I hope." Silas smirked.

"No, a real one." Micah stepped closer for a better look. The huge tiger filled up most of the truck bed. Its massive paws were larger than Benjie's head. A single red bullet hole was drilled through its forehead between the golden eyes.

It felt surreal, staring at a tiger up close in the middle of a suburban neighborhood. "Where in the world did it come from?"

"Probably the zoo," Gabriel said. "People still want to hunt exotic game, even in the apocalypse."

"Do you think it's modded or the real thing?" Finn asked.

"No way to tell." The only differences between modded and unmodded were the creatures' disposition and temperament. Scientists genetically modified apex predators to be as docile as sheep. The elites enjoyed parading their pet cheetahs and leopards around their marble mansions.

"I wanna see!" Benjie squealed from behind them.

"Hush," Amelia said. "I'll show you. Hold on."

"Keep moving." Jericho gestured for them to follow him. "Whoever did that didn't leave it here without a reason."

Both doors of the truck slammed open and two men burst out. Before Micah could get his own gun up, the men trained semi-automatics on them.

"Don't move!" the first man said. He was dressed in a jean jacket and a 'Truckers Unite' baseball cap turned backward. He wore a face mask and gloves. "Guns down on the ground! Now!"

Jericho swore under his breath. He lowered his weapon. The others did the same. Gabriel slid behind Jericho, hiding his cuffs. It was smart. Who knew how these guys would react if they knew Gabriel's true identity? Micah wiped his sweaty palms on his pants.

"Hands up!"

Micah obeyed. His glasses started to slide down the bridge of his nose, but he didn't move. His heartbeat jackhammered in his ears. "We're friendlies."

The second man stepped forward, patting them down with one hand, still aiming his gun with the other. Then he stepped back. "Always better to be safe than sorry."

"Name's Gonzales," the first man said. He was a Mexican-American guy in his late twenties with long hair bound in a knot at the base of his neck and a broad, friendly face. The second man—an Irish guy in his thirties with a russet-orange beard and sharp, twitchy eyes—introduced himself as Russell, no first name.

"You live in the neighborhood?" Horne asked.

"We're around," Russell said evasively. "We just changed a dud tire. That's how you got the drop on us. But when we saw you and your kid, we thought we'd introduce ourselves."

"What's with the tiger?" Finn asked.

Gonzales grimaced. "Soon as the world started coming undone, folks went crazy. A bunch of animal activists released the animals from every zoo, shelter, and wild animal sanctuary in the country, it feels like. Now we got 'em wandering around like Georgia is a damn African jungle."

"Good thing most of 'em are mods." Russell patted the tiger's hindquarters. "Easy as cake to take 'em down."

"You using it for meat?" Micah glanced at the tiger. He hoped not. It seemed tragic to see such a magnificent creature killed for any reason. He couldn't imagine eating it.

"Nah. The Headhunters got a thing for pelts."

Micah tensed. "You're with them?"

"No, but they're traders," Gonzales said. "We've gotta have things to trade."

"Makes sense," Horne said agreeably. "We've all got to survive somehow."

"Where are you folks headed?" Russell's voice was affable, but his gaze shifted from Jericho to Horne to Gabriel and back again. It made Micah uneasy.

Jericho hesitated for a fraction of a second. "The FEMA regional medical center."

Both men took a step back, their expressions hardening. "You got the sickness?"

Micah pointed. "Those two back there might have been exposed. We're being cautious."

Gonzales nodded. "Smart move."

A gust of wind blasted them, almost knocking Micah's glasses off. He shifted to keep his balance as leaves swirled angrily around his feet. The sky boiled with a mass of storm clouds now.

"Why haven't you guys headed to the safe zones?" Micah asked.

"We figure we'll hunker down 'til the government gets things back online." Gonzales raised his voice over the wind. "No reason to trust 'em any more than we have to. They screwed things up plenty. Besides, we've got what family survived with us already. Most of the world lost everybody that mattered. Without the ones you love, people tend to go real cold, real fast."

Lightning lit up the underbelly of the storm clouds glowering on the horizon.

Gonzales pointed at something over their shoulders. "We gotta be on our way, but you should watch your back."

"What do you mean?" Micah asked, even as the hairs lifted on the back of his neck.

"Watch the wildlife, especially those damn dogs. You're being hunted."

Before Micah could ask what they meant, thunder crashed overhead. Lightning sizzled the sky. The trees creaked and moaned.

"And get yourself inside. Storm's coming quick!" Gonzales twisted his cap so the brim protected his face. "These houses are all diseased. There's an empty warehouse a quarter mile up Wickingham Lane on the left, plenty big enough for your group."

"Thank you!" Micah called after them. The men hurried back into their truck, started the engine, and drove away, swerving to avoid the cars stacked along both sides of the road.

The first fat drops of rain struck Micah's head and shoulders. Lightning clawed at the sky, way too close.

"You heard them. Let's move!" Horne yelled. They hurried along the road, cresting a small hill before turning left on Wickingham Lane, a road infested with weeds and potholes. By the time they spotted the warehouse, they were running. The sky blackened. The rain fell harder, slapping their exposed faces.

They dashed inside, wiping water from their eyes and shaking out their hair.

The warehouse was dim and empty, the dark shapes of forklifts and hovercarts slumped somewhere in the back of the vast space. Plastic sheeting covered several doorways wide enough for semi-trucks to back into. It smelled like sawdust and something old and rotting.

Micah checked to make sure everyone was present and accounted for. Amelia and Benjie sat shivering against a wall half-finished with drywall. He moved within a dozen feet of them, wishing he could come closer, give Benjie a hug and let Amelia know she wasn't alone.

He blinked in the dimness. It was hard to see anything, but Amelia seemed paler than he remembered. He couldn't tell if rain or sweat beaded her forehead. "You okay?"

"I'm fine," she said with forced brightness. "Just freezing, you know?"

"I have a Mylar blanket in my pack. I'll get it."

She shook her head. "You won't get it back. It'll be infected."

"I'll be fine." He tugged his pack off his back and twisted it to get at the zipper. His wet glasses slipped down his nose, and he shoved them back in place with his palm. "I'm too manly to get cold."

She grunted. "Is that how science works these days?"

Before he could respond, a noise came from behind them. A soft rustling. Something scraping against concrete.

Amelia's eyes widened. She heard it too. The hairs on Micah's neck prickled.

He whipped around, searching the shadows deep inside the warehouse. The wind-whipped trees outside mixed with streaks of lightning made the shadows dance and waver.

One shadow seemed to separate itself from the others. It moved independently, neither dancing nor wavering. It skulked.

"Amelia, don't move." Ice flushed through his veins. His heart constricted.

Yellow eyes peered out of the darkness. First one pair, then another, and another, until at least a dozen gleamed. And still, there were more.

A low growl emanated from the bowels of the warehouse.

They weren't alone.

19

GABRIEL

Gabriel didn't hear them at first.

He stood a few steps from Jericho and several others at the front entrance of the warehouse, watching the trees thrash in the storm. His clothes were soaked, his hair wet against his scalp. Rain dripped down the back of his neck, but he didn't try to wipe it off. The water soothed his bruised, chafed wrists.

The black sky reminded him of the hurricane that battered the *Grand Voyager* before it sank, consumed in smoke and flames. Lightning split open the clouds, lighting up the warehouse in pulsing flashes. A crash of thunder hit so close it shook the cement floor beneath his feet.

"Dogs." His brother's voice came from somewhere behind him.

The next crash drowned him out. Then came another sound. A low, vicious growl. Gabriel spun around, peering into the dark.

He saw them in a flash of lightning. A glimmer of eyes and teeth. More than two dozen shapes slunk low to the ground. The creatures were coming at them from the left, the right, and from behind in a loose circle. They were stalking them. Hunting.

Gabriel gritted his teeth, his pulse leaping. His hands balled into fists. He was helpless without a weapon. His eyes met Micah's. For once, he saw no resentment or recrimination, only a wary, growing fear.

"Stay calm," Micah said.

Gabriel nodded. They were outnumbered. Only a few in their group knew the first thing about defending themselves from anything. There were packs of strays in Gabriel and Micah's neighborhood, but they'd usually gone after smaller, weaker prey. Pet dogs and cats, raccoons and rats, occasionally a small child.

Once, Gabriel clubbed a rabid mutt who attacked him for the prefab beef in his grocery bag. Usually a shout and waving hands or weapons would scare them off if they grew too bold. But this was different. He saw it in the way they moved, the strange, unblinking intensity of their gazes.

"Dogs," he said to Jericho, who hadn't heard Micah over the thunder. "Behind us."

Jericho stiffened. "How many?"

"Too many." Between crashes of thunder, he heard several muffled growls. He scanned the warehouse again. Now that his eyes were accustomed to the dark, his gaze snagged on the fluffs of fur scattered across the floor.

He made out the faded imprints of hundreds of scuffed, dirty paws. There were a few small bones here and there, squirrels or chipmunks, and a pile of bloody chicken feathers in one corner. His throat tightened. "This is their lair."

Silas's typical sneer froze on his face. "I hate dogs."

"You hate everything," Willow said, but there was an edge of concern in her voice.

One of the dogs, a husky, crept within a dozen yards of them. Gabriel liked dogs. But he didn't like these dogs. He stared at the husky with growing unease.

"Here, doggy, doggy," Celeste called.

Willow shot her a look. "Celeste, stop it!"

"What? They're just dogs. Where's that nasty faux-meat jerky we had?"

Willow slid her knife out of its sheath. "I don't think they're hungry."

The husky's jowls writhed in a snarl, its eyes like two demon eyes in the night. It looked wolfish, predatory. "Actually," Gabriel said, "I think they are."

Jericho gave a sharp jerk of his chin. "I need everyone to calmly and carefully form a circle, facing outward. Arm yourselves and be ready to fight. We have visitors."

"Or, more accurately," Finn said, "we're the visitors, and the hosts aren't so happy to see us."

The group hurriedly formed a circle, Jericho crouched on Gabriel's left, Finn like a mountain on his right. He watched the husky stalk closer in the pulses of lightning.

"Benjie!" Willow gasped, pointing.

Gabriel's gaze flicked from the husky to the far wall, where Amelia and Benjie pressed themselves against a steel beam as a retriever and two bulldogs advanced on them. "Don't move!"

Micah gripped Willow's arm to keep her from running after her brother. "We'll get him, I promise. Just stay still."

"This is an excellent time to see if food might do the trick," Elise said tersely.

Nadira reached into her pack and pulled out the last of their prefab beef jerky. She flung it at the dogs. They yelped and howled, scrambling for the food, plunging over each other. The dogs devoured it within moments, but it gave them the time they needed.

Lightning split the sky, lighting the hard planes of Jericho's face. He whirled, his rifle up and sighting the dogs. He shot once, twice. He missed. A dog barked. The growls grew louder.

Silas spun and shot at a hunched shadow streaking by only a few feet away. They were spirits in the darkness, shifting like oil in water.

Gabriel recognized a few German shepherds, several pit bulls, a snarling golden retriever, a Siberian husky, a couple of mutts, and two Rottweilers. They darted in closer, growling and snapping, but still hesitated to attack.

These dogs were former pets, most still with collars. But there were a few mutts that must have been strays for years, their skeletons showing through their mangy fur.

A gangly gray creature slunk closer. Its ratty tail hung low, its ribs gaunt, a jagged scar arcing from above his eye socket down across his muzzle. His eyes blazed savagely.

Scarface, Gabriel thought. Their leader.

Something wasn't right about them. They were driven mad by starvation or disease; Gabriel didn't know or care which. But they were scavengers now, used to feeding on prey already sick or dead. They weren't used to taking on humans at full strength. They stalked and circled and growled, darting in for a nip or a slash of fangs before leaping back.

Maybe they didn't want to attack. Maybe they just wanted the humans to leave their lair alone.

"You think they'll run if we act like the predators?" Micah said, echoing Gabriel's thoughts.

As if Scarface read their minds and strongly disagreed, the large stray gave a savage growl and sprang at Nadira with a snap of its fangs.

Nadira screamed and fell back, collapsing the circle.

Gabriel lunged at Scarface with a roar, ramming into the beast with his lowered shoulder. Taken by surprise, Scarface rolled and skittered back on its feet, hackles raised, growling. Something dripped from its mouth.

Jericho yelled something, the sound obliterated by an explosion of thunder overhead. The rain slammed against the metal roof, spilling over the doorways in a gray curtain.

Finn bent to help Nadira. Micah turned and shot at a German shepherd closing in on Finn as he yanked Nadira to her feet. The bullet ricocheted, skimming the outside of Gabriel's thigh.

Micah shot again. The dog howled and fell, then jerked itself back to its feet, limping with one bloody hind leg.

"Stop shooting!" Gabriel shouted. "Stop shooting! There's ricochet!"

Silas flipped his rifle and used the stock as a club. Micah pulled a hammer out of his belt. Elise and Nadira gripped their knives, but their blades were far too short. The dogs would tear their throats out before they could use them.

A retriever lunged at Jericho. He smashed the animal's snout with the butt of his rifle. It yowled and staggered back, shaking its head, its mouth foaming.

The other dogs were the same. Some with only a tinge of white flecked in their slobber, others with jowls dripping with red-streaked foam, the fur of their chests and front legs matted with it.

The realization hit him with a sickening jolt. The dogs were infected. If they bit anyone, it was likely a death sentence.

He searched for Amelia. She stood frozen, still as a statue against the wall, two dogs barking viciously at her but not yet attacking. Benjie was no longer beside her.

He scanned the dark warehouse. A streak of lightning revealed movement against the far wall. Benjie climbed on top of a forklift. He screamed and flailed his arms at two shepherds trying to leap onto the machine.

A righteous rage filled him. Death was coming for him and he yearned for it. But he wasn't going to die like this, chained up like a dumb animal, completely helpless. He wasn't going to stand by and let another little kid get killed. He wasn't going to abandon Amelia. *Not again.*

He scanned the warehouse, spotting several lengths of two-by-fours leaning against a forklift. He turned to Jericho, thrusting his handcuffed wrists at him. "Free me! Let me help!"

Jericho hesitated for a fraction of a second. Then he pulled the key from the cord around his neck and unlocked the handcuffs. "If you try to run, I'll kill you."

Thunder exploded. In the next flicker of lightning, there were three dogs after Benjie, snapping at his legs. They were growing more daring. A pit bull snarled at Gabriel's feet. Gabriel kicked the dog with all his might. The pit bull howled and fell back, dazed.

"I'm coming with you!" Micah raised his voice above the rain pounding the roof.

"You go for Amelia, I'll get Benjie." Gabriel headed for the pile of two-by-fours. Out of the corner of his eye, he glimpsed Micah racing for the dogs circling Amelia, his grip tight on his rifle.

Micah had a handle on it. His brother was stronger than Gabriel gave him credit for. He could protect Amelia.

Gabriel reached the woodpile, snatched up a two-by-four in each hand, and raced for the forklift. The thought only entered his head for a moment—*you can run.*

In the chaos, he could easily escape, fleeing into the forest where Jericho wouldn't be able to find him. He could end it all on his own terms, finally stopping the storm of shame, loathing, and hatred he endured every moment of every day. *Or you could even choose to live, free from these people, from justice and judgment . . .*

The temptation flared—a bright beacon flashing in the darkness for a brief moment—and then a scream brought it crashing down. He would consider his options after everyone was safe. For now, he could do something. His white-hot rage had an outlet—those damn dogs. So help him, he would destroy every single one before he ran off into the woods like a yellow-bellied coward. Gabriel was many things, but a coward wasn't one of them.

Nadira screamed to his left. She backed away from a viciously barking retriever. The retriever crouched, its ears laid back against its skull, foam drizzling from its slavering fangs.

It launched itself at Nadira. She stumbled and fell, her arms raised to protect her face. The dog leapt on her chest, about to go for her throat—but that's as far as it got.

Gabriel angled himself at Nadira and lunged, swinging hard and nailing the beast in the head with a loud crack. It slumped on top of Nadira and didn't move. Gabriel aimed a kick at a skulking terrier who yelped and skittered away. He dropped the wood, leaned down, and jerked her to her feet. "Are you hurt?"

She shook her head, her eyes wild. Her headscarf was knocked askew. Her palms and elbow were scraped. Her pants were ripped over her left thigh.

"Did it break the skin?"

She hastily fixed her headscarf. "I don't think so."

"Follow me." He thrust one of the two-by-fours into her hands. "On my count, get Benjie, climb inside, and close the doors."

"But he's—"

There wasn't any time to worry about the possibility of infection. Not with the very real threat of mauling or death by dog attack. "Don't touch him and keep your mask on! Now, go! I'll take care of the dogs."

His anger blazed with a white-hot fury that burned the darkness from his mind. He raced for the forklift, screaming like a madman as he ran.

The shepherds and the Rottweiler dropped to all fours and turned toward him, snarling, red-flecked foam dribbling from their muzzles. Two more mutts came at him from the left.

He sprang into the middle of the pack, using the board as a club, nailing one dog in the ribs, another in the haunches, and the last square in the head. The dog crumpled and fell, limp and lifeless.

The other dogs smelled blood. Gabriel stumbled back, startled, as the dogs lunged in, barking savagely, and attacked the fallen one. His stomach lurched, but it would give them the time they needed. "Go!"

Nadira raced past them and climbed into the forklift. She grabbed Benjie's arm and pulled him inside. There wasn't room for Gabriel. He hadn't expected there would be.

He slammed the door shut and turned back to face the dogs.

The Rottweiler advanced, head lowered, snarling, blood staining its fangs and lips.

"Come on, you filthy, ugly beast!" Gabriel lifted his club. "Come and get me!"

20

WILLOW

Willow couldn't find Benjie. In the chaos of the attack, everything was slinking shadows and bursts of lightning. Thunder crashed, wind shrieked, the rain pelting the roof like stones. The storm roared so loud she could hardly hear.

And over everything, screams and shouts of terror, and the dogs slinking closer like silent demons from hell. It felt like some terrible, distorted nightmare.

The circle was broken. Every person defended themselves. Only, Benjie couldn't defend himself. *They're your responsibility. Take care of them.* She had to protect him.

She spun around, searching for her brother, shouting his name, peering into shadows. She darted aside as a great dark shape leapt past her, snarling and snapping its jaws inches from her left leg.

The lightning created a stuttering strobe effect. With each flash, the chaos of the warehouse froze like a flashbulb—dogs running, crouching, snarling. In the next flash—people backing against each other, lashing out with two-by-fours, knives, and the butts of their rifles.

Fear plowed through her. "Benjie!"

She felt hot breath on her arm, smelled wet fur and something rancid. She turned slowly, so as not to startle the creature into attacking her. A German shepherd stood less than three yards away, its eyes trained on her, the hackles on its back raised, tongue lolling as it panted.

Her *lola* taught her what to do near strange, aggressive dogs when she was little. She made Willow practice with Benjie and Zia. *Stand as still as a tree.* Benjie would stand on one leg and giggle until he lost his balance and fell over, knocking into Zia and sending them both tumbling to the floor, laughing hysterically as they tried to take Willow down with them.

Her heart lurched in her chest. She couldn't think about that now. She had to focus. She had to *survive*.

The German shepherd growled, slinking closer.

She froze, her gun clutched in her right hand, her arm flat against her side. Her muscles trembled with the focus it took not to bolt. She stared below the dog's eyes, not meeting its gaze.

In between flashes of lightning, the shepherd advanced a step. Then another. A low growl rumbled in its throat. Its jowls lifted in an ugly snarl. She saw the foamy blood on its blackened lips. She could guess what it meant.

This was no ordinary dog.

It wouldn't care if she was still as a freaking tree. It would tear her apart anyway. "Stay back," she murmured. Slowly, she lifted the gun, bringing her left hand to close over the grip, willing her fingers not to shake, trying desperately to focus, to *think* over the thunder and the screams, through the panic spiking through her.

She remembered what Jericho told her. No safety. Aim, press firmly, and shoot.

This dog was someone's pet once. Like the one at the gas station. She'd never hurt an animal before in her life.

But this was different. This dog raged with diseased fury. Whatever gentleness had once been a part of it was gone now. She couldn't let sentimentality make her hesitate. She must be strong.

Lightning flashed again. The dog snarled, teeth gleaming. It crouched, bristling and slavering, ready to spring at her, its eyes glittering with malice.

She pulled the trigger. The shot echoed like a blast, ringing in her ears. The shepherd howled and hurled itself sideways, shaking its head furiously. It was startled, not hurt. She missed.

She wasn't good enough with the gun. If she shot again, she'd miss again. This time, the dog would be ready for her.

She turned and ran.

Her feet pounded against the concrete floor as she fled for the back of the warehouse. Another huge doorway loomed against the back wall on the left, hung with nothing but plastic sheeting.

Maybe the dogs would hate the rain. Maybe that shepherd wouldn't follow her out into the storm, and she could swing back around and reenter from the front to find Benjie. It was worth a shot.

A bolt of lightning revealed a slavering mutt skulking directly in her path. It was huge, with matted gray fur and a nasty scar carved across its face. In the strobed lightning, it seemed like some malevolent beast leaping out of the depths of Hades to devour her.

Her veins turned to ice. Thunder roared overhead. Her heart hammered, her chest burning. She charged it, hoping to scare it like she scared the Shepherd. She screamed wordlessly and waved the gun.

At the last second, the stray darted to the side but twisted its head and lunged for her leg. She felt its teeth snag her pants. She stumbled, slamming to the floor on her hands and knees. The gun knocked from her hands and skittered over the concrete.

She felt a heavy weight and sharp nails digging into the back of her thighs. The thing climbed on top of her.

She rolled, flipped onto her back and kicked, connecting with something hard that gave way with a yelp.

There was no time to search for the gun. She scrambled to her feet and bolted.

The stray barreled right behind her. Its nails scraped the floor, its jaws snapping at her heels.

Fear throttled her. She couldn't breathe.

It didn't matter, she was almost there. The doorway towered in front of her, the storm-battered world just beyond the billowing plastic sheet.

She struck the sheeting with outstretched arms and plowed through it. Rain pelted her face, the wind whipping her, nearly bowling her over. The trees thrashed, some bent sideways. Above them, thunder cracked the sky. The boom was so loud she felt it in her bones, felt a shuddering in her teeth.

The stray tore through the plastic with a head-shaking snarl and in seconds snapped at her heels again. Two other dogs scurried right behind it.

Her boots hit a mud puddle. She flailed in the slick mud before her feet flew out from under her. She went down hard.

The dog crashed into her, knocking her flat onto her back. It scrambled to a stop and came hurling back toward her, jaws hinged open to bite.

She flung up her arms. She'd try to seize its head and plunge her fingers into its eye-sockets. She never in her life thought she'd die like this, but she sure as hell wasn't going down without a fight.

The stray never reached her.

A huge black shadow streaked across her body and slammed into the stray head-on. The thing bowled the dog over and they rolled in the muddy grass. The two other dogs—a pit bull and a husky—leapt back, ears laid flat.

Willow scrambled into a crouch and froze, staring in shock at the scene before her. The stray sprang to its feet, but the other creature was faster. He launched himself at the stray.

Lightning shattered the sky, revealing massive shoulders and haunches, black fur clumped with mud and dripping with rain, tall ears, and a long, narrow muzzle.

A wolf. The huge black shadow was a freakin' wolf.

The wolf twisted and lunged, snapping its jaws and ripping open the side of the stray's face as he passed. The dog yelped and staggered back, stunned.

But the wolf wasn't done. He came barreling in again and slammed his shoulder into the stray's side.

The dog stumbled. More swiftly than Willow thought possible, the wolf plunged in and opened a gash deep in the dog's throat. Blood gushed down its neck and chest. The stray whimpered and fell onto its side in the mud, its skeletal sides heaving as it struggled to breathe.

A few seconds later, it shuddered and went limp. It was dead.

The wolf nosed the dog, grunted, and lifted his head. He growled once at the two dogs now cowering in the mud. They turned tail and fled back into the warehouse.

The wolf turned and looked directly at her.

She climbed to her feet. The trees groaned as a branch fell with a sharp crack only a dozen yards from where she stood. Rain slashed against her, dripping water into her eyes. The wind lashed her wet hair into her face and yanked angrily at her clothes.

She didn't move. She didn't run. She stared at the wolf. The wolf stared back.

He was enormous, bigger than any wolf she'd ever seen, even the docile modded ones. His shoulders easily reached her waist, his massive head even taller.

He stood less than ten feet away. If she tried to flee, he could reach her in a single bound.

She willed herself not to panic. She wasn't a threat when the wolf had the dog to battle. But now? Would he see her as prey? Was he sick, like the other dogs? No foam dripped from his jaws. Maybe he was immune. But still.

The hackles along his spine were raised, but he didn't growl or snarl. He simply stared, unmoving, his yellow eyes seeming to say something she couldn't understand.

She sensed movement to her right. She was loath to take her focus off the wolf even for a second, but if there was another threat—another dog, a pack of them, a human predator—she needed to know. She shifted her gaze to the tree line.

A figure stood between two swaying pine trees. It wore dark pants and a camouflaged rain slicker, the hood shielding the face in shadows. The figure pushed back the hood. She glimpsed dark eyes, a round face, and sleek black hair. A girl.

She was short, though taller than Willow. She was Asian, not Filipino like Willow, but Japanese maybe, and looked about sixteen. She wore a backpack and held a hoverboard in one hand.

The girl whistled. The wolf bounded to her side, vanishing into the shadows but for his yellow eyes, still peering intently at Willow.

"Who are you?" Willow asked over a rumble of thunder.

But fear and urgency overcame her curiosity. The rest of her group were still fighting for their lives inside the warehouse. Maybe that wolf could help them, if that girl could tell it what to do. "Can you help us? My friends, my brother—" She gestured behind her.

The girl pointed past her shoulder. Willow turned and saw three trucks heading down the road toward the warehouse. Her stomach dropped. Rescue? Or something else? She glanced back at the girl.

The girl raised her finger to her lips.

She didn't understand. Be quiet? Why? What did she know? Where did she come from? Who was she? And why had she and the wolf saved Willow? "Help us!"

But the girl shook her head soundlessly and stepped back, fading into the shadows between the trees as easily as her wolf.

21

AMELIA

Amelia pressed her spine against the steel beam behind her. It was the only thing keeping her up. Her breath came in shallow pants, the front of her shirt drenched with sweat from the fever burning through her. The headache hammering her skull brought waves of dizziness with it.

If not for Micah, she'd be lost. He stood several feet in front of her, aiming his rifle at a black Labrador prowling only two yards away.

He pressed the trigger. The dog staggered, whimpering. Blood dripped from its haunches. "Get out of here!"

A chow chow turned toward them, sniffing the air. The lab fled, lurching on its wounded hind leg, but the chow chow reached it and brought it down.

Amelia looked away, her empty stomach heaving. It wasn't just the sight of the fighting dogs. Lightning pulsed harsh and blinding. She squeezed her eyes shut against the pain spearing through her eye sockets.

Micah frowned. "Amelia! What's wrong?"

She shook her head, forcing her eyes open. He turned toward her, forgetting in the chaos that she was infected, that she was as dangerous as the dogs. Even with her mask and gloves, she was still a threat to him, to everyone she cared about. "Stay away!"

He took a step back, shifting his concerned gaze from her to the dogs and back again. They were busy with the Labrador, for a moment at least.

Near the entrance, Jericho stood back-to-back with Silas, defending Amelia's mother, Finn, and Horne from a pack of five. Gabriel fended off three dogs in front of a forklift with Benjie and Nadira safely inside. She didn't see Willow anywhere.

"What's wrong?" Micah asked again, his face creased with worry.

She saw it reflected in his eyes. She looked as bad as she felt. The fever that started two days ago was worse, along with the irritating tickle in the back of her throat that made her cough constantly. She knew what it meant. She hadn't told anyone, not yet. She couldn't bear to see the look on Silas's face, or her mother's. Her mother still hoped.

The fever flared, flushing through her body with a white-hot fury. Her skin melted off her bones. Her vision blurred and wavered, flames licking the corners of everything. Dizziness washed through her in waves.

"You're sick," Micah said dully, answering his own question.

She coughed into her mask, pain blazing behind her skull. Sweat dripped down her forehead. She wiped it away furiously. "A migraine." As if that could deceive him.

"When it rains, it pours," he said with forced lightness, but she knew him enough now to recognize the tremor of dread in his voice.

She grunted. "It doesn't matter if we're going to die here anyway, does it?"

A mutt locked eyes on them and snarled. Micah aimed his rifle. He fired and this time the dog went down without a sound. Two others sprang at it. "We're not gonna die here. I promise you that."

The sound of engines roared over the thunder and pounding rain. Before Amelia could form a coherent thought or register surprise, a gray, dirt-streaked truck plowed through the plastic sheeting over the entrance and burst into the warehouse.

The truck squealed to a stop in the center of the floor, two more trucks following close behind, spraying mud from their tires. Four men leapt out of the back of the first truck, armed with handguns and nail-spiked baseball bats.

They hurled themselves at the dogs with a shout.

The passenger door opened, and the guy with the tiger in his truck, Gonzales, poked his head out. "Come on! Get in!"

Jericho grabbed Amelia's mother. He and the others raced to the trucks and clambered into the second truck bed. Two of the men ran for the forklift, scattering snarling dogs as they went.

Micah gestured at Amelia. "Let's go!"

She pushed off from the wall, but only made it a few steps. Heat boiled her insides. Dizziness seized her, pain exploding inside her head. She staggered.

Before she could stop him, Micah darted in and grabbed her waist. "Lean on me. Hurry!"

She tried to jerk away. What was he thinking? She was infected; she could kill him. He was too close. She turned her head and coughed violently into her mask. "Micah, stop!"

But he shook his head, his brown eyes flashing with determination behind his glasses. "I'm not leaving you. Just don't cough on me, okay?"

He tightened his grip on her side and dragged her toward the truck. They stumbled, a terrier snapping at Amelia's feet. She managed to kick it hard enough to send it sprawling.

They reached the gray truck, and Micah thrust her up. She grabbed the side and hoisted herself over the side even as her vision blurred with white spots.

"She's sick!" Micah warned Gonzales, who leaned half-outside the truck, yelling at everyone to hurry the hell up. "Put everyone else in the other trucks!"

Russell adjusted his own mask, his ruddy face blanching, but he nodded.

Amelia crawled into the furthest corner away, attempting to touch as little as possible. She watched the two men with spiked baseball bats knock aside a couple of dogs as Gabriel helped Nadira out of the forklift. He hesitated, then lifted Benjie gingerly and set him down. He turned to the trucks, spotted Amelia, and gestured to Benjie.

Benjie nodded and raced to the gray truck. Amelia forced herself to focus, to hold on to consciousness. Even Benjie shouldn't be in this truck with her. He wasn't coughing. She was the one on fire, the virus burning her up from the inside.

"Stay on that side!" she croaked. "Don't get near me."

Benjie climbed in and hunched into the opposite corner, pulling his knees tight to his chest and wrapping his arms around himself. He shuddered violently.

Amelia longed to go to him, to hug him and tell him everything was okay. But she couldn't. It wasn't worth the risk. "You're okay, Benjie. You're safe."

Gonzales ducked back in the truck. The vehicles reversed and started to back up. "Go, go, go!"

Benjie stared at her with wide, shocked eyes, his hair standing up all over his head. "Where's Lo Lo?"

Amelia caught sight of movement at the back of the warehouse, the flash of a round brown face and flying black hair. Willow sprinted toward them.

"Wait!"

The gray truck slammed its brakes. Silas stood up in the rusted-out Ford, his rifle aimed at a dark shape lunging at Willow from behind. He took out the pit bull just as Willow reached the truck. Micah and Finn reached down to haul her up.

Tires squealed as the trucks spun in a circle in the center of the warehouse and roared out into the night. The trees on either side of the road bent and groaned. The truck jolted as it bounced over fallen tree branches.

Lightning zigzagged across the sky, searing the backs of her eyelids. Rain struck her face. In her fevered mind, it seemed to hiss from the heat roiling off her.

The pain descended on her like a pulsing, living thing, clawing at her brain, dipping her body in flames. She tried to sit up, but the metal side was too slick to grasp, her arms weak and floppy. Dimly, she heard Benjie crying.

She collapsed into unconsciousness as the fever took her.

22

MICAH

By the time Micah woke the next morning, the sun shone through a heavy layer of white clouds. A rooster crowed somewhere nearby.

He grabbed his glasses from the nightstand and left the small, bare room he shared with Finn and Willow—a scarred wooden floor, two narrow beds (Finn offered to take the floor, since he'd never fit on the mattress), a dresser, and a curtained window—and made his way to the cafeteria, still wiping sleep from his eyes.

Fog drifted around his legs, obscuring most of the features of the place Gonzales had taken them after rescuing them from the warehouse.

Their arrival last night was a frantic blur of darkness and rain, shining headlights, glimpses of darkened buildings, and strange faces and voices. The battle in the warehouse exhausted him. He'd passed out within moments of hitting the mattress.

They were at some kind of farm commune. Their leader, Harmony Willis, had promised them a real breakfast, so it couldn't be that bad.

"Welcome to Sweet Creek Farm," Harmony said as he entered the cafeteria. The long rectangular building boasted concrete floors, rough-hewn walls, a metal roof, and a few dozen farm-style tables.

He felt strangely disconnected from his surroundings, like he still couldn't quite believe this wasn't a dream.

"Would you like some milk?"

"Huh?" he asked.

Harmony was a white lady in her mid-sixties, with long gray hair and intelligent brown eyes set in a handsome, angular face. She wore pressed slacks and a flowy silk shirt that looked more fit for a high-end boutique than a farm, though her feet were encased in a pair of battered work boots.

Gonzales, the guy who'd saved them last night, leaned against the wall behind her, his arms crossed, an unlit cigarette dangling in one hand. They both wore gloves and masks.

"Milk?" Harmony repeated, raising arched eyebrows.

Micah didn't want to be impolite. Besides, hunger gnawed at his empty stomach. "Thank you."

Harmony set a glass of thick, cold milk down on the farm table in front of him. For a moment, Micah stared at it in disbelief.

"It won't drink itself," Silas smirked from further down the long table.

Micah picked up the sweating glass and gulped it down in one swallow. It tasted sweet and thick, smooth and soothing on his tongue. Real cow's milk, like he hadn't tasted in years.

"That's more like it," Harmony said with a smile.

"What is this place?" Micah asked.

"My father built it over twenty-five years ago. He envisioned a self-sustaining community free of violence and the intrusion of the government. We formed a community of like-minded individuals. The rest, as they say, is history. After he died seven years ago, I took over to keep his dream alive."

"Why did you save us?" Micah asked.

Harmony's smile widened. "In these difficult times, that's a good question. We know all those who appear innocent aren't always what they seem. However, my father's dream was to build a community in a land where community has been forgotten."

"Some of us still believe in good old-fashioned Southern hospitality. We don't invite everyone our scouts come across, but Russell told me about you straightaway when he returned from hunting. He didn't realize the dogs had re-infested the warehouse. It's less than a quarter mile as the crow flies from our compound, so we keep an eye on it."

"We tried to clear it last week." Gonzales shrugged. "They came back."

"When he realized he'd sent you into a trap, Russell begged me to take a few trucks to get you out."

"I guess we're real lucky that Gonzales has a conscience." Jericho nodded at Gonzales.

Gonzales dipped his chin. "Don't abuse our hospitality, and we'll be straight."

Micah took another sip of milk and glanced around the table. Gabriel sat at the far end, his hands folded on the table, free of cuffs, a long-sleeved waffle-knit shirt covering the bruising on his wrists.

Gabriel met his eyes with a hard smile. But Micah knew him. He recognized the anxiety underneath, that coiled restlessness that set Micah's teeth on edge and filled him with foreboding. Why hadn't Jericho handcuffed him? Didn't Jericho recognize how dangerous his brother was? He jerked his gaze away.

Jericho, Elise, Horne, Willow, and Silas were seated and well into a breakfast of scrambled eggs and pancakes. He'd slept late; even Finn and Celeste were already up. Benjie and Amelia weren't here; they'd been quarantined in separate buildings last night.

Micah rose to his feet, fresh fear jolting through him. It felt like waking from a pleasant dream to realize you were still trapped in a nightmare. After they'd escaped the dogs, they found Amelia unconscious in the back of the truck, her face white and sweating, her skin on fire. "Amelia—"

Beside Jericho, Elise flinched.

Harmony refilled his cup from a pitcher and handed it to him. "She's in our infirmary, remember? She's safe and as comfortable as we can make her."

"Infirmary?" Micah said dumbly, glancing around the room.

Harmony sat down across from him and folded her hands on the table. She wore bright tangerine nail polish beneath her plastic gloves. She seemed grandmotherly at first glance, but there was strength in the sharpness of her posture, a wary intelligence in her eyes. She was the leader of this place for a reason.

"We added a three-room infirmary when we built this place two decades ago," she said. "We've got three patient rooms and a small surgical theater for minor injuries. Once the virus hit, we sealed off the rooms for quarantine."

"Can you save her?" Elise's shoulders hunched, her face haunted.

"There isn't anything that can save her now, but we can make her comfortable."

Gabriel's jaw tightened. Elise's pallor paled even further. Micah winced. Harmony's words were true, but he hated hearing the words spoken aloud.

But Amelia was strong. She'd lived with epilepsy her whole life. Surely, she could fight this stupid disease. "What about a cure?"

Harmony shrugged helplessly. "There isn't one."

Silas stood up abruptly, shoving his chair back, his expression a rigid mask. Without a word, he stalked out of the cafeteria and slammed the door behind him.

"Excuse him," Elise said weakly. "He's had a rough time." As if the rest of them hadn't.

For a second, Micah longed to meet Gabriel's gaze and roll his eyes, like they'd done for years. But he couldn't. Their brotherly camaraderie was long gone.

"But the FEMA camps." Elise bit her lower lip. "That's where we're headed. They said—"

Russell grunted. "You don't wanna go there."

"But the fliers—" Elise sputtered. "They said there's a treatment."

Harmony met Elise's gaze. "Not everything the government says ends up being true."

"We have to take her there." Elise's hands fluttered to the hollow of her throat.

Harmony adjusted the mask over her face. She closed her eyes for a moment. "When my grandson got sick, that's where we took him," she said very quietly. "He didn't come back."

Elise stilled. Willow's eyes took on a wild, haunted look. She wrapped her arms around herself. Micah knew they imagined Amelia and Benjie in the same circumstances. There was so much death, so many people who'd suffered huge loss. "I'm so sorry."

Horne cleared his throat. "Things change. It's been weeks. Surely, the WHO, the Department of Defense, and every country's health organization are working around the clock—"

"Are you sure?" Harmony asked. "We haven't seen them."

"Well, why wouldn't they be? I'm sure they're on the brink of a breakthrough." He glanced around and wrinkled his nose in distaste. "We need to get out of the boondocks and find actual civilization."

Micah bit the insides of his cheeks, fighting down a flare of irritation. People like Horne had never experienced the inconvenience of hunger or the frustration of an indifferent government. He didn't have a clue what it was like to be in a situation where no one came to save you. Micah tried to have sympathy for everyone, but some days—and some people—were harder than others.

"We're taking Amelia and Benjie to FEMA," Jericho said. "We could use your help, but we're going with or without it."

Harmony nodded heavily. "Some people must see to believe. Here is the one thing I ask. Go see it for yourselves before you try to transport that suffering girl. It's one-hour west by car. The main road is so congested with abandoned vehicles, you'll never get close, but there's an access road I can show you. It'll be almost entirely clear, and it's through woods and fields, safer than the open highways. Still, it is a dangerous journey."

"Fine." Horne rose from his seat. "Let's go right now. We can be back and out of here by tonight."

"We'll see," Harmony said. "I will lend you a couple of trucks and one of my men on one condition—*if* you wait and leave first thing in the morning. If you choose to take her to FEMA, you can return in the afternoon, get your people and your things, and head out immediately."

"Why not now?" The sooner they got Amelia and Benjie to the FEMA center, the sooner they could stop this thing. Even if the chance was slim, they had to take it.

Gonzales tugged down his mask and lit a cigarette. "Trust me. If we run into trouble, we'll be thankful for every minute of daylight we have. It's foolish to travel anywhere at night."

"Then we'll do as you advise." Micah didn't wait for Jericho's response. They needed all the help they could get. If it would save Amelia, he'd do anything. "Thank you for your offer."

Jericho shot Micah a look. He cracked his knuckles and sighed. "Fine. We leave at dawn."

Nadira sat up straighter in her seat, folding her hands on the table. "Thank you for your hospitality. We know how much time and effort it takes to feed us and provide shelter. I would like to contribute any way that I can."

Harmony smiled warmly at her, wrinkles appearing at the corners of her eyes. "We do have farm animals to tend to and some fences that need mending."

Celeste made a face like she'd bitten into something bitter. "You don't have service bots for that?"

Harmony's smile widened. "Here at Sweet Creek, we believe that physical labor is good for the soul."

"My soul is just fine," Celeste muttered.

An African-American woman bustled out of the kitchen carrying a huge bowl of pea pods. She set it in front of Harmony and gave them a small wave. She was in her forties, her short hair tied back in a bandana. "I'm Anna. Formerly a gourmet chef. I whip up most of the food here."

After pleasantries and introductions, she went back to the kitchen.

Harmony dumped the pea pods onto the table and began shelling the peas into the now empty bowl. "Feel free to help."

Micah, Nadira, and Willow grabbed a handful of pods and started shelling. Celeste stared at the pea pods like she'd never seen such things before, like preparing food was a foreign concept, a thing reserved for servants and metalheads. To her, it probably was.

"What do you know about the state of things?" Nadira asked.

"The military told us very little," Elise said.

Harmony's face darkened. "That's to be expected, I suppose. Dozens of travelers have passed through over the last few months. I worked as a secretary in a pediatrician's office before the bioterrorist attacks.

"The government called in the National Guard to arm the hospitals and clinics. Curfews went into effect in every major city, but that didn't stop people from looting pharmacies for antibiotics and pediatric offices for antivirals that didn't work. Travelers were quarantined in tent cities outside airports. Stadiums were seized by the government and used as quarantine centers."

"What about the bodies?" Micah adjusted his glasses. He tried to imagine what it must have been like, but couldn't. It was too huge, too awful, like some terrible nightmare he couldn't wake up from.

Harmony flexed her fingers, glancing at the manicure beneath her gloves before tossing a handful of shelled peas into the bowl. "For a few weeks, the Department of Health commissioned body-collection teams to travel around and load the bodies into vans. That didn't go over well with the surviving family members. The collection teams had to be protected by drones and guards in combat gear. But after a few more days, there were fewer and fewer family members to complain. And one day, the white vans stopped coming."

"What about the CDC? Haven't they developed a treatment?" Elise asked anxiously. The pea pod in her fist split open, green goo oozing between her fingers.

"The CDC fell." Gonzales leaned against the wall and took a drag of his cigarette. "The vloggers showed it happening in Atlanta. If anyone had the vaccine, it would be them, right? Some people believed the government was withholding the cure. They went mad. Hundreds of people camped out in front of the CDC. After a week, it was thousands.

"The National Guard was overwhelmed. They even shot citizens. But it didn't matter. The mobs kept coming. They closed the CDC, and the remaining workers had to be airlifted by chopper from the roof."

Micah rolled a pea between his fingers. The things Harmony and Gonzales said were shocking. The world had been bad for a long time. Armed gangs had ruled the streets of his neighborhoods for years. Violence and chaos weren't anything new. But this was on a mind-boggling scale. "Is the government still functioning?"

Harmony shrugged. "There are rumors. Once the government shut down the internet and demanded self-imposed quarantines, we were cut off from the rest of the world. Without telecommunications, it's impossible to know. Judging by the last newsfeed reports, things aren't good. The panic and rioting in the major cities was so severe the military pulled out, abandoning Chicago, Tampa, L.A., and who knows where else."

"Where are the other safe places?" Nadira asked. "Surely, there must be some."

"Three weeks ago, they did those chopper flyovers, dropping red and green pamphlets," Gonzales said. "They directed the sick to the FEMA regional centers, the well to designated safe zones."

"Why didn't you go?" Micah asked.

"We've always been the independent type. It's how we want it. And we've done fine on our own." Harmony glanced back at Gonzales, signaling the end to the conversation. "Gonzales can show you how we do things."

Gonzales pushed himself off from the wall. "Why don't I show ya'll around? I expect you'll be wanting to take a shower soon."

Celeste's hand shot up. "Me first!"

Willow rolled her eyes and exchanged an irritated glance with Micah.

He shrugged. "I'm sure we'll all get a turn."

"Ten bucks says she uses up all the hot water," Willow muttered.

"I'm penniless." Finn turned his pockets inside out. "But I can bet the bag of Skittles in my pack."

"You're on," Willow said. "Benjie loves Skittles."

"Not as much as I do," Finn said.

Willow cocked her eyebrows. "We can see that."

"I'm touched." Finn gave her a gentle shove, nearly knocking her over.

She shoved him back. He didn't budge. "You're like some kind of ginormous mountain troll, aren't you?"

"As long as I get to eat Skittles, not goats."

Willow rolled her eyes. "These days, you never know."

Micah grinned as he followed Finn, Willow, and the others outside. Sweet Creek Farm included a dozen or so buildings surrounded by a forest thick with pine, maple, and oak trees.

"These are the living quarters, the mess hall, and the workshop." Gonzales pointed at various buildings that looked like small warehouses, each one or two stories with metal roofs. He walked along a gravel path, leading them past a garage filled with trucks and cars, with a small charging station next to it.

"You planning on selling any of those electric vehicles?" Horne asked, his eyes lighting up. "I may know a buyer."

Gonzales grunted. "No need."

Horne's face fell. He glanced back longingly at the vehicles as Gonzales moved the group along. "Back here are the farms and the hydroponic fields. We grow most everything—wheat, corn, potatoes, and vegetables inside greenhouses to protect them from the blights."

Further down the path, a handful of cows and goats grazed inside a small pasture. A girl no older than ten tossed chicken feed in a large, fenced yard, three dozen chickens squawking, ruffling their feathers, and pecking the ground at her feet. In one corner stood a large chicken coop. The girl tugged at her overalls as she smiled and waved at them. Gonzales introduced her as Gracie, Harmony's granddaughter.

"How many people live here?" Micah asked. These people had been here long before the Hydra Virus turned the world to chaos.

"We had around fifty people here for the last decade, but we've taken in about thirty more in the last several weeks." Gonzales eyed them. "Don't know how many more we can accommodate."

"We won't be staying longer than tonight," Jericho said. "After we verify the FEMA center, we'll be on our way."

Micah shot him a glance. Why was he so quick to shun the offered hospitality? As long as they could help Amelia and Benjie, why not stay for a while? There was food, water, and shelter here, and more importantly, normal people who didn't try to kill them. Surely a few days of rest could only be a good thing.

"Suit yourself," Gonzales said. "Though we do ask you to pitch in and pull your weight as long as you're here."

"Not a problem," Micah said.

"We aren't afraid of hard work," Nadira said.

Celeste crossed her arms over her chest and scowled. "Speak for yourself."

"I'm pretty good with medical stuff," Nadira volunteered.

"Good to know," Gonzales said. "I'm sure Mrs. Lee would appreciate your help. Now, here's our solar-powered well system . . ."

Micah allowed Gonzales and the others to pull ahead. He fell into step beside Gabriel. He hadn't spoken directly to his brother in weeks. He pushed his anxiety away. "Why aren't you in handcuffs?" he asked in a low voice.

Gabriel cocked his brows. "Why? You concerned I'll escape the firing squad, brother?"

Micah bristled. "Answer the question."

Gabriel shrugged. "Jericho knows he needs the manpower. Besides —" he lowered his voice even further, "Gonzales and that other guy didn't notice me the first time we met. You think these people would let us inside their gates with a dangerous prisoner in tow? Jericho is smart. We're already bringing the infected in with us. A terrorist would break the camel's back, or whatever."

Micah hated that Gabriel was right. He kicked a stray piece of gravel off the path. "What are you planning to do?"

A muscle jumped in Gabriel's cheek. "Who says I'm planning to do anything?"

"Please don't hurt anyone else."

Gabriel's mouth contorted. "The New Patriots didn't release the virus. You have to know that—"

"Don't you ever stop lying? Or have you forgotten how to speak the truth? I know what you did. We all know you helped kill all those people—" He couldn't finish. A lump formed in his throat. Dangerous emotions rose within him. If he didn't tamp them down, they'd overwhelm him. He wasn't afraid of his feelings, but he couldn't deal with them here in front of everyone. He still didn't know how to deal with them. That was the problem.

"I did plenty of harm," Gabriel said in a rush. "I'm not saying I didn't. But I didn't do that. I did not kill all these people. You know me."

But Micah had heard that before. He blinked hard behind his glasses. "I don't know you. I don't know what to believe."

Gabriel spread his arms. "Believe in us."

"I can't," Micah forced out, struggling to keep his voice low. "That's over."

"Ask Amelia, Micah. She knows the truth. Ask her—"

But Micah turned and strode up the path, away from his brother. He joined Willow, Finn and the others listening to Gonzales drone on about hydroponics.

He bit the inside of his cheek and brushed his brother's words out of his mind. He was only trying to drive a wedge of doubt and distrust between Micah and Amelia. He wasn't falling for it.

Thoughts of Gabriel only filled him with impotent anger—and regret, sadness, and resentment, all hopelessly tangled with the love that still survived somehow. He thought of the *Old Man and the Sea*, of Santiago and his great fish, how he loved and respected it but needed to kill it anyway.

Was it a lesser sin to kill what you loved, or a greater one? Micah loved Gabriel still, in spite of everything he'd done. He would never kill his brother, but could he kill off his love? Strangle his affection for Gabriel so it didn't hurt so damn much every single day?

It would be easier if love wasn't in the way. If he could hate as easily as Gabriel seemed to. He'd lost his brother, even though he stood less than three feet away.

He shook the thoughts from his head. He carried that heartache with him, always. But he needed to think about the present now. He needed to focus on things he could do something about.

"This is an amazing place," Elise said, though every word seemed forced. Her mind was consumed by other things, just like Micah's.

"What about fortifications and defenses?" Jericho scanned the complex. "I don't see perimeter fences or watch towers."

"We don't need them." Gonzales headed back the way they'd come.

Micah hurried to catch up. He pushed thoughts of Gabriel out of his mind. "What do you mean, you don't need them?"

"From what we've seen, the world has gone to hell in a handbasket," Finn said. "Actually, I think it skipped the handbasket altogether."

"Everyone needs protection," Willow said. "What about the gangs?"

"We have protection." Gonzales spoke in a clipped tone as he picked up his pace. "We're a peaceful people. Here, we believe violence against man only begets violence. Other than a trip alarm to warn us of the occasional stray dog or various other wildlife, which we dispatch with bats or a bullet if required, we don't need anything else.

"Besides, we're naturally isolated," Gonzales continued, a hint of defensiveness in his voice. "We're back in the woods, with only the single dirt road entrance. Until the attacks, we'd buy and sell supplies with the town up the road. There's seldom a need to travel to Macon or Atlanta. We aren't bothered much. Most of the people we see now are the ones our scouts find and choose to invite here. Now, if there are no other questions, I'll take you back to your quarters to wash up."

Jericho allowed Gonzales to pull ahead of them. "I don't like this.

No defenses? No security perimeter or night watch? That doesn't make sense."

"What do you expect?" Horne sniffed. "These people choose to live like the last century never happened."

"They said they're a peaceful people," Nadira said, glancing up at Gonzales. "There's nothing wrong with that."

"I agree with Nadira," Micah said. "Maybe we should take them at face value."

Jericho's brow creased. "We'll be gone by tomorrow night, at any rate. Until then, be ready for anything."

23

GABRIEL

"Take me with you," Gabriel said the next morning at dawn. He watched Jericho shoulder his rifle, then check his gun holster and the knife sheaths he'd hidden on various parts of his body.

Jericho insisted Gabriel sleep cuffed and bound within Jericho's quarters. It was an uncomfortable night. Gabriel rubbed the aching muscles of his shoulders and lower back. "You know you can't leave me," he said again.

Jericho grimaced.

"This was your idea." Though he hadn't protested when Jericho told him to hide his identity. He'd hoped a day of freedom might quell that edgy, caught-in-a-trap feeling of captivity he despised—he was wrong.

Jericho glowered at him. "An idea I'm regretting."

"It's too late now. You can't leave me unsupervised and free to wreak havoc while you're gone."

Jericho sprang in front of him. Gabriel hadn't even seen him move. Jericho seized the front of his shirt and jerked him to his toes. "If you so much as sneeze the wrong way, so help me—"

Gabriel longed to shove him away, but he resisted. The derision seething in Jericho's gaze matched his own. *Don't turn your back*, he wanted to snarl. He hated being a prisoner. He hated the dread and self-loathing eating away at him. He'd been tempted to run more times than he could count yesterday. But deep inside, he knew he couldn't. Not yet.

He still needed to say goodbye to his brother. The conversation they had yesterday disintegrated into frustration and anger. He needed to find a way to show Micah everything he couldn't seem to say out loud. *I love you. I'm sorry. Always.*

He couldn't leave while Amelia lay dying. Something—some last remaining thread connecting him to his old life, to his old feelings—wouldn't let him. He could wait until she—until she died. It wouldn't be long. He blinked at the pang that shot through him. "Scout's honor."

Jericho released him. "No weapons."

Gabriel shrugged and followed him out the door. The sky faded to midnight blue, still salted with stars, the first fingers of dawn beginning to color the horizon. Last night, Jericho ordered Horne and Finn to stay back and keep an eye on things—like either of them would be any help if things went sideways.

Horne made a grand show of protesting, puffing out his chest and boasting of his skills, but he knew the truth as well as Gabriel. The real danger waited on the road. And Horne had no interest in real danger. He was like every other blathering, puffed-up elite—a coward at his core.

"Let's roll," Jericho said.

Micah, Silas, and Elise waited by the trucks, along with two Sweet Creek men: Gonzales and Russell, the white guy with the backward baseball cap and the sharp, shifty eyes. His gaze lingered on Gabriel, sizing him up. Gabriel disliked him instantly. He knew the type—a man familiar with cunning and violence.

"Don't know why we needed to get up at the butt-crack of dawn," Silas grumbled. He glanced at Gabriel. "Nice face. You look like a piñata who lost a fight with a bat."

He shrugged, refusing to let Silas get under his skin. "I'm clumsy."

Silas smiled. Like Declan Black, his smiles never reached his eyes. They were just stretched skin and a vicious flash of teeth. "You ever have a day where you want to set someone's face on fire and put it out with a fork?"

"What's your deal, man? Were you dropped on your head as a baby?"

Silas's smile widened, empty of any emotion but contempt. "The question is, how many times?"

"You're insane."

Silas slouched, shoving his fists into his pockets. "That's a matter of perspective."

"Enough." Elise shot Silas a warning glance. "Today of all days, please."

Silas leaned in close as he sauntered by, purposefully bumping Gabriel's shoulder. "What doesn't kill you, disappoints me."

He gritted his teeth, reining in his anger. Silas just wanted to get a rise out of him. He wouldn't give him the pleasure.

Gabriel climbed into the backseat of the cab with Jericho and Elise. Russell and Gonzales took the front, while Micah and Silas sat in the open truck bed on bales of hay. Gabriel's fingers twitched. He longed for a weapon. As long as Jericho was around, he wasn't likely to get his hands on one.

The first hour passed uneventfully. The truck bounced along an overgrown access road with weeds as high as Gabriel's knees. Twice, they stopped and moved fallen branches.

They passed a few abandoned cars, but the truck maneuvered around them easily. The group lowered their masks and ate granola bars in silence before pulling them up over their mouths and noses again.

A few deer bounded across the road, chased by a sleek, distinctly feline shadow. "Was that—?" Gabriel gaped, peering at the spot where the creature vanished in the underbrush.

"If you were about to say a panther, you would be correct." Russell snapped his gum. "The one upside of the apocalypse: the greatest hunting of your life."

Gabriel wouldn't want to stumble across an enormous cat like that alone in the woods. "Are they all modded?"

Russell shrugged. "Most."

Fifteen minutes later, they turned onto a paved road. The vehicle carcasses were more numerous here. Gonzales drove off the shoulder several times to avoid hitting them. He slammed his brakes and Gabriel jolted against his seat belt.

"Dog pack." Gonzales laid on the horn. Six dogs—most of them strays, one that looked like a collie, another a shaggy mutt but wearing a blue collar—slunk sullenly across the road. The collie paused in front of the truck and glared up at them, its ears laid flat, blood-foamed jowls twisted in a snarl.

Gonzales slammed the horn again. The dog moved unhurriedly, pausing on the shoulder to watch as they edged past. The hairs on Gabriel's neck prickled. The same disquieting unease he felt in the warehouse rustled beneath his skin. "They have no fear."

Micah poked his head through the opened back window. "How long before the virus kills them?"

"It doesn't," Russell said. "They're some kind of reservoir host. The virus don't kill 'em; it only makes them mean. And deadly. We thought at first it was the starvation making 'em aggressive. But it's something more. It's like rabies—the disease wants to spread itself, so it does somethin' to the dogs' brains, makes 'em want to bite. Don't know what, but it ain't pretty."

Gabriel repressed a shudder. Yet another manifestation of a world gone mad. He turned his gaze back to the road.

Soon they were passing stores and restaurants, all vacant, most with smashed windows. He thought of the infected dogs in the warehouse turning on their own. This is what Declan Black and his corrupt government minions had wrought. They'd turned on their own, too. The destruction of billions, of entire countries, the age-old story of a power grab gone terribly awry.

So much devastation, suffering, and death. The New Patriots tried to stop all this. The methods of their leaders were brutally violent, but the cause Gabriel believed in would've fought this with a righteous fury.

Were there any New Patriot factions left? Were they still fighting? Was there a government left to fight?

From where Gabriel stood, there didn't seem to be much of anything left to fight for.

Russell checked the GPS on his SmartFlex and made another left. A car moved far down the road ahead of them. It likely carried an ill passenger as desperate as they were to find a treatment, to reach salvation.

"There." Gabriel pointed as they crested a hill. In the distance, the FEMA regional medical facility rose above the horizon. It was an enormous white tent surrounded by a small city's worth of smaller tents.

Gonzales pulled the truck behind an abandoned SUV parked half-off the road and handed Jericho, Elise, and Gabriel a pair of binoculars. "Take a look before we get too close."

Gabriel stepped out of the truck and held the binoculars to his eyes. From their vantage point, he could see several armed military trucks beyond a checkpoint zooming with dozens of drones and copbots, along with several soldiers dressed in hazmat suits overlaid with combat gear. Beyond the guards, a blue crackling plasma fence offered an additional line of defense.

That didn't make sense. This was a medical center, not a government facility or military base. Why so much security?

Three vehicles waited to enter the checkpoint. A man and a child of six or seven stood before the first vehicle. Even from a distance, he could see the girl was ill. She leaned limply against her father, her head down. A couple of soldiers spoke to them, swiping details into a holotablet.

Gabriel lowered the binoculars. "Something isn't right."

Jericho frowned in agreement.

"He's right," Micah said from the truck bed. "Why does it look like they're trying to keep people out?"

"They aren't." The realization struck him like a punch to the gut. "They're keeping people in."

Elise shook her head. "That doesn't make sense. Why would the government—?"

"You should know better than anyone what a government is capable of," Gabriel snapped before he could help himself.

Elise's face paled. She looked at him, her eyes beseeching, silently begging him. Silas gave him a baleful glare.

He'd kept their dirty little secret. But not for that woman or her son's sake. And not for Declan Black, a traitor to his own country, his own people. For Amelia. For the terrible things he'd done to her that he could never take back.

He gave the slightest nod before turning away, his jaw clenched. He felt no pity for Elise. She was Declan Black's wife, the epitome of the corrupt elite. Still, she was suffering. She was Amelia's mother. For that, he would not make things worse for her.

"We didn't care much for the thought of our loved ones sick and dyin', locked up inside that place without even a hand to hold," Russell said. "After they wouldn't let Miss Harmony back in to see her grandson, we knew it wasn't the place for us. Thought you should decide for yourselves before the choice gets taken from you."

A shout echoed from the checkpoint. Gabriel raised the binoculars. One of the soldiers scanned the wrists of the man and girl. The second soldier stared at some sort of handheld scanner.

The first soldier gestured for the man to back up. The second soldier tugged the girl's arm, leading her past the checkpoint. She swayed, almost collapsing, and cried out. The man reached for her, but the soldier blocked him.

The man yelled again, trying to get to the girl. The second soldier hurried her toward the enormous white tents of the FEMA regional medical center.

Sensing the elevated distress signals in the man's voice and actions, four drones zoomed over, activating their pulse lasers and blaring a warning he couldn't make out. The man stumbled back and fell to his knees, lifting his arms as if begging.

A great invisible hand seized Gabriel's chest and squeezed. Rage filled him. How dare they separate a parent from their child? How could they be so heartless? What *was* this place? If he had a weapon, or even better, a tank, he'd storm in and shoot every soldier within sight. "That's why they have heightened security."

"Can't we do anything?" Micah said.

Gabriel recognized the pain in his voice. Where Gabriel felt fury at this injustice, he knew his brother's soft heart was bleeding like a wound. He resisted the urge to go to him like he would when they were kids. That time was long past. Now thoughts of his love for Micah brought only piercing pain—and a tidal wave of guilt.

Gabriel shook his head. "We can't do a damn thing. Not unless you have a suicide wish," he said between gritted teeth. Which, ironically, he did.

"Let's go." Silas touched the holster at his side. Gabriel noticed a tremor in his fingers. Since they arrived, Silas had gone from sardonic and taunting to silent and sullen.

Gonzales tapped his unlit cigarette against his chin. "One of those drones could detect our body heat."

Jericho turned toward the truck. "We're out of their sensor range, but we should still bug out."

Elise seized his arm. "We can't leave. What about Amelia?"

"You saw the same thing we did." A part of him wanted to soften the blow, but there was no point. All these pampered elites needed to recognize the world for what it was—a cold, brutal place devoid of justice. There was nothing fair in this world. There hadn't been for a long, long time. "You want to leave her there? You might never see her again."

Her expression contorted. "What about the *treatment*?"

"Mother," Silas said sharply. "There's no way in hell we're leaving her here. You know that."

"But she'll die otherwise." Micah's bronze skin went ashen.

Gabriel cleared his throat. A thought niggled in the back of his brain, one that wouldn't go away. But he couldn't pinpoint exactly what it was. "There's something else about this place, something that's bothering me."

"It gives me the heebie jeebies," Russell said.

"More than that." Gabriel gazed down the road at the carcass of a red sports car. All the doors were opened. The seats were slashed, the stuffing spilled onto the floorboards. "If we're gonna even consider leaving one of our own here, we need to know exactly what this place is."

Elise turned her pleading gaze on Jericho. "Please."

Jericho cracked his knuckles. "All right. We'll do some recon. But no promises."

24

WILLOW

Willow blinked back the tears as she hugged her brother for the first time in nine days. It felt strange through the bulky personal protection suit she wore—like her whole body from head to toe was encased in a silicone glove—but she would take whatever she could get.

Benjie squeezed her back fiercely.

Her heart swelled. "Oof! Don't break my ribs. You're getting too strong for your own good." She pulled away so she could get a good look at his face.

"Sorry, Lo Lo." He gave her a goofy, lopsided grin that made her heart ache. His eyes were bright. His light brown skin wasn't discolored or burning with fever. He sat cross-legged on his bed, alert and wide-awake, his worn playing cards in his hands, his hair a tousled mess as usual. He seemed okay.

They were in a white tent set up inside a small room, with an airlock in front of the door and a HEPA air filtration system. The walls of the tent seemed to be breathing, distending and deflating as the stale air was sucked out and fresh air filtered inside.

Inside the tent, plastic covered the floor. There was the bed Benjie sat on, a sink with several biohazard bins beneath it, a small night-stand, and a single blue plastic chair.

"Have you eaten?" Willow asked Benjie. "Do you want me to bring you something? They have real butter here. Can you believe it?" Earlier in the morning, she actually helped to churn that butter with the little girl, Gracie, and Anna, the woman who ran the kitchen. She'd mucked out some stalls and fed the chickens, then spent the afternoon training by herself. Silas and Jericho were still scouting that FEMA place.

A pang of guilt stabbed through her at the thought of Silas. He'd been quieter ever since Amelia got sick, but even more hostile, if that was possible. He was an asshole, but he cared for his sister. Amelia was unconscious with a fever of one hundred and six in the next room, while Benjie was bright-eyed and healthy.

She pushed the thoughts away. She'd lost too much already. She refused to feel guilty because her brother wasn't sick yet. She'd trade anyone's life in a heartbeat for Benjie's.

Benjie pointed at the empty plate on the nightstand next to the bed. "Miss Harmony brought me eggs and cinnamon bread. I ate three whole pieces, and she said I could have more when she comes back!"

Willow raised her eyebrows. "Harmony visited you?"

"Yep." He thrust a handful of face-down cards at her. "Pick a card, any card. Mister Finn couldn't even figure it out, and he's super smart."

"Eh, he's marginally intelligent," she said, unable to stop smiling.

Benjie made a face at her. "I bet you five dollars you'll pick the ace."

"You don't even have five dollars."

He shrugged. "Finn will lend me some, I bet."

"Mister Finn," she corrected. Benjie talked about Finn like he was some sort of superhero, capable of conjuring anything out of thin air. She didn't mind. Finn was her friend. She hadn't spent a night away from him since their first day in quarantine. She didn't care whether he was a pacifist; she still felt safer—and happier—around him. That he and Benjie adored each other only warmed her heart more.

"Pick one, *Ate*," Benjie said, using the Filipino term for 'older sister'.

She picked a random card. Sure enough, it was the ace. A fierce, aching love filled her. "Look at you, magician-in-training."

She leaned in and pressed her forehead against his. It was awkward with her helmet, but she didn't care. She gazed into his sweet, beautiful eyes. "I love you, you know. Bunches and bunches." She repeated the phrase their mother used to say when she tucked them in and kissed their cheeks at bedtime.

"I love you, too, Lo Lo."

She tickled his ribs with her gloved hands. "You're lucky I can't take this helmet off and cover you with kisses."

"Eww!" he squealed, giggling.

After playing with him for as long as she could stand the stifling suit, she promised to check on him later and moved to the doorway, where the nurse, Mrs. Lee, waited for her.

Mrs. Lee wore the same PPE gear as Willow. She was a polite but efficient Chinese woman in her thirties, her black hair cut blunt to her chin, and she was short—even shorter than Willow.

"Before you leave, you need to go through the decon chamber," Mrs. Lee said briskly.

Willow nodded. She passed by it when she entered. She glanced at Mrs. Lee, almost afraid to ask. "It's been nine days . . ."

Mrs. Lee's expression softened. "Your brother remains symptom-free. He still shows no signs of infection, no persistent cough, no fever. We don't have advanced equipment here to monitor antibody and viral levels in the blood, but if he's still symptom-free by tomorrow morning —day ten—I think it's safe to release him from quarantine."

Willow could have hugged her, she was so happy. Hope filled her— a hope so huge she was almost afraid to let herself believe it. "That's— that's fantastic."

She heard a noise down the hallway behind a door on the left. Someone coughing violently. She glanced at Mrs. Lee, confused.

Amelia was in the room on Benjie's right. She assumed the third room was empty.

Before Mrs. Lee could say anything, the door to the room opened. Harmony shuffled out, her expression tense beneath her helmet's visor.

Before the door closed again, Willow glimpsed a skinny teenage boy with a shock of red hair and freckles sprinkled across a pale, drawn face. Nadira sat beside him in a protective suit, mopping his forehead with a damp cloth. His body trembled, drenched in sweat, tendons standing out on his neck and arms, handfuls of sheet clutched in his fists.

"Who is that?" Her stomach tightened.

Harmony sighed heavily. "My fifteen-year-old nephew, Carson. He was exposed several days ago when a stray dog bit him on a scouting mission. We followed emergency procedures and quarantined him immediately. We were hopeful the dog wasn't infected . . . but yesterday, Carson started showing symptoms."

Willow crossed her arms, hugging herself against the chill running down her spine. She thought about the dog with the scar that attacked her in the warehouse. She'd be infected along with Amelia and this boy Carson if not for that wolf appearing out of nowhere.

"I lost my daughter, Gracie's mother, a month ago," Harmony said. "Carson's parents refused to come here when this whole thing started. By the time they believed it was real—it was too late."

Willow didn't know what to say. Harmony's story was tragic, just like her own. She shuffled her feet and cleared her throat. "I'm sorry."

Harmony leaned against the wall and stared down at the gloved fingers of her suit, examining them as if she were imagining the manicure with the bright orange polish underneath. When she spoke again, her voice took on a raw edge. "Sometimes it feels like you're barely holding on. What is there to live for, if not family?"

"I don't know."

"Keep your loved ones close, Willow. I'm praying Benjie is safe."

Her eyes lit up for a moment, her gaze sharp. "He's a very special boy. So bright and full of life."

Willow forced a smile she suddenly didn't feel. Something shifted in the room; she felt colder than she had a moment ago. "I think so, too."

Harmony left after Willow promised to help Gracie gather the eggs and feed the chickens before dinner. "There's always more work to be done," she said with another sigh.

Willow turned back to Mrs. Lee. She thought about Rihanna again, how glassy her eyes were the last time she'd seen her. How Amelia hardly coughed before collapsing yesterday after their escape from the warehouse, her body burning with heat. And the boy in the room next to Amelia, shaking and sweating. "What happens after the fever?"

"At the clinic in town where I worked, we followed the reports from the World Health Organization's Global Public Health Information Network." Mrs. Lee spoke as if she were reciting from a holotablet at a doctor's office. "There's a seventy-two-hour incubation period. On day four, mild coughing and sneezing sets in, not enough to feel sick, just enough to efficiently spread the contagion.

"As the disease advances through its latter stages, onset is acute with high fever, breathing difficulties, chronic coughing, and hemorrhaging from days ten through eleven or twelve. Bleeding occurs mainly from the mouth and eyes, but also the ears and other orifices. Respiratory failure and death come between days ten and fourteen.

"Some patients experience an adrenaline surge during the bleeding phase—they claim to feel better and try to escape confinement. It's the virus's last-ditch effort to spread itself."

Willow remembered how Rihanna claimed it'd just been a stupid cold, then just the flu. She'd resisted medical treatment. She didn't think she needed it. She didn't want to waste her mom's precious money. "It spread so fast because it mimicked other illnesses."

"Correct." Mrs. Lee's mouth contorted. "The bioterrorists were maliciously clever. The bat influenza was already an epidemic, with millions of people complaining of colds, fevers, fatigue, and headaches. The engineered virus mimicked the same symptoms. Normally the key to containment is contact tracing—find patient zero, make a tree of everyone they had contact with and everyone those other people had contact with. In this situation, the CDC couldn't do that. There were too many patient zeroes."

She paused, swallowing hard. "Every day, the infected thought they only had a cold, so they continued to go out. They still touched their noses and mouths four times an hour, touching other surfaces at least three times an hour, on average. They flew on airplanes, went shopping, picked up their kids from school. By the time the first infected were sick enough to seek medical attention on day eight and nine, it was already too late."

Willow shivered as they walked toward the decontamination chamber. "How many people died here?"

"Some. More than we'd like. Not as much as other communities."

"And—what about everywhere else?"

"It wasn't until two weeks in that the government and health agencies started to realize the staggering death toll. The virus is highly contagious with an extremely high mortality rate. By that point, hundreds of millions were infected and still spreading the virus like wildfire.

"Millions of people dropped like flies, more than the health agencies could even keep track of. They enacted the curfews and the travel bans, cordoned off cities and tried to separate the sick, but it was too late. On day eighteen, over one billion people died."

She smiled grimly. "That's the day the world as we knew it stopped working. No segment of the population was spared—doctors, government workers, soldiers, the poor and elite alike, military bases, government centers, exclusive gated communities, it didn't matter. Day twenty was the last day of vlogger broadcasts and newsfeed updates. They announced half the world's population was dead."

Willow felt cold all the way to the marrow of her bones. "Half the world's population is dead?"

Mrs. Lee cocked her head, studying her. "No, dear. That was day twenty, as I said. This is day fifty-five."

Willow's brain filled with sludge. It couldn't seem to figure out the pieces of the puzzle. It felt like working out the worst math problem ever invented. She swallowed. "What—what does that mean?"

"Before the net went out, an epidemiologist from the CDC gave an interview on the newsfeeds. According to their projection models, within the next thirty to sixty days, ninety-four to ninety-six percent of the population would be wiped out. The holoscreen went dark less than five minutes later. It never came back on."

Willow stared at her, uncomprehending.

"Two to three percent are likely immune," Mrs. Lee continued. "But many of them have died or soon will due to the abrupt lack of health care—think of people with diabetes, cancer, pacemakers—plus accidents and other secondary diseases caused by millions of decomposing carcasses polluting water supplies.

"Another two to three percent are not immune but have protected themselves through isolation and early precautionary procedures. Several small towns were able to effectively seal themselves off and expel outsiders and anyone showing symptoms. Out of four hundred million Americans, less than ten million are still alive. How the rest of the world has fared, no one seems to know."

She couldn't handle any more information, not right now. It was too much.

She thanked Mrs. Lee and moved through the decon chamber in a daze. Inside a sealed chamber with pressurized air, she stripped her suit and placed it into a container marked 'ultrasonic cleaner and sterilizer'. She dropped the gloves and paper booties into a biohazard bin, then stepped inside a tall aluminum box and turned on the disinfectant foam shower.

She sealed the door behind her, then stood naked and shivering in front of the heat blowers in the clean room. After she dressed in black utility pants and a loose pine-green T-shirt, she stepped into the sunlight, blinking.

All around her, people were caring for animals, preparing meals from scratch, or tending to hydroponic farms. It was like she'd stepped back a hundred and fifty years or more, but for the clothing and the occasional hovercart whooshing between buildings.

The sun still shone. The sky dared to be blue. A squirrel chattered at her from a nearby tree, whose leaves burned a dazzling orange and crimson. Nature would continue on without them, she thought dimly. The earth didn't care about any of them—not her *lola*, not her aunts and uncles, not Rihanna or any of her school friends.

How many of them were dead because they were poor? The terrorists unleashed the virus in the poorest communities. Their hospitals and medical centers were the first to be overwhelmed, the first to be guarded by soldiers refusing the sick at gunpoint.

When people sought help for their sick mothers and grandparents and children in neighboring counties, the very checkpoints touted to save lives became the snares that doomed them. Entire neighborhoods were quarantined, trapping people in infected zones and virtually guaranteeing their fate.

She couldn't begin to imagine the horror.

She moved without knowing her destination, her heart a ball of fire in her chest.

25

MICAH

Micah and the others abandoned the truck behind a thick copse of trees further down the road and headed into the small town surrounding the FEMA center. Everyone carried guns, even Gabriel.

They followed Jericho as silently as they could as he jogged between houses, crossing overgrown lawns and clambering over fences, keeping the rising spire of the largest tent always in sight as they circled to the rear of the facility.

They crouched as they ran across the parking lot of a dated apartment complex about six stories high, the paint a faded, peeling dark brown. There was a strange stench in the air, like something singed or burning. They hugged the wall and crept to the end of the last row of buildings.

"Damn it," Jericho said.

Past a low fence that bordered the apartment property was a huge open field, and beyond that, the plasma fence perimeter. There was far less security on this side.

Still, two drones patrolled the fence line with a single human soldier standing at a lookout station built into the top of the fencing.

They couldn't reach the guard or disarm the drones without crossing the field. They would be too exposed.

"What do we do now?" Micah whispered.

Russell spat out his gum. "Nothing to do."

"We'll try the far side," Silas said.

Elise shook her head. "That's the same. A huge open field all around that plasma fence. There's no getting close."

"We could crawl through the grass," Micah offered.

"Maybe at night." Jericho frowned. "There's still no way to get inside the fence. The only entrance I've seen is the one crawling with soldiers."

Micah stared at the fence. A humming noise came from inside, followed by a loud beeping. He could make out huge, lumbering shadows behind the crackling blue plasma. Some sort of electric machines.

What were they doing? What was happening in there? The hairs stood on the back of his neck. If only they could—

The apartments. He spun around, shielding his eyes as he gazed up at the aging complex. "We climb."

"What are you mumbling on about?" Silas said.

"We can't get inside or see through the fence. But maybe we can see over it."

Jericho shoved his goggles over his eyes. He raised the rifle. "This could be dangerous. Stay behind me, be quiet, and for the sake of all that is holy, stay on your toes, people."

Micah fixed his glasses, checked his gloves, and adjusted his mask, making sure it fit tight over his face. Adrenaline flooded his veins. He breathed deeply and whispered a silent prayer as they made their way around to the front of the building.

The door was locked, but the glass top half was busted out. Jericho reached inside and unlocked it. The door swung open.

They stepped inside, their feet crunching on broken glass. The fetid stench struck them like a solid wall. It was overwhelming—like rancid meat, rotten eggs, and raw sewage, the foul reek of decay and death.

Micah flung his hands over his face mask, as if that would help.

Three bloated, putrid bodies lay decomposing in the small foyer. One splayed on the floor directly in front of them. Two others leaned against the stairs, arms flaccid, heads lolling, like grotesque dolls.

Jericho lifted his fist, then gestured them silently toward the stairs. Acid burned the back of Micah's throat. He could taste the rotting stench in his mouth. He choked back the nausea writhing in his gut.

He needed to keep it together. This was for Amelia. He could do this. He forced his gorge back down as he stepped gingerly over the bodies and the puddles of their assorted bodily fluids.

They climbed up the first flight of stairs, still covering their mouths and noses. The only sound was his own breath against his mask, the rapid thud of his heartbeat, and the distant hum of whatever machines were at work inside the FEMA perimeter.

They climbed the second flight. A soft dripping noise plop, plop, plopped from somewhere. Rust-colored handprints stained the railing.

Sweat slipped down the back of Micah's neck. There'd been so much life here only a few weeks ago. Families, children, people longing for a better life. Now this place was a tomb. His fingers tightened on his rifle.

On the landing of the third floor, Jericho paused, lifting a closed fist. The group froze behind him. Micah strained his ears. He heard a faint, mechanized whine from above them.

Jericho lowered his mask to whisper, "Drone."

Micah's pulse raced. He looked up the stairwell and saw nothing but more metal grate stairs, the landing, and a glimpse of an empty, shadowy hall to the right.

Jericho crouched, gesturing for the others to do the same. "It's an older model. The newer ones are dead silent. They'll kill you before you know they're there."

"Where is it?" Micah asked.

"Fourth floor." Jericho cocked his head. "Sounds like it's further down the hall, inside one of the apartments."

"What do we do?" Elise's face turned bone-white, but her voice remained steady.

"As soon as we're on the same floor, the drone will be able to read our heat signatures."

"Too bad we don't have your drone," Micah said. "It could save our asses again."

Jericho's lips twitched into a grim smile. "Alas, the Navy confiscated it."

"So, we shoot the drone or knock it out the window." Russell hefted the spiked bat he brought. "Easy peasy."

"These militarized drones are all connected to a centralized cloud, a hive mind," Jericho said. "The second we attack it, it will send a signal to alert the other drones and send the soldiers our exact GPS location and thermal image screen shots."

"But the net is out." Micah bit the inside of his cheeks. He couldn't bear to just crouch here, letting every worst-case possibility loom large in his head. They needed to move.

"A government facility like this will have a local system online, I guarantee it." Jericho grimaced. "If I had an electromagnetic pulse shredder, I could deactivate it from here."

The mechanized whine grew louder.

"We're screwed, then," Silas muttered.

"The sensors are usually at waist and chest level," Gabriel said. "We can crawl."

Micah shot him a glance. "Usually?"

"He's right." Jericho jerked his finger to his lips. He spun and crept up the stairs like some deadly spider.

Micah helped Elise and then followed behind Gabriel and Silas, holding his breath, his gloved hands touching the stair treads stained and infected with who-knows-what. He prayed his gloves wouldn't rip, willed his roiling stomach not to turn on him, not now.

They crawled up the stairs to the fourth-floor landing, rounded the corner and kept going, silent and terrified. They didn't stand until they reached the sixth and last floor.

The walls were grungy, trash scattered across the dingy carpet. Darkness bathed the long, narrow hallway, the only light streaming from an opened door midway down the hall.

They moved swiftly to the open door. Jericho and Silas slipped inside, guns up, quickly clearing each room before gesturing for Micah and the others to follow.

The apartment stank but not of death. The owner hadn't died here, or at least, not recently. The singed smell was stronger, like something burnt. The group crowded around a sliding glass door that led to a tiny balcony.

Micah peered through his binoculars. He was right. They were high enough to partially see over the plasma fencing. And what he saw made his blood turn to ice.

Behind the white tents but within the perimeter of the fence was a wide expanse of field—or rather, what used to be a field. Dozens of mounds of dirt were pushed up all over; other sections were flattened down with pressed dirt.

Three automated digger machines dug a fresh pit. A second huge pit was already finished. Two more machines were stacking in long, floppy shapes wrapped in some kind of plastic.

Bodies filled the pit. Human bodies. Micah staggered, a sickening dizziness washing over him.

Jericho gripped his shoulder. "Keep it together."

"Those are mass graves," Elise said.

"They're burning them first, then burying them." Silas pointed to a third pit along the west side, where another digger dumped a load of dirt. Micah made out piles of ash and glinting shards of bone.

He shook his head, his brain refusing to compute what his eyes had already told him. Surely, he was wrong. This had to be some kind of mistake. The government was corrupt. Everyone knew that. But this? "No."

"These aren't treatment facilities." Gabriel's eyes burned with fury.

"They're waste disposal centers," Silas said.

"We thought they were up to no good," Gonzales stammered, "with them refusing to let anyone in or out. But this—I never imagined..."

"It's brilliant, really," Silas said woodenly. "Promise treatment to get the sick to come to you. They're going to die anyway. This way, you're able to properly dispose of hundreds of thousands—millions—of bodies that would otherwise be decomposing everywhere, making the job of clean-up and reconstruction that much easier."

Beside Micah, Elise let out a moan deep in her throat. She stared down at the pits. She didn't move, didn't speak.

Jericho touched her shoulder. "We found what we came for. It's time to go."

Micah tore his gaze from the bodies. He felt a bone-deep weariness all the way down to his toes. He was sickened, revolted, and gripped with a desperate need to be anywhere but here.

He followed Jericho numbly, unaware of putting one foot in front of the other. How could they do such a thing? Promising treatment—promising hope—to sick and desperate people, only to trap them in a death camp. It sickened him. It enraged him.

Jericho halted on the landing to the third floor, raising his fist. The whine of the drone was close. Too close. Red laser beams crisscrossed the hallway, the drone's sensors seeking heat, searching for a target.

A bullet pinged the wall above Micah, raining crumbs of drywall down on his head.

Jericho whirled and shot the drone. It screeched and careened into the wall. Silas added two more shots before the thing finally clattered to the carpeted floor. The metal disc shuddered, and the lights spinning over its metallic surface stilled.

Gabriel pushed Micah. "Go, go, go!"

They raced down the stairs, their feet pounding the metal grating. Micah leapt over the dead bodies in the foyer and burst out the front door into the blinding sunlight. The two perimeter patrol drones were zooming closer. Gun ports descended from their reflective bellies with a whirring sound, barrels swiveling toward them.

They bolted across the parking lot. A rain of bullets busted up the pavement inches from Micah's feet. Pain jolted him as a chunk of asphalt struck his shin.

He looked for Elise to see if she needed help. She ran even with him, maybe even a little ahead, her expression steady and focused.

Silas took aim as he ran and took out the closest drone as it hovered eight feet in the air, recharging for another spray of bullets. It sputtered and fell to the ground with a metallic clanking sound.

They reached the last apartment building before the tree line. If they could reach the woods, they'd have a chance. Micah whirled, squeezed off a shot and missed.

A bullet whizzed past his head. He twisted, craning his neck, and glimpsed the soldier behind him, creeping in the tall grass between the buildings.

His glasses slid down his nose but there wasn't time to fix them. He grabbed Elise's arm and jerked her around the front corner as another bullet struck the wall and disintegrated a hunk of cement.

"You okay?" he asked.

She nodded, breathing hard.

"I'll cover you!" Jericho ducked behind an SUV, shot out the windows in a rain of glass, and pumped a hail of bullets at the soldier. The soldier flattened himself in the grass, taking cover. "Go, Elise! Now!"

Micah checked to make sure Elise was with him and ran into the trees, his heart slamming against his ribs, his side aching. He tripped over a root, branches slapping his face, and stumbled.

Elise leaned down, seized his arm, and yanked him up.

Russell and Gabriel sprinted past them. They dodged, weaving between tree trunks. No more shots followed them.

Still, they didn't stop running until they reached the truck a mile and a half later.

Gonzales leaned against the trunk of a towering oak tree, gasping. "They don't seem too interested in pursuing intruders."

Gabriel reloaded his magazine and slapped the stock. He scanned the forest behind them. "We'd be dead if they did. We're lucky as hell."

"What about Amelia?" Elise wrung her hands in front of her chest. Her dark curls were pulled back in a tight bun. A few loose tendrils clung to her sharp cheekbones. She was a woman used to keeping it together, but the possibility of losing her daughter threatened to undo her.

Micah wished he could offer her some comfort. He understood the pain she must be feeling. He knew better than anyone what it felt like to love someone you couldn't save. He shoved his glasses up the bridge of his nose with his thumb. "Amelia's a fighter, Mrs. Black. She's beaten worse things."

Elise gave him a tremulous smile. "Thank you."

Gonzales glanced at Micah, his brows knit, his mouth working, but he didn't say anything. Russell spat on the ground and stared vacantly at the trees. Silas sharpened his hunting knife against a rock, his expression stony.

Jericho jogged back through the trees, unharmed, his brown skin gleaming, the front of his shirt damp with sweat. He slapped the side of the truck. "Let's roll."

Micah climbed into the back of the truck with Silas. He didn't stop shaking for hours. He prayed silently under his breath for Amelia, for all the dying people trapped in those white tent prisons. He would have nightmares for the rest of his life from the terrible images seared into his mind.

They hadn't found what they'd hoped for, but at least they'd escaped. At least they were alive. More and more, survival was its own accomplishment.

26

WILLOW

Willow peered through the sights and aimed at the center target she'd scrawled on the paper tacked to the hay bale. She widened her stance the way Silas taught her, her fingers curled around the gun's grip, her second hand clamped over the butt to steady her aim.

She breathed deeply, narrowing her focus until the red circle in the center filled her vision. She channeled all her worry and tension into executing the perfect shot. She squeezed the trigger.

The shot went wide, punching into the white right corner of the paper. "Damn it!" She resisted the urge to hurl the gun itself at the target.

"At least you hit the hay bale," said a voice behind her. The girl who fed the chickens, Harmony's granddaughter, Gracie, leaned against the fence. She had dark hair bound in braids and golden-brown skin. She was a serious, solemn little girl, not sweet and goofy like Benjie. Still, Willow liked her.

She holstered her gun with a sigh. "Maybe someday I'll hit the target."

"You will." Gracie tugged on her overalls. "Gran says I don't need to know about guns other than to stay away from 'em."

Willow cocked her eyebrows. "That's good advice. What are you, ten?"

Gracie nodded. "I know how to milk a cow."

"That's a pretty awesome skill to have these days. Maybe you can teach Benjie after dinner."

Benjie had been cleared from quarantine that morning. Willow had knelt and wrapped him in her arms, pressing her forehead against his for long, glorious minutes, relishing his warmth, his sweet smile, his little-boy smell, the way his beautiful dark hair stuck up all over his head.

He'd wriggled out of her grasp, giggling. Several dozen hugs and more than a few tears later, Willow finally let him out of her sight.

Now, Benjie and Finn lounged on a blanket on the grass outside the cafeteria while they practiced some new sleight of hand method. Even Harmony took a break to sit with them. Benjie proudly showed her every magic trick he knew.

But Amelia was still sick. So was Harmony's great-nephew. She felt a twinge of guilt at her own joy when others were still suffering. But Benjie was alive. She refused to feel guilt over that. "I'm sorry about Carson."

The girl bit her lower lip. "I didn't see him much. He lived in Raleigh until a few weeks ago. He's nice, though. He finds me Twizzlers on his scouting trips."

Willow pushed her hair behind her ears. "I'm sorry. I heard one of the dogs got to him."

"Yeah. They're all mean, now. I'm supposed to whistle if I see one." She pointed to a red whistle hanging from a string around her neck.

"That's a smart idea. You ever see a wolf around here?"

"There's a wildlife preserve ten miles that way." Gracie pointed west. "Gran says a few crazy people let them all out. But they're mostly modded, so they aren't dangerous."

Mostly, Willow thought wryly. "Thanks for your help."

Gracie gave her a shy smile. "I'm glad you're staying."

"It's not for long." Willow was glad, too. Benjie was safe now, but

Amelia wasn't. And this little farm with goats and chickens, real food, and soft mattresses seemed like an oasis after the last several weeks—heck, after the last several years. She was happy—thrilled, elated—that Benjie was okay, but after Mrs. Lee had revealed the staggering casualties of the Hydra Virus, it was hard to feel anything but a numb, horrified shock.

When the group had returned from their recon trip late yesterday afternoon, they met in the cafeteria with their people and several of Sweet Creek's leaders, including Harmony, Gonzales, and Russell.

The room fell deathly silent after the news about the FEMA center. FEMA's promise of treatment was too good not to believe, at least a little. Every single person in the room had allowed themselves to hope. Now there was no possibility of a treatment. Not for Amelia, not for any of them.

Willow's mouth had gone dry, her eyes gritty as Elise wept and Silas stared unblinking at the wall. They were the rich and powerful elites, and yet they were all in the same place now, desperate and grieving for loved ones they could do nothing to protect.

Harmony and her people rose respectfully. "We'll give you some time," she said quietly before she left the cafeteria. "You are welcome to stay here as long as you need."

For a long moment, no one spoke. Micah slumped with his head in his hands. Finn's face went ashen. Nadira's lips moved in a silent prayer. Celeste's eyes were wide and glassy as she picked despondently at her nails. Gabriel looked furious, a tic jumping in his cheek, his fists about to punch through the table.

Willow couldn't sit. She stood against the wall, her arms wrapped around her ribs to keep herself from shaking.

"We should leave," Jericho said. "It's not safe."

Elise's hand fluttered to the hollow of her throat. "No. They're taking care of Amelia."

"It's not going to matter. She's going to—"

"You think I don't know?" Elise's expression filled with tension, her lips pressed into a thin line. "Give her a chance to rest in peace. That is all I ask."

Jericho's mouth hardened. "Elise—"

Horne pushed back from the table and smoothed his blonde hair. He'd found pomade from somewhere and styled it into tousled spikes. "While I appreciate the sentiment, we've got to get ourselves to a safe zone. A real one."

Gabriel scowled. "For once, I agree with this asshole. We don't know these people. They have no security, no defenses."

"What he said." Horne's teeth gleamed. "We all care deeply for your daughter, Elise, but it's not like they can even cure her here. She has a better chance at a military base or civilian safe zone with a hospital."

"She'll die before we get there," Willow said.

Gabriel's hard gaze settled on her. "It isn't safe here."

"Nowhere is safe!" Willow said, her anger rising. They could leave today and get ambushed on the road by those Headhunters or some other gang tomorrow. Here, at least, they could feel somewhat normal. They could eat their fill every meal and have time to practice and train. Every night they stayed here, they grew stronger. "What does a few days matter?"

"Willow is right," Micah said. "We can't drag Amelia or Benjie on the road with us. And we're not leaving Amelia. This place is safe. These people are good people. We need to stay here until . . ." He let his words trail off, unable to say it aloud.

Elise seized Jericho's hand. "I'm begging you."

Jericho looked at Elise for a long moment, his gaze drifting down to their entwined hands. His expression didn't change. He didn't pull his hand away, either. "Fine. We will stay . . . as long as we need to. But no longer."

Elise let out her breath. Willow did the same.

"This is the right thing," Micah had said. "We need this."

The thing Willow had needed more than anything was Benjie. And she'd gotten him back.

A cool breeze blew her bangs into her eyes. She shoved them behind her ears and turned to Gracie. "Thank you for everything you've done for us. We really do appreciate it."

"You're welcome. It's good to have another kid here." Gracie grinned, her nose wrinkling—just like Zia used to do.

Fresh pain speared Willow's heart. Before she could stop herself, tears sprang into her eyes. "I'm sorry, Gracie. I'm—I have to go." She spun away from the hay bales and Gracie's confused expression and walked hurriedly down the gravel path toward the greenhouses and the woods beyond.

She sucked in a breath, blinking rapidly. She needed to keep it together. She felt like the seams of her soul were stretching, threatening to burst. Her mom was gone. She'd lost Zia. She'd give anything to bring her back, to right her wrong.

But she couldn't. Zia would forever be dead, and it would forever be Willow's fault. If she ever lost Benjie, too . . . she couldn't think like that. She'd fall apart with no way to put herself back together again.

But Benjie was safe. He was okay. She would keep him that way.

She pulled her jacket tighter around herself and turned sharply, heading back toward the residence halls. She would find Silas or Jericho and get them to train her harder. She wouldn't stop until she could hit the bull's eye, bring down an assailant, and fling a blade at a target and strike its beating heart.

This was a tough world, so she just had to be tougher. If it took a warrior to protect Benjie, then she'd become one.

27

AMELIA

Amelia's brain was on fire. Her body throbbed with heat. Fever dreams gripped her, jerking her beneath the surface of liquid fire.

She was drowning, drowning, drowning in the nightmare that always came for her, owning her, destroying her again and again. In her white-hot delirium, she couldn't distinguish between dream and reality.

She was trapped in that awful place, Kane leering over her with his stinking tobacco-breath, his meaty fingers clawing at the straps of her dress, those vicious snake eyes that wanted to hurt her, that relished hurting her.

She tossed and turned, crying out, but the dream wouldn't release her. Kane rose above the bed, his fingers closing around her neck, his image stretching, leering, a grotesque shadow shrieking her name.

The shadows of Gabriel and Declan Black writhed beside him, their eyes demon-red, boring into her. Their teeth gleaming like flames, cackling in maniacal laughter. They were hurting her, killing her, agony streaking through her head, cracking her skull open, splitting her into pieces—

"Amelia!"

She woke with a gasp. The demon still leered over her, filling her vision—

"Amelia!" Hands seized her shoulders and shook her. "Wake up. It's me!"

She shut her bleary eyes and forced them open again. Her mother leaned over her. Her mother, not Kane, not some nightmare demon. Her mother wore a bulky personal protection suit. A full respirator mask covered her head, a square of glass revealing her anxious face.

"Amelia." Her voice sounded tinny through the mask. "It was a nightmare. You're awake now."

She smiled weakly, the terror draining from her veins. It was a dream. Just a dream. But this—the unbearable heat, the disease plowing through her body, liquefying her from the inside out—this was horrifically real.

Her mother pulled up a chair and sat hunched next to the bed, Amelia's limp hand clutched between her gloved ones. "How is the pain?"

Everything hurt. Everything burned. Her eyes felt like they were being pierced with needles. A war raged inside her body, a war she appeared to be losing. She drifted in and out of consciousness, carried on a river of molten lava. "How long have I been here?" she croaked.

"Three days."

Her mother could have said weeks or months, and Amelia would have believed it. Pain had a way of stretching time. Each ticking second was agony.

Her mother pursed her lips. "I've wanted to talk to you for a long time, sweetheart . . . I thought if I gave you your space, you'd come around. I thought you needed time."

Amelia turned toward the wall and coughed. "I guess we've run out of time."

"Don't say that," her mother said fiercely. "Please."

"Okay."

"You don't have to talk. Will you listen to me?"

"Doesn't look like I have much of a choice, does it?" She was being difficult, like Silas. Even in her delirium, she recognized that. It made her feel guilty.

Her mother shook her head. "I know you're angry with me. You have every right to be. But there are things I didn't get to tell you before. I'm going to tell you now. I want to tell you how I met your fa—Declan."

"I know." She'd heard the story a hundred times: how they just happened to meet at the hotel where he'd presented his findings on an experiment with epilepsy patients, how fate brought them together, Declan Black whisking her mother off her feet, how he'd saved them both.

"You don't." Her mother wiped a cool cloth across her forehead and checked the IV fluids dripping into Amelia's right arm. "I came from a poor family. My parents died young when the cholera epidemic hit twenty-five years ago. My grandma claimed she couldn't afford to raise me, but she just didn't want the burden of a child. I bounced around the foster system until one day, I decided to run. The streets are a vicious, dangerous place for a girl, especially if you have something men want—like beauty."

She paused, biting her lower lip. "But I found a way. I'm not proud of some of the things I did, but I survived."

Amelia could do nothing but stare at her mother, stunned. For a moment, the burning fever seemed to fade for a moment. She never imagined her graceful, intelligent, beautiful mother as anything but a noble, aristocratic elite, a queen of society. She'd never said a word differently.

"Then one day, I realized I was pregnant," her mother continued. "I was twenty. I had no family, no one to call my own. I was all alone in a harsh world—until I felt you growing inside me."

She paused again, her face contorting. "It would have been easier to end things, but I knew. I knew you belonged with me. But I couldn't keep sleeping in tent cities and scavenging for my next meal. When I was four months pregnant, I fled New York City. I went back to my grandmother and begged her to take me in. Because I was pregnant, she agreed. She wasn't a good woman, Amelia. She was selfish and didn't know the first thing about love. But I felt I had no choice. You were more important."

Amelia half-wondered if she was still delirious and this was some bizarre dream. She forced her arm to move—it was so heavy, so exhausting to tell her brain to make her muscles stretch and contract —and reached inside her shirt for her charm bracelet. The platinum metal was warm from her own smoldering skin.

She pushed the point of the violin into the tip of her finger, keeping her focused, keeping her present. If this was real, she wanted to drink up every word. Her mother was finally speaking the truth.

"You transformed my life." Her hand fluttered to the hollow of her throat. "I never knew love like the love I had for you."

"Mom—" She started, but she didn't know what else to say. Black spots flickered in front of her eyes.

Her mother brushed a damp tendril of hair back from her face. "I need you to hear this, Amelia. I know I was wrong not to tell you before. So please, let me tell you now."

Amelia fell silent. She nodded.

"You were six weeks old when you had your first seizure. I rushed you to the hospital and they diagnosed you with a mutation of Dravet's Syndrome, the deadliest form of epilepsy. I was devastated. I couldn't lose the one good, perfect thing in my life. I couldn't believe there wasn't a cure, not in this day and age. I started reading science journals, scouring the net for anything remotely related to researching epilepsy.

"That's when I stumbled on an article Declan wrote about his research, studying the effects of utilizing nanoparticles on medications crossing the blood-brain barrier in epilepsy patients. I found a conference where he was presenting. I stole my grandmother's savings and spent it on the finest dress and haircut I could afford. I went to that hotel and waited for him."

Her hand lifted to the hollow of her throat. "I told him about you to pique his interest, and then I did what I had to do to make him fall in love with me."

Amelia's eyes widened. "You—seduced him?"

"Use whatever words you prefer. I did whatever I needed to do to save you."

"So . . ." Amelia tried to get her sluggish brain to work, to fit the facts together like puzzle pieces. But they still didn't fit. She dug the tip of the violin against her fingertip. "You never loved him."

"Love for him never factored into my decision," her mother said, an edge of iron in her voice. "He saved you with the medication he created. I convinced him to use it on you, even though the FDA wouldn't approve it. I *knew* it would work. And it did."

"He terrorized all of us!" She thought of Declan's hard, unflinching gaze, his lip curled in contempt, wielding his words as a weapon as she cowered before him, weak and terrified. That same familiar fear she'd suffered her entire life knifed through her. She shuddered.

Her mother squeezed her hand. Her gloved fingers were cold and rubbery. "I had to make a choice, Amelia. Stay with a hard, brutal man and have my precious daughter alive and well, or flee and cut out my own beating heart. You needed that medication, and I could only get it from Declan. You'd be severely mentally impaired or brain-dead without it."

Or dead, Amelia thought blearily. "You could have stockpiled the medication, stolen the formula—"

"Declan Black is many things, but he isn't stupid. He kept the formula and the medication in a highly secured location. He doled it out month by month, only three auto-injectors at a time. It was all I could do to get the extra bottle to keep in my purse." She leaned over the bed and wiped a strand of hair from Amelia's sweating face.

Darkness swirled at the corners of her mind. It was too much to take in, too fast. Her foundation shifted beneath her, things she believed her whole life suddenly disintegrating to nothing but dust between her fingers. "Mom—"

"It was the hardest decision of my life to stay with a man like

Declan Black, to watch helplessly as he hurt me and my children over and over, day after day. Little by little, year after year, the abuse wore me down, too, until I didn't even recognize myself. I—I nearly lost myself. But I *endured*. Do you understand? I endured."

All this time, Amelia blamed her mother for the pain she'd suffered. She believed her mother was a coward, too weak to defend herself, let alone her children. Amelia's own fear had blinded her from seeing clearly. Even with the fever roaring through her, she could see clearly now. Amelia tried to speak, but her throat was thick with emotion.

"You once asked me how I could stay with a monster. I hope you can understand now. Everything I've ever done, I did for you."

Use what you have, her mother told her once. It helped Amelia survive Kane. It helped her mother survive a cruel marriage. Her mother had only herself—and she'd willingly sacrificed herself to keep Amelia alive. Tears squeezed between her eyelids.

Her mother wiped them away. She leaned in close, her hands on either side of Amelia's face. "But I'm not sorry," she whispered. "I will never, not for one second, be sorry."

"I'm the one—that's sorry," she whispered.

Her mother shook her head. "No. Don't be sorry, darling. Be strong."

28

MICAH

Micah took the night shift at Amelia's bedside. The tent walls billowed silently around them like a cocoon. The PPE suit he wore was hot, bulky, and uncomfortable. But Amelia's suffering was worse. It was the least he could do to make sure she was never alone.

This was their sixth evening at Sweet Creek Farm, the eleventh day since the infected man coughed blood in Amelia's face. He couldn't believe how little time had passed. Every day seemed like a month.

It was the beginning of November, only two months since the *Grand Voyager*'s departure from the Manhattan terminal that fateful day in September. Only sixty days for the world to be irrevocably shattered.

Amelia groaned, trapped in another restless dream. Her face was chalk-white, sweat filming her forehead. Tendrils of damp hair stuck to her neck and cheeks. She stank of sickness, the fever-heat emanating off her in waves.

She twisted, moaning and flailing, almost yanking out her IV. "No, no, no!" she whimpered, her eyes rolling frantically beneath her lids.

"Amelia!" Micah squeezed her hand, steadying her arm to protect the IV.

She woke with a gasp. Her eyes were red and wild when they

focused on him. She jerked her hand out of his grasp. "Don't touch me!"

He pulled his hands back, lifting them in a gesture of surrender. "It's okay. You're okay. You're safe."

She was trembling like a bird. Micah longed to wrap her in his arms. He started, shoving the thought out of his mind. He couldn't think those things. Amelia wasn't his, and she never would be. He knew that, accepted it. Still, he cared for her, more than he wanted to admit.

He'd felt something when he first heard her play the violin in the Oasis dining room, her bow sweeping over the strings, her fingers coaxing out each sweet, vibrant note as the haunting song thrummed through his bones, filling him with awe. When he looked at her, he saw beauty, not just in her face, but in her soul.

Gabriel would tease him for that, he thought ruefully, before remembering afresh that he'd never get to share such feelings with his brother again.

Sweat rolled down the sides of Amelia's pale, stricken face. She sucked in a ragged breath and shook her head. "I'm sorry."

"Was it him?" he asked softly.

She didn't answer. She didn't need to.

He knew who haunted her. "He can't hurt you anymore. He's dead, remember?"

She closed her eyes. "Not in my head. Not in my dreams."

Micah's gut twisted. Kane was still inside her like a poison. Anger rose in him, so white-hot it was nearly hatred—for Kane, who was dead and beyond vengeance; for Gabriel, for turning her over to that monster; and for himself, for trusting Gabriel with her safety in the first place. His belief in his brother had almost gotten her killed.

"You're safe now." The absolute irony of those words did not escape him. She was the furthest from safe she could possibly be.

She didn't answer, only stared up at the tent ceiling, panting, her eyes glassy. She squeezed something in her right hand. Someone—

probably Elise—had taken the charm bracelet from the leather thong around her neck and given it to her to hold.

"Do you want water? More pain meds?"

"No, thank you."

He watched her face carefully. "Everyone sends you their love. Even Horne and Celeste."

"Ha," she said. "I doubt it."

"Finn wanted to come in, but you know . . ."

The corner of her mouth twitched. "He couldn't fit inside the suit."

"Exactly."

"Silas." It wasn't a question. He could tell by the tension in her expression that she hadn't expected him to come, but it hurt her anyway.

Micah scrambled for something, anything, to say to take that pain away. "Silas, ah, had a project he was finishing—he said he's planning to come—"

"You're a terrible liar, Micah."

He shifted uncomfortably, biting back another flash of anger. Silas had disappeared after the FEMA fiasco. Micah hardly saw him for meals, and even then, he sulked alone at a table in the corner. He didn't doubt that Silas was suffering, grieving in his own way. But Silas couldn't abandon Amelia just because he couldn't deal with it. She needed him. "I'm sorry. But he should be here."

She gave a resigned sigh. She knew her brother better than anyone, after all. "Tell him I'm not angry, okay? He'll need to hear that."

He wanted to argue with her, but how could he? "I'll tell him. I promise."

"Tell me something beautiful," she said after a moment.

"What do you mean?"

"You've got all those books filling your head. Books I always wanted to read, but it was my music that filled me." Her fingers clutched the violin charm. "But I can't hear it now. It's like the notes are fading. So give me something else."

"Okay," he said, thinking. "You are braver than you believe, stronger than you seem, and smarter than you think. But the most important thing is . . ." He hesitated on the last line, but said it anyway. "Even if we're apart . . . I'll always be with you."

She gave him a tiny smile. "That's brilliant. What literary giant said that?"

"It's from *Winnie the Pooh*."

She snorted, then managed a strangled laugh. "Why am I not surprised?"

He resisted the urge to grab her hand. "You can talk to me, you know." He wanted to do something to let her know he was there for her. But she wouldn't let him, even now, even as sick as she was. Even as she was dying. As much as it hurt him, he had to accept that. "I'm your friend. You can trust me."

She remained silent for a long moment. "Do you still believe in forgiveness?"

"Yes," he said slowly, considering. Once upon a time, he would've said yes immediately. Not anymore. "Though it depends on the context, the person, and their motivation."

"Leave it to you to complicate everything," she mumbled.

Micah forced a smile. "I try."

"Well, you give great deathbed advice."

His eyes burned. "Amelia, don't—"

She waved her hand weakly. "It was a joke. A pretty lame one, I guess."

"Seriously lame."

"I was never very good at funny . . ."

"I'm pretty sure that's not a requirement of friendship."

Her gaze met his, her brow wrinkled in pain. Her eyes were so bloodshot they were almost crimson. "What about Gabriel?"

He flinched. "I don't know. It's different. With him, there are . . . extenuating circumstances."

"I think he's the definition of extenuating circumstances." She turned her head and coughed into a white hand towel.

"Are you okay?"

She ignored his question. "Will you ever forgive him?"

"I . . ." His heart twisted. His thoughts and feelings about his brother were too dark, tangled, and confusing. *Just us. Always.* He didn't want to think about that now. "I don't know."

She coughed again, a deep, wet, rattling sound that raised the hairs on the back of Micah's neck. When she drew the towel back from her lips, it was splattered with blood.

"Amelia—"

"I don't want to talk about it." She folded the towel and laid it on her chest. If she saw the blood, she ignored it. "I think I'd do a lot of things differently . . . if I had the chance."

"Me, too."

"But not everything . . ." She closed her eyes, exhaustion lining her face. She rubbed her charm bracelet. "I wish I could play the violin again. I want to hear it—" she placed her hand over her heart, "—here."

"I know." It wasn't fair. None of this was fair. He watched a single bloody tear track down her cheek. The hemorrhaging had started. The beginning of the end.

Helplessness washed over him. He wished he could promise her something—that he could protect her, could take away the pain. Everything he wanted to say would sound stupid or ridiculous. So much was meaningless in the face of true suffering. "I'm gonna sit here, okay? I'm not going anywhere. I won't leave."

Time passed. He couldn't keep track of the minutes ticking away, marking the last hours of Amelia's life. The thought made his heart constrict. She was too young. Too talented and brave and beautiful.

It was a long time before he saw her wrinkled brow relax, the tension in her face finally melting to unconsciousness.

After a while, Elise came in and sat next to him. Even through her protective helmet, he could see her pain and exhaustion. "You're a good boy," she said quietly.

He didn't know what to say to that that didn't involve tearful blubbering, so he said nothing. He stared at the white walls until his vision blurred, praying for Amelia long into the night.

It seemed like his prayers bounced off the tent ceiling and fell back into his lap, just as useless as he felt. But there was nothing else he could do, so he prayed anyway.

———

Micah woke to shouting. He leapt to his feet, adrenaline flushing through his veins. For a frantic moment, he didn't know where or when he was.

His glasses half-fell off his face, and he tilted his head back to slide them into place. He glimpsed white fabric walls, the plastic-covered floor, and Amelia, silent and motionless in her bed.

The nurse leaned over the bed, trying to roll her onto her side. Elise stood on her other side, yanking the auto-injector from Amelia's pouch on the bedside table. Amelia was unnaturally stiff, her face blue-tinged and masklike, eyes closed, her tongue lolling out of her mouth.

"How do I help?" Micah cried.

Elise grabbed the auto-injector and plunged it into Amelia's neck. Amelia's body went rigid.

"What do you think you're doing?" the nurse asked in shock.

"Stopping her seizure," Elise snapped.

"You can't stop a tonic-clonic seizure!"

"This can." Elise placed the used injector into a medical waste disposal container and dropped it into the biohazard bin next to the sink. "If we caught it fast enough."

Micah stared at Amelia's taut body in horror. She looked stretched, her tendons standing out, her muscles straining. "What can I do?"

"We wait." Elise gripped his arm.

After a dozen agonizing seconds, Amelia gasped, writhed for a moment, then collapsed, her eyes rolling into the back of her head.

Elise placed her on her side, tilted her chin up, and checked her airway. "She's unconscious but breathing."

Micah pressed his fingers to her wrist to be sure. Her pulse thudded weak but present. Her skin burned hotter than he thought possible in a human being.

The nurse stared at Elise suspiciously. "How did you do that? What did you give her?"

"It doesn't matter now," Elise said, exhausted. "That was the last one."

"Won't she need more?" Micah asked.

Elise wiped the faint streaks of blood smearing the corners of Amelia's eyes. She gazed at him with a wearied, haunted expression. "Only if she lives."

29

WILLOW

Willow caught a glimpse of movement at the tree line, a flash of red. She scrubbed her face with the back of her arm and looked again.

Silas stepped over the trip wire and slipped away between the trees. It wasn't the first time he disappeared for no reason. Where the heck was he going? What was he up to?

They trained that morning and afternoon, but Silas was unfocused and cruel. The second time he'd nailed her in the ribs with a 'practice' kick hard enough to knock her breath from her lungs, Jericho stepped in and rebuked him.

Silas only curled his lip. "Why would I waste my time with a gutter rat, anyway?" And he'd stalked off.

For once, she didn't blame him. He was angry and hurting. This awful waiting around for someone to die put everyone on edge.

She headed toward the trees before she could think about what she was doing. As she passed the last greenhouse, she grabbed one of the spiked baseball bats the Sweet Creek people used to fend off infected wildlife. She might need it in the woods.

She followed him at a distance, keeping his red shirt in her sights as she stepped over tree roots and eased past unwieldy branches as thorns tugged at her pantlegs. The leaf canopy towering far above her wore fiery shades of yellow, burnt orange, and crimson. The shadows were thick and dense, the air cool on her cheeks. She pressed the nodule sewn into her sleeve, adjusting the settings of her auto-warm sweater.

Fifteen minutes later, he disappeared. She turned, searching the forest, the bat gripped in her sweaty hands. She listened to the sounds of birdsong and the soft creak of branches rubbing against each other in the breeze.

A twig snapped behind her. She spun, bat up, heart pounding. She half-expected to see a panther or some other exotic creature, or even the huge black wolf that saved her at the warehouse.

A deer stood ten yards away, sniffing the air, large ears swiveled toward her. It stared at her for a moment before bounding away through the trees.

Willow sighed.

She heard another sound, a series of dull thuds and cracks. She kept the bat up and crept toward the noise. She stumbled into a small clearing with a log cabin in the center. The noises were coming from inside—banging sounds, followed by muffled curses.

She circled the cabin until she reached the front, then crept hesitantly through the front door, which hung open on its hinges. Dust swirled in the light streaming through scummy windows, a fine layer silting the small kitchen's counter, the table, the sofa and the wooden coffee table.

No one had been here in a long time.

Something slammed against the other side of the living room wall. An old-fashioned painting of a bear in a mountain stream fell to the floor with a dull thud.

Maybe this wasn't such a good idea. If it wasn't Silas in there, she was in trouble. But she was committed now. Willow took a breath and entered the dark hallway. She leaned around the doorway of the first bedroom and peeked inside.

She glimpsed a bed with a patterned quilt shoved into a corner, a dusty dresser, and a faded blue rug. Silas faced the wall, repeatedly punching and kicking it with his bare, ungloved fists. The drywall was cracked in several places, white chunks crumbling to the hardwood floor at his feet.

His mask was yanked down around his neck, his expression fierce. He slammed his fist against one of the cracked spots with a growled curse. The drywall splintered. Blood streaked his knuckles and splattered the dull yellow wall.

"Silas!" She stared at him, stunned.

He leapt back, stumbling against the dresser as he ducked into a crouch, fists up, ready to fight. When he saw her, his mouth contorted, emotions crossing his face so rapidly she couldn't read any of them. He stood up and wiped his fists against his thighs.

"What the hell?" he snarled, a raw edge in his voice. "What are you doing here?"

She lowered the bat to rest against her leg. "I could ask the same of you."

"You stalking me? Is that it?"

She wanted to sneer back at him, but something about the situation, the glassy sheen of his eyes, the way his upper lip imperceptibly trembled, gave her pause. She stared at him for a long moment. "No."

He glowered back at her. "No one said you could follow me. You're trespassing."

She raised her brows. "Oh, do you own this cabin?"

"Go away."

She shrugged. "I don't feel like it. Why are you out here bashing walls?"

"Don't you ever get the hint? I don't want you here." He turned away, his mouth twisting— but not in contempt or derision. His eyes went glassy.

He was an asshole, but he was also a human with real feelings, no matter how he tried to mask them with sarcasm and cruelty. He might despise everyone else, but he loved his sister. Willow knew better than anyone how grief manifested itself in strange ways. Rage tangled so easily with sorrow.

"It's okay," she said. "It's okay to be sad about Amelia."

He whirled on her, teeth gritted. "Shut up! You don't know anything!" He shoved past her, knocking her against the door frame, and strode down the hall to the living room.

Willow followed him. He didn't want easy platitudes any more than she did. She thought of Zia, who she'd lost, who she'd failed to protect. She felt that impotent rage, that familiar wave of grief and shame she'd fought for seven eternal weeks.

She swung the bat as hard as she could. It struck the living room wall with a resounding crack. Drywall spidered, crumbled chunks dropping to the floor.

Silas spun and stared at her.

She held out the bat, handle first. "More satisfying, less painful."

His mouth twisted like he was about to spit out some biting, asinine comment. But he didn't. He reached out and took the bat. He turned to the wall and stared at the hole she made.

Silas swung, gouging his own hole.

"Again," Willow said.

He swung again and then again, slamming the bat against the wall, the spiked nails biting out deep chunks of drywall. A fine white dusk clung to the damp sheen of his arms and face.

He handed the bat back to her. Together, they destroyed the entire wall until it was nothing but jagged holes, exposed framing, and a tangle of wires. They didn't speak. They didn't need to.

With every satisfying crack, with every crater she created, with every reverberation from the impact trembling up her arms, with every bead of sweat that dripped into her eyes and every shriek torn from her throat, she felt the pain like a throbbing wound, opening wider and wider.

Memories assaulted her—Zia grabbing her hand, grinning mischievously.

Whack. Zia's snorting, shoulder-shaking donkey laugh.

Smash. Zia dancing and singing dorky karaoke songs at the top of her lungs.

Bang. Zia's crumpled face as Willow shouted, "I don't want you around!"

Crack. Zia staring, unseeing, her eyes blank and lifeless as a doll's.

And then her mother's voice, always haunting her. *They're your responsibility. Take care of them.*

She hadn't. Willow stumbled back, gasping, her eyes burning.

Silas seized the bat and took a vicious swing that tore out a three-foot chunk of drywall. His knuckles were still bleeding, the bat handle flecked with red. "If she dies—" He made a sound in the back of his throat, like the tortured whimper of an animal caught in a trap.

Willow stared at him. She saw her own grief and guilt drowning in his eyes. If she were Micah, she'd say something brave and pithy. If she were Finn, she'd make a joke to lighten things up. If she were Nadira or Benjie, she'd enfold him in a comforting hug. Even Amelia, coolly aloof, was still sensitive in her own way.

But she wasn't them. And she didn't know what to do. She had her own guilt, her own pain. She didn't know any way to survive it other than to claw her way through, one desperate handful at a time. Her nerves felt raw, exposed. She said the only thing she could think of. "I know."

He nodded.

That was enough.

They stood there in the center of the log cabin, filthy and drenched in sweat. She didn't know what it meant. She doubted this made them friends. She was pretty sure she still hated him. But as they made their way into the fading sunlight and headed back through the trees, they walked side by side.

30

AMELIA

Amelia opened her eyes. Her head hurt. Her body felt like it'd been pelted with rocks and then pushed through an incinerator. Everything felt heavy, sluggish, bruised.

She turned her head. Early morning sunlight shone through the window she could make out on the other side of the tent wall. In the dim shadows, her mother slumped in the chair in the corner, dressed in her protective suit, her head flung back against the wall. She was sleeping, her face lined with exhaustion.

Amelia pushed herself to a sitting position. Waves of dizziness crashed over her. She blinked against the white spots sparking across her vision. Pressure thudded against the back of her skull.

She felt dirty all over. Her skin was itchy and filmed with dried sweat. She touched her bare arms.

She wasn't hot to the touch. She felt weak and exhausted and aching all over, but fire no longer blazed through her. The fever was gone.

Wonder filled her, an emotion so extraordinary she wasn't even sure she recognized it. She was so close to death, she felt it tugging at her soul. But she wasn't dead. She was alive.

She considered waking her mother, but she wasn't ready to talk to anyone. Not yet. She glanced around the room, her gaze landing on the side table beside the bed. A pair of utility pants and a long-sleeved shirt were folded neatly, her SmartFlex charged and resting on top of the shirt. The clothes she wore at the warehouse were gone, likely burned.

Her mother had done that. A burst of warmth filled her chest. Even in the face of enormous odds, her mother refused to give up hope, ensuring everything was prepared for when her daughter awoke.

Amelia's pouch with the auto-injector lay open and empty beside the clothes. She shivered. She must have started seizing. She hadn't suffered a full tonic-clonic seizure, or she wouldn't be thinking coherent thoughts. But now she had no protection against the next one.

She couldn't allow herself to think about that. She was alive. That was what mattered now. Tomorrow's problems would come tomorrow. Today, she was alive.

Her fingers closed around the charm bracelet still in her hand. She spread her fingers and watched the diamonds glitter in the light. She wasn't who she used to be. She wasn't that scared, weak little girl. She wasn't her father's daughter, not anymore.

Her mother wasn't who Amelia had believed her to be, either. In a blink, she'd transformed. Amelia could, too.

She wasn't Gabriel's patsy, wasn't Kane's victim. She wasn't a rich princess who couldn't protect herself. She'd survived all that. She survived the Hydra Virus. If she could defeat a killer disease, she could defeat Kane's ghost. She could rise above Declan Black's sordid legacy. She didn't have to hang onto anything from the past she didn't want to.

Her belt lay coiled on the other side of her stack of clothes, the knife sheath still attached. She leaned over and slid out the blade. She held it in her hands for a long moment.

She could be someone else, someone new. Herself—only better, stronger, braver.

Before she could overthink it, she grabbed a hunk of her hair. She held the blade against the pale strands and sawed. She cut again and again and again, long tendrils drifting down until a heap of white-blonde coils rested in her lap.

She didn't stop until her choppy layers fell unevenly around her ears. She felt her scalp with her hands, the cool air kissing the back of her neck.

She didn't do it for her mother or to protect herself from all the evil, lecherous men out in the world. She did it only for herself.

Amelia let her mother sleep a while longer. Her mother would figure it out when she saw the pile of hair on the rumpled blankets. She dressed silently, holding the bed to maintain her balance on her weak, rubbery legs.

An uneaten granola bar and an apple lay on a tray at her mother's feet. She ate them hurriedly, letting the calories give her precious energy. She shuffled out of the room.

Nadira walked down the hallway, carrying a biohazard bin, which she almost dropped when she caught sight of Amelia, her eyes growing huge.

Amelia raised a finger to her lips. "My mother is sleeping."

"You're better! Praise Allah!" Nadira set the bin on the ground. "Everyone else is at breakfast. They'll be so happy!" She frowned. "You're weak. Let's get through the decon chamber. I'll help you."

A few minutes later, Nadira slung her arm through Amelia's and led her out of the building into the bright sunlight. Amelia blinked and shielded her eyes. She and Nadira made their way haltingly along the gravel path leading to the largest building.

Inside, the cavernous room buzzed with the hubbub of a hundred and fifty people eating and talking. Her stomach cramped as the smells of eggs, real butter, and pancakes filled her nostrils. Nadira helped her walk slowly among the rows of tables.

"Amelia!" Micah leapt to his feet a few tables away.

The din stilled. Everyone stared.

Finn's face broke into an enormous grin. "Get your skinny butt over here, girl, so we can suffocate you in a group bear hug."

It was Benjie who got to her first, barreling into her and nearly knocking them both to the floor. Nadira barely kept her on her feet.

Benjie wrapped his arms around her and squeezed as tight as he could. "I can't breathe," she said, unused to so much human touch. After a moment, she placed her arms around his small shoulders and gently hugged him back. It felt good. It felt right.

"I don't understand." Silas stood in front of her, his hands dangling uselessly at his sides. His typically sullen expression gave way to confusion. In his gray eyes, disbelief warred with something akin to joy, if her brother could feel such a thing.

He was beautiful. She loved every jagged edge and bristling part of him. She loved Benjie with his messy hair and huge, trusting eyes. She loved kind-hearted Micah and giant, goofy Finn and all of them, Willow and Nadira and Jericho—and in that moment, she didn't feel even an iota of pain or bitterness for Gabriel's startled, hard-edged face.

She smiled broadly. "I got better."

"That's impossible." A woman stood up from the head of the table where Jericho, Willow, Nadira, and the others were seated. She wore mud-splashed work boots, leggings and an elegant, lace-embroidered tunic.

She must be Harmony, the leader her mother had told her about. The woman's face was deeply weathered, her gray hair pulled into a braid down her back, her deep-set eyes staring warily at Amelia like she was some kind of ghost.

Amelia glanced around at the strangers all looking at her, their expressions a mix of awe, bewilderment, and even suspicion. An unsettling feeling niggled at her mind. This was a bizarre reaction, and not the one she expected.

"Haven't ya'll seen someone sick get well before?" Finn flashed one of his crooked smiles. Only a few people smiled back.

"No, we haven't," Harmony said.

Amelia froze. "What do you mean?"

The cafeteria went dead silent. Amelia felt the stares of a hundred and fifty pairs of eyes.

"How many survivors are here?" Silas's gaze narrowed as he shifted from Amelia to Harmony and back again.

"None," Harmony said.

The way the woman looked at her sent a cold chill slicing through her spine. She gripped Nadira's arm for balance. The room began to spin, her legs going weak. "None from this compound?"

"No. No one else. The Hydra Virus shows no mercy. Everyone dies in the end. Everyone." Harmony stared at her, a strange, wild look in her eyes. "You're the first survivor."

31

GABRIEL

Gabriel hadn't taken his eyes off Amelia since she'd entered the cafeteria like some miraculous angel, only with purple bruises beneath her eyes and her glorious hair chopped into a short, jagged fringe.

She lifted her chin, skinny as a wraith from the sickness, but still the strong, determined girl Gabriel knew from the bowels of the *Grand Voyager*. She was still the girl who'd gotten the drop on him, then handed him the knife she'd held to his throat seconds before, offering him her trust, a second chance, everything. And he'd thrown it all away.

His joy and relief swiftly gave way to harsh reality. She still wanted nothing to do with him. Her gaze flickered to him once, then danced away, landing on Benjie instead, who'd leapt from the table and rushed into her arms with a jubilant shout. It'd felt like a savage punch to his gut.

Gabriel clenched his jaw. How dare he wish for anything else? Yet he did. Every fiber of his being longed to tug her jagged hair back from her face and kiss her long and hard. She was alive, and for that he was grateful.

He deserved nothing but spite and contempt from her, he knew that. He deserved death by a thousand cuts for the betrayals he committed, the part he played in the deaths of innocents. But he still couldn't stop his dark and traitorous heart from loving what he could never have.

"We need to leave immediately," Jericho said, jerking Gabriel back to the present. "It's more crucial than ever that we get to Fort Benning. They'll have medical facilities."

"They'll use the antibodies in her blood to develop a vaccine, or hell, even a cure." Horne raked his hand through his hair, grinning broadly. "I always knew that girl was special."

"Wait." Harmony held up a hand. She gestured at Gonzales, who bent next to her as she whispered something in his ear. He nodded and walked swiftly out of the cafeteria. "Of course, you must go. But please, stay one more night. Get a few more warm meals in your bellies. Take today to gather the supplies you'll need for the journey. At dinner, I'll have Gonzales show you the best route to take. A hundred miles of lawlessness lies between you and Fort Benning. You need to be prepared."

"That's my vote," Micah said.

Gabriel had no vote. He said nothing, though leaving immediately seemed the wisest choice by far. He watched the scene warily, taking everything in.

"Besides," Harmony said with a wink at Benjie, "Benjie can help me and Gracie milk the cows and gather the eggs."

Benjie nodded eagerly. "Can we, Mister Jericho? Please, Lo Lo?"

"I could definitely use another spaghetti dinner," Willow said.

"Me, too." Finn gave another one of his enormous burps. "I'll never turn down an offer of more food."

Harmony ruffled Benjie's unruly hair with a grandmotherly affection. Benjie giggled, his eyes bright. This place was good for the kid. He looked happy, the way a kid should.

"What do you say, Jericho?" Harmony asked, her voice unusually high. She looked more haggard than usual. The lines in her face were deep, and her eyes held a sadness that belied her chipper tone. She must be burning candles at both ends, caring for her dying nephew even as she ran the compound.

"We'll stay one more night," Jericho said grudgingly. He didn't look pleased about it. "We leave at dawn."

"Thank you for your hospitality and generosity." Micah adjusted his glasses and grinned, dimples appearing in his cheeks. "You're very kind."

Harmony glanced down at her hands. She rubbed her polished nails beneath her gloves. "We all do what we must."

This all seemed so easy, too easy. He'd learned from hard experience that truly kind people were rare enough that they might as well not exist.

It seemed too good to be true. But no one else batted an eyelash, not even Jericho.

"We need to gather our supplies and repack everyone's packs." Jericho glanced at Harmony. "And we'd like to offer something for transportation and more ammo. We've got a couple of valuable SmartFlexes."

Harmony raised her gray eyebrows. "Not so valuable anymore."

"Gold and precious gems will always hold value," Gabriel said.

Harmony stood, pushing her chair back from the table. Her gaze flicked to Benjie, who held an ancient relic of a quarter, in the middle of showing Gracie how to hide it behind her ear. "True. Some things will always be valuable. Priceless, even . . ." she faltered.

"Do you feel all right?" Micah asked.

She swallowed and wiped a bead of sweat from her brow, even though the cafeteria wasn't warm. Her voice wavered. "I'm sorry. I'm upset about Carson lying sick in that room." She cleared her throat. "I'm fine, really. Why don't you guys head over to the kitchen? Anna and Gonzales will load you up with water, fresh bread, and cheese. I'll check with Russell about any nearby usable vehicles our scouts may know of."

Jericho nodded. "Gabriel and Micah, come with me. Silas, keep training Willow. The rest, pack your things and then help Sweet Creek with whatever they need. We leave tomorrow at dawn."

Gabriel followed Jericho down the gravel path toward the residence buildings. The sun hid behind a stack of gray clouds, a chill in the air. Brown leaves crunched beneath their boots. Winter was coming.

He rubbed his chafed wrists. As soon as they were out of sight of the compound tomorrow, Jericho would cuff him, and he'd be a prisoner again. Death was coming for him, but he was still determined to face it on his own terms. He refused to die at the hands of a cruel, corrupted government with more blood on its hands than any New Patriot.

He was guilty of his own heinous crimes, but not the ones they'd hang him for. Amelia was alive and well. His brother was safe. No one needed him anymore. He'd escape tonight at dinner, when Jericho was preoccupied with preparations.

All he needed was a gun, a bullet, and a head start.

———

"Here's the likeliest safest route." Harmony spread an old-fashioned paper map on the table. "It's faster to take Interstate 137, but far more dangerous. Skirt the highway by taking Edgewood Parkway past Buena Vista and Cusseta. From Maple Grove, you can cross over and only have a small stretch of highway between that point and the base. You'll hit some suburbs, but that's the best you'll get."

Gabriel gritted his teeth as he stared at the red line she'd drawn over the giant, multi-colored spider's web of roads across the paper. No wonder people only used GPS. Who could figure out anything from such a complicated mess?

"Russell found two older model trucks without bioscan verification, so they're hackable if you know what you're doing."

"I do." Simeon had taught him many skills. His chest tightened as a memory of his mentor flashed through his mind—Simeon's wide, stunned gaze as Gabriel pulled the trigger, the way his body fell, crumbling like his bones were water. Gabriel balled his hands into fists.

"Their batteries are dead." Russell chomped noisily on his gum. He slouched against the wall, his arms crossed over his skinny chest, his gaze darting around the room, never landing on anyone for more than a few seconds. "We can tow them here and charge them. A fresh charge should take you halfway, at least. After that, you're on your own."

"Thanks." Jericho placed Amelia's gold-plated, diamond-encrusted SmartFlex in the middle of the map. "Will this do in trade?"

Harmony raised her brows. "I'm impressed. Thank you. Why don't you grab Micah and Gabriel and help Russell tow those trucks? He'll need it."

Gabriel liked Gonzales well enough. He held his own on the mission to the FEMA camp. Russell, though, had sly, shifty eyes. He reminded Gabriel of a ferret, cunning and wily. There was something in the man's gaze he didn't like. But he'd be free of all of them by tonight. What did it matter? "I'll go."

"And me," Micah said.

Nadira came out of the kitchen carrying a small denim backpack. She wore a simple blue dress that matched her headscarf. A smudge of flour dusted her right cheek. She handed the pack to Gabriel. "I packed some lunches for you: goat cheese with barley bread and beets."

He took the pack and slung it over his shoulder. "Thanks."

She stepped closer, her gaze intense as she studied his face. He fought the urge to look away, that disquieting sensation that she could see straight to his black, twisted heart settling over him. "What do you want?"

She lowered her voice. "In Islam, those who do deeds of righteousness earn their redemption—combined with Allah's grace, of course."

He glanced across the table, but Jericho, Micah, and Harmony were still bent over the map, finalizing their plans. "I thought you didn't know if you believed."

She smiled. "I have found my faith again."

"What does that have to do with me?"

"I see the good things you are doing. You saved me and Benjie in the warehouse when you could have fled. You went to the FEMA center and discovered the truth. Now, you are volunteering to get the transportation we need."

"What's your point?"

"You're a better man than you think you are."

"I highly doubt it."

She touched his arm gently. "The Qur'an says that you can earn your salvation, Gabriel. This is how you do it."

His fingers tightened on the straps of the backpack. He resisted the urge to recoil, to snarl something ugly, to flee. "I don't think you understand," he said through gritted teeth.

She wiped at the smudge of flour with the back of her hand and smiled sweetly at him again. "I do. Like I said before, I'm praying for you."

He turned away from her. "You really shouldn't."

She didn't say anything further. After a moment, she walked quietly back to the kitchen. He pushed their unsettling conversation out of his mind. He didn't believe in Allah or God or salvation or any of it. Her words didn't matter. They were meaningless.

Tonight, it would all be over.

———

A few minutes later, they were ready to leave.

"Let's head out." Russell pushed himself off the wall. He shot Gabriel a hard, appraising glance, then looked away. "We'll be back by dinner."

As they headed for the garage, Gabriel fell into step beside Micah. "You should watch out for that one," he said quietly. "He's shifty."

"So are you," Micah retorted.

Gabriel raked his hand through his hair in frustration. "Something isn't right about all this, this place. They're just gonna hand over two working trucks? Precious commodities like that?"

"Why do you doubt everything and everyone?" Micah whirled on him. Wavy tendrils of black hair fell into his eyes.

"You have to be prepared for anything—"

Micah's eyes flashed. "Or maybe the dishonest always assume others are like them."

"I'm telling you, there's something off with that guy." He bit back his frustration. "Why aren't you listening to me?"

Micah shook his head. "Sometimes, good people are just that—good people."

"And sometimes they're not. I'm trying to help you."

"I don't need your help." Micah shoved his glasses up the bridge of his nose with his thumb. "You're the most dangerous person here, Gabriel. Don't you see that?"

Gabriel raised his hands placatingly. "Look, I get that things can never go back to how they were with us. I know what I did—" The little girl flashed again through his tortured mind, her lemon-drop bathrobe, that small, still face haloed by dark hair. "—And I know what I didn't do. I don't expect you to forgive me."

Micah hesitated, a shadow crossing his face. They both remembered how many times Gabriel had played off his brother's innate goodness to get what he wanted. But this time was different. There was no absolution for him. Micah couldn't give that to him even if he wanted to. He knew that now. "I want you to know that I'm sorry—for everything."

Micah didn't speak. He lowered his head and stuffed his hands into his pockets against the chill. He kicked a rock off the path and they both watched it skitter into the weeds. Ahead of them, Russell backed a tow truck out of the garage.

They wouldn't be alone for much longer, and Gabriel was running out of time. He knew it was a lost cause, knew it in his head but his heart was a different matter. The words tore from his throat. "Just us."

Micah looked at him. Gabriel saw the little boy he used to be, the round cheeks, the huge, trusting eyes. He waited for it. He could die with peace if he could only hear that word one more time. *Always.*

"I'm sorry," Micah said. "I can't."

His brother hurried up the path after Jericho and Russell, leaving Gabriel behind.

32

WILLOW

Willow wiped sweat from her brow and took a deep breath. She circled Silas in the center of the small clearing near the hay bales behind the compound. The muscles of her legs and arms ached. She couldn't remember being this tired or this sore. But she sure as hell wasn't going to admit it.

"Focus." Silas spun the wooden stick he was using in place of a knife.

She tightened her fingers around her own stick. "I am!"

Finn, Amelia, and her mother were working with Benjie and Gracie in the small garden in front of the cafeteria, pulling weeds and gathering turnips and other weird-sounding fall vegetables for dinner. Celeste was supposed to be working, too, but she'd believe it when she saw it. Willow would rather train to fight any day.

Nadira watched them spar for a while before wandering off to find a private spot to pray. Willow had met plenty of religious people in her life, but none seemed as genuine as Nadira and Micah. They believed different things, but they both tried to be good people. That had to count for something, especially in this world.

Jericho, Gabriel and Micah were still off collecting the trucks. After packing the slim contents of her backpack, she found Silas. They'd been at it for over two hours.

"Come on. We don't have all day." Silas lowered his stick and tapped it against his thigh.

She studied his body movements. He seemed wide open, his stance loose and slouching, his attention on taunting her rather than defending himself. She lifted her stick and lunged at him.

Silas spun and easily deflected her attack. She came at him again, swinging hard. In one swift move, he dodged beneath her outstretched arm, darted in close, and thrust his stick against her throat. "You're dead."

"Damn it!"

"With every strike, look for what your attacker is leaving vulnerable." He shoved the stick until it pricked her skin. "There's always something. Your enemy won't play fair. Neither should you."

She batted his stick away and rubbed the stinging scratch on her neck. She had scrapes and bruises all over her body. "You don't have to be such an asshat about everything."

A sly smirk played across his lips. "You're too soft, little girl. Wanna cry and give up?"

She blew her bangs out of her eyes and crouched back into her fighting stance. "I'm just getting started."

"Me too." He whacked her across the back of the knees, knocking her off her feet.

She landed hard on her tailbone, pain exploding through several body parts simultaneously. "Oww! You just broke my . . . everything."

He flashed her a wicked smile, his eyes glinting with amusement. "My apologies."

She sucked in a breath and glared up at him. Now that Amelia was well, Silas had returned to his arrogant, sardonic, infuriating self. He'd made no mention of their afternoon breaking walls in the cabin, and neither did she. Some things you didn't need to talk about. Besides, it was much easier to hate him.

She gritted her teeth, tasting blood. "Again."

An hour later, her stomach growled too loudly to ignore. She couldn't get enough of the real food they served here. It was terribly unfortunate how long it took to grow, harvest, and then prepare actual fruits, vegetables, and grains. She missed fast food, even if most of it was prefab crap.

"Ready to quit so soon?" Silas taunted.

"Not a chance." Though she felt more like curling into a ball and nursing her wounds than enduring another round with Silas the sadist. But she would never admit it. She wiped the sweat filming her forehead. "I need some fuel first."

But she never got the chance. The rumble of a dozen engines broke through the sounds of birds, trilling insects, and squawking chickens. Motorcycles. Willow whipped her head toward the noise. "Do you think it's them?"

Silas's face went hard. "Only one way to find out."

Only one thought shot through her mind. *Benjie.* "Come on!"

Silas slung his rifle over his shoulder and loped toward the front of the complex, heading for the cafeteria. Willow raced after him, her pulse thudding in her throat. Maybe they were driving past. Maybe it was another group. Maybe they were harmless. But the apprehension that gripped her warned otherwise.

They rounded the corner of the cafeteria and reached the garden as the first biker appeared, roaring up the long, winding driveway leading to the compound.

"Someone's coming!" she called breathlessly.

Harmony crouched next to Benjie, holding a half-full basket as he picked leaves of Swiss chard, kale, and collard greens. She straightened and shielded her eyes. Her lips pursed. "I hear them."

"Who is it? Are they dangerous? Do we need to run?"

"Settle down, dear," Harmony said calmly, though a line appeared between her gray eyebrows. "Let's not upset the children."

Gonzales rested on his hoe. "They're traders."

Amelia stood beside her mother, a handful of basil leaves in her fist. Nadira picked herbs next to them. Finn and Celeste lounged on a checkered blanket, playing an old-fashioned game of chess. A handful of Sweet Creek people were busy picking apples from several trees shading the small garden. And Horne sprawled on the steps of the cafeteria, eating an apple.

They all paused and watched the growing cloud of dust. A dozen bikers followed the first. Willow's veins flushed cold as she recognized the animal pelts flapping behind them. "They're Headhunters."

"You trade with *them*?" Celeste asked incredulously. "Have you met them? They threatened to kill us. Two of them shot a family dead on the highway—"

"Hush your mouth." Harmony smiled sharply, but the smile didn't reach her eyes. "I'm sorry, honey. But we've dealt with these people for years. They must be . . . handled correctly." She smoothed her long, flowery dress and straightened her shoulders. "It's best to go with the flow. Trust me on this."

Gonzales shot Harmony a look but said nothing. Several Sweet Creek people whose names Willow didn't know watched them from the other side of the garden, their expressions confused and wary.

Benjie whimpered. He clutched a handful of turnips in one hand. Harmony's face softened. "Come here, child. You too, Gracie." Both children went to her. She dropped the basket and put one arm around each of their shoulders.

Willow hated how vulnerable she felt. She and Silas were the only ones with weapons, and she hardly knew what she was doing. "Benjie, maybe you should come here."

"Everything will be fine," Harmony said smoothly. But an intense, almost frantic look flickered in her gaze, an anxiousness that raised the hairs on Willow's arms. Dark circles rimmed Harmony's eyes like bruises. She didn't like the way the woman's arm tightened possessively around her brother. She didn't like it at all.

Willow glanced at Silas. His eyes were narrowed in suspicion, his mouth flattened. "What the hell is going on?"

Horne stood up and cleared his throat. He raked his hand nervously through his hair. "We don't want any trouble, now."

"There won't be," Gonzales said as the Headhunters parked their bikes in the gravel drive twenty yards away. He glanced at Harmony again with a frown. "Right, Harmony?"

"The Headhunters protect us in exchange for resources," Harmony answered.

Willow's skin prickled. "What kind of resources?"

"What is this?" Anna said from beneath an apple tree. She glanced warily at the bikers. "This isn't the normal scheduled pick-up. Why are they here?"

But Harmony didn't answer either of them. A dozen Headhunters sauntered up the gravel drive, several without masks or gloves. They carried various weapons—rifles, knives, a few with pulse guns. They all wore those hideous pelts across their shoulders, their faces lean and hard, their eyes glinting dangerously.

The bottom dropped out of Willow's stomach.

"Well, well, well," said one, stopping only a few feet from Willow. He was tall, with a barrel of a chest and digital tattoos squirming across his meaty arms. He was handsome in a formidable way, with a strong, stubbled jaw, brown hair shorn close to his skull, and intelligent gray-blue eyes that seemed to take everything in with a single glance. He wore a striking white wolf pelt draped over his shoulders like a cape. The fur reached to his shiny black boots.

"What do you want?" Silas rested his hand on the stock of his rifle.

The leader clucked his tongue. "That's no way to make introductions. You must be one of the new ones. The fresh meat, so to speak."

A few of his men chuckled.

"You're early," Harmony said tensely. "I thought we agreed—"

The leader held up a hand, silencing her. "Introductions, first. This is Bones." He gestured at a burly man beside him with lanky ash-brown hair to his shoulders, a bristling beard, and a craggy, acne-scarred face. He held a pistol in his left hand and carried some kind of specialized cooler in his right.

"And this is Razor." He pointed to a gaunt man with a cadaverous face and dull, sunken eyes. He cradled a pulse gun in his arms, looking every inch a cold-blooded killer.

"As for me, you can call me Cerberus." He gripped a slasher—a plasma rod—in one hand, tapping it against his opposite palm. Slashers were military-grade weapons, highly illegal for citizens. One touch would melt the skin off your bones.

"The hound dog of Hades," Finn said.

Cerberus smiled wider. "Very good. This generation still reads. In case ya'll haven't figured it out by now, we're the big dogs around town now."

"And you're the alpha," Amelia said in flat voice.

Cerberus's eyes snapped to her. His gaze drifted over her body and lingered at her hair. His lip curled. "A quick study. Impressive."

"You've caught us a bit off guard," Gonzales said amiably, though his hands were curled into fists at his sides. "But we're happy to get you whatever you need."

"I'm sure you will," Bones sneered.

"Well, get it and be on your way already," Silas said.

Gonzales flashed him a warning glance, but Silas ignored it. Willow's pulse quickened. Without Jericho, Silas was attempting to step into his shoes and act as their leader. But he wasn't as strong or as intimidating as Jericho. Instead, he came off as a smart-mouthed punk.

"Watch where you're aimin', boy," growled a burly Headhunter wearing a Rottweiler pelt. "Put that thing down."

Silas didn't move.

"Too bad you aren't as quick as your girl here." Cerberus flicked his left hand, and Razor leveled his pulse gun at Celeste and Finn, who sat frozen on the blanket. "That wasn't a request."

"Hey now!" Horne raised his hands in a placating gesture, trying to look dignified. "There's no need for all that. Silas, be reasonable and put down your gun."

Silas shot him a contemptuous look, but he obeyed, holding out the rifle and lowering it to the grass.

Willow didn't breathe. Tension rippled in the air. She didn't take her eyes off Cerberus. He looked like the kind of guy who smiled cheerfully while wrenching out your teeth with pliers.

"Much better." Cerberus nodded at Razor, who lowered his pulse gun. "We're all civilized here, aren't we?"

"Maybe we can take this inside," Harmony said.

Cerberus ignored her. "We're here to offer our services. We're traders and service providers. Communities like Sweet Creek here exchange their resources in fair trade for services rendered. In this case, protection from thieves, marauders, and various unsavory criminals. Isn't that right, Harmony?

"Yes," she said, her voice tight. 'That's right."

Willow blinked. That explained why they didn't need fences, guards, and patrols. The Headhunters did the work for them, keeping the town clear of thieves and other undesirables. But in exchange for what?

"We take our resources and trade them with other like-minded communities. That's how things work now. And the best thing about it?" Cerberus paused for dramatic effect, his eyes gleaming. "No taxes."

Willow's group only stared at him. The Sweet Creek people said nothing. Anna crossed her arms over her chest and glanced nervously between Cerberus and Harmony. Several of the others quietly retreated, slipping away between the trees.

Cerberus moved past Willow, ignoring her as he strode into the garden, crushing herbs beneath his boots, his white-furred pelt sweeping behind him. He paused in front of Elise. "My, my. You truly are a lovely specimen, even for your age. We don't see many ladies of your caliber these days."

He pointed his slasher at Celeste. "Stand up, girl. What do you think we might get for you?" He moved to Nadira, who trembled, twisting the front of her blouse in her hands. He tugged on her headscarf until it loosened. Her black hair tumbled around her shoulders. "Or you?"

Willow stilled. Her mouth went dry. He spoke of Elise and Celeste and Nadira like *they* were the resources. It hit her like a sickening punch to the gut. The Headhunters traded in people. And Harmony and her group just sold them out. "You can't do that!"

"We can and we do." Cerberus's voice went cold. "There's no law to prevent us, not anymore. 'He who is unable to live in society must be either a beast or a god.' Aristotle said that, did you know? What are we, men? Beasts or gods?"

Several Headhunters howled. The eerie sound sent chills skating down Willow's spine.

"You hear that?" Cerberus pumped his fist, his eyes sparking. "We're both. And the only law any of you answer to now is to us."

"I'm sure we can work out a deal that satisfies both parties," Horne stammered, the whites in his eyes showing. "We have Smartflexes—"

Cerberus smiled warmly at him. "How thoughtful of you. But I'm afraid we've already come to a prearranged agreement."

Gonzales turned to Harmony, his mouth gaping. "You did this?"

Harmony ignored Gonzales. She held Gracie and Benjie tightly, her face ashen, her jaw set. Her eyes went shiny and hard. "Remember our deal for the boy."

Willow spun toward her. "What deal? What are you talking about?"

"I'll take good care of him, I promise." Harmony met her gaze furtively then quickly looked away.

Understanding fell swift and terrible. The woman not only sold them out to the Headhunters, but she planned to steal Benjie, too.

"You bitch!" Willow lunged for her.

A Headhunter swept in before she could take five steps. He swung his fist and caught her solidly across the mouth, knocking her on her ass. Her head spun, her ears ringing.

"Down, dog," he said with a cruel laugh.

"Now, Scorpio, let's not ruin the potential merchandise," Cerberus warned in a jovial tone.

She licked the blood from her stinging, split lip. The pain was nothing compared to the helpless rage sweeping through her. "You can't do this!"

"I'm sorry." Harmony grimaced as if in pain. "There is always a cost for safety."

"You aren't the one paying it!"

Harmony squeezed Gracie's shoulder. "I have to protect my family."

"Benjie!" Willow cried in desperation. "He's mine! He's *my* brother!"

But Harmony had already turned away, taking Benjie with her.

33

MICAH

The tow truck was halfway up the long gravel drive when Micah heard the first scream. He rode in the backseat of the cab next to Gabriel. Jericho drove with Russell in the passenger seat. The first truck—a fifteen-year-old scratched and dented Ford—was hitched to the back.

"What was that?" A chill crept through him.

Russell shrugged. "Probably a coyote or somethin'. Got a lot of 'em around here." But an uneasiness edged his voice. He rolled up the window.

Beside him, Gabriel stiffened. Keeping his hand low behind the seat so only Micah could see, he pointed up the road. They couldn't see the compound yet, but a dozen motorcycles were parked on the shoulder a few hundred yards ahead. Headhunters.

Micah's heart leapt into his throat. Amelia, Benjie, and all the others were unarmed and unprotected. Only Silas and Horne were there to defend them.

Gabriel gestured silently, pointing at the gun holstered at Micah's waist. He slanted his eyes toward the back of the seat in front of him. Micah knew what his brother wanted.

He stole a glance at Russell. The man slouched in the passenger seat, like before, but his shoulders were tensed. The pistol he'd held loosely in his lap was now surreptitiously angled at Jericho.

The realization lodged like a splinter in his gut. Gabriel was right. This was a setup. A trap. Why else would Russell take their best fighters with him on an errand he could've done himself? The vehicles were bait.

As soundlessly as he could, Micah slid out his gun and handed it to Gabriel. He didn't like it, but he saw little choice. He would have to trust his brother. Gabriel sat the closest to Russell and could lift the gun behind the seat, catching him by surprise.

Which he did, so swiftly that Micah barely registered his movement. Gabriel pressed the barrel against the back of Russell's head. "Don't move."

Jericho slammed the brakes without a word. He must've suspected something, because he didn't hesitate or ask a single question. He grabbed his rifle, jumped out of the truck, and circled to the passenger side. "Step out of the vehicle, nice and slow, both hands up. You've got two guns aimed at your head, so I wouldn't try anything tricky."

Russell cursed under his breath. "What the hell you doin', man?"

"Shut up and move." Gabriel prodded him with the gun.

Russell obeyed grudgingly.

Micah reached over the front console, took the man's pistol, and stepped down onto the weed-infested gravel road. He kept the gun pointed at the ground.

Gabriel had Russell on his knees, his hands raised, his gun aimed at the man's head. His body was taut, his muscles coiled, his face carved in stone. Micah barely recognized him. But he didn't know his brother, not anymore.

Gabriel jammed the barrel of the gun against his forehead, knocking Russell off balance. "What the hell are the Headhunters doing on your property?"

Russell's hands shook. "Man, chill out. How should I know? We do trades with them."

"What kind of trades?" Jericho leveled his rifle at Russell's chest.

Russell flinched. "Look, it's not what you think. They don't hurt nobody if you give 'em what they want."

"And what the hell do they want?" Gabriel took a step back and kicked the man in the stomach. Russell doubled over with a groan. His baseball cap fell to the gravel road with a soft thud.

Micah felt sick. He hated this. He hated every second of it. This wasn't who he was. It wasn't who Gabriel should've been. They were raised better than this. *Be good. Be brave.* His mother's last words echoed in his mind. "Gabriel, we don't need to do this."

Another scream drifted through the trees.

"Hell yes, we do." Gabriel clicked off the safety. "We're wasting time."

"The girl!" Russell grunted. "They want the girl who lived. They'll leave the rest of you alone, I swear."

Gabriel stilled.

"Gabriel—" Micah warned, afraid of what Gabriel intended to do. "You don't have to kill—!"

"Too late." Gabriel pulled the trigger. There was a soft popping sound. Russell dropped like a stone.

Micah's stomach roiled in horror. "You didn't need to do that—!"

"What were we supposed to do with him?" Gabriel glared at him, eyes blazing. "Let him warn the Headhunters that we're coming? Do you want to live through this? How about Amelia and the others?"

"We could've thought of a way!"

"He sold us out," Gabriel said. "He's not innocent."

"There's no time." Jericho lowered his rifle. "We need to regroup. We're outmanned and outgunned. They have our people. The tow is electric, so they likely didn't hear the engine. The only thing we've got going for us is the element of surprise."

Gabriel seized his shoulder. "Micah! We need you. Are you with us?"

Micah nodded numbly. He tore his gaze from the crumpled body. He couldn't focus on that now. He hated violence and death, but he wasn't naïve anymore. He'd seen firsthand what the Headhunters were capable of. His friends were in danger: Amelia. Willow. Benjie. Nadira. All of them. He saw the girl lying on the road in his mind's eye, shot for no reason. Sometimes good people had to do things they weren't proud of to protect the people they loved.

"I'm with you."

They hurried back into the tow truck, backed down the driveway, drove down a side street lined with maple trees exploding with fall color, and parked. Micah bit the inside of his cheek, every nerve on edge, his mind consumed with terrible possibilities. "What's the plan?"

"We're kicking ass and taking names, that's the plan." Gabriel was jumpy, on edge, still amped from what he'd done to Russell. His eyes blazed with that old familiar passion Micah knew so well. Gabriel was ready to fight, and he wasn't going to back down for anything.

"We risk our own people if we go in there with guns blazing," Jericho said grimly. "There's a dozen of them to three of us. Four if Silas still has his rifle, but I doubt it."

"You're right," Gabriel said. "We need to be smart. We will be smart."

"We need a distraction," Micah said. "A diversion. Like one of Benjie's sleight of hand magic tricks."

"Yes, but what?" Sweat beaded Jericho's brow. The tension in his jaw betrayed the anxiety below the surface. As cool and controlled as he always appeared, he was nervous now. He cared what happened to Elise, Amelia, and the others. "We're running out of time."

Micah had to think. Every second that passed wasted time, time when their friends could be hurt or worse. He gazed frantically out the windows, his gaze skipping from the road to the overgrown grass to the trees to the abandoned sedan in front of them, its tires blown out, to the empty gas station down the road.

He stared at the gas station, his pulse jumping. "The dogs."

"What about them?" Gabriel asked. "Spit it out."

Micah twisted in his seat to face the others. "We use the dog pack as a diversion. The warehouse is two miles by road but less than a quarter mile through the woods."

Jericho cracked his knuckles, frowning. "How are we gonna herd a pack of rabid dogs?"

Micah sighed as he adjusted his glasses. "I don't know."

"I do." Gabriel's eyes sparked. "With bait."

Dread and apprehension coiled in his stomach. It could easily backfire. The dogs were wild, rabid, infected. They couldn't be controlled. The dogs were as likely to bite one of their own people as a Headhunter. And Micah couldn't ask his own brother to act as bait, no matter what he'd done. The plan wouldn't work. "Don't be stupid."

"Stupid is all I've got left," Gabriel said.

Micah felt the seconds ticking by like a time bomb. The longer they waited, the smaller their window of opportunity. "It's a dangerous play."

Gabriel only grinned, his eyes lit with a dark, pulsing energy. "My favorite kind."

Abruptly, Jericho stiffened. He looked past Micah, at something out the passenger side window.

A great black wolf stood in the middle of the road.

Before Micah could react, Gabriel clambered over him and leapt out of the truck. "Wait!" He scrambled after his brother. "That's Willow's wolf!"

Gabriel lowered his gun. "What the hell—?"

A girl stood at the wolf's side. In his shock, Micah hadn't noticed her. She looked Japanese-American. Her sleek black hair fell to her chin. She stared at them with dark eyes shining with a crafty intelligence that matched her wolf's. She wore a camouflaged rain slicker, the hood pulled back, and a faded backpack with a hoverboard sticking out of the partially zipped top compartment.

She strode toward them without fear, even though they were all armed. The wolf sauntered behind her. He was huge, his yellow eyes watching Micah warily.

She spoke her first words as a fact, not a question: "You need help."

34

AMELIA

It would never end, Amelia thought dimly. She would never be safe. None of them would ever be safe. The rest of their lives would consist of fleeing from one life-threatening crisis to another. Her body hadn't yet recovered from the virus, and now here she was again, staring into the face of a killer.

Cerberus gazed down at her, a predatory grin spread across his face. "And what will we get for you?"

"Leave her alone," Silas snarled, reaching for the gun on the ground.

Razor raised his pulse gun and aimed it at Silas's head. "I wouldn't try that if I were you."

Silas backed off. Beside her, Nadira wept quietly. Willow slumped on the ground, blood dripping down her chin. Everyone else stood frozen in shock and fear.

"Take me instead." Her mother stepped in front of Amelia.

"No!" She'd just gotten her mother back. They finally understood each other. She couldn't bear to lose her now. "Mom, you can't—"

Cerberus laughed mirthlessly. "Never had a volunteer before. But why not? The more, the merrier."

"You can't take her!" Finn said.

"In case you haven't noticed, we can do whatever we want." Cerberus scanned the group. "But don't worry. We won't take all of you. Just a choice few. Your women are particularly enticing. This one —" he trailed his finger along Nadira's trembling jaw, "—will fit into the new order of things quite nicely, I think. You already know how to serve, don't you?"

"Let's be reasonable, here," Horne tried again.

Cerberus turned a gun on him. "No one suggested you should speak."

Horne's face went white, and whatever remnant of courage he'd summoned fled. He backed away, hands up in surrender. "I don't want any trouble."

Razor seized her arm. Amelia tried to twist away, but his grip was iron.

"Leave her be." Her mother's eyes blazed. "Don't you dare touch her!"

"It's good to see familial bonds are still alive and well," Cerberus said. "If you agree to come with us freely, no funny business, I promise we won't harm your daughter. How's that for diplomacy?"

"I'll do anything," her mother said.

Amelia's heart ached at the terror lacing her mother's voice. "Mom, don't do this—"

"Shut up!" Razor said, but he dropped her arm.

Cerberus gestured at Bones. "Load her up."

Two men seized her mother's arms and dragged her across the grass and gravel to the parked motorcycles. Amelia watched them, horrified. This wasn't happening. This wasn't real. They'd survived so much. It couldn't end like this.

Cerberus stepped in front of Amelia, blocking her view of her mother. "You're a lovely little thing, aren't you? Too skinny, but we could fatten you up. I could find a good home for this one, couldn't I, Razor? Oh, yes, we could teach you to be a proper woman."

His eyes were a gray-blue, the color of cold winter seas. Predator eyes. Like Kane's. The demon of her nightmares swelled inside her, a thing of fangs and claws and bone-crushing terror.

"You said you wouldn't hurt her!" Silas said hoarsely.

"Ah." Cerberus lifted one finger. "I said I wouldn't harm her, not that I wouldn't *take* her." He fingered a jagged chunk of her hair and frowned. "Who gave you this ghastly haircut?"

She felt it then, that seed of strength deep inside her. She knew fear. She knew pain. She'd known them her whole life. And she was stronger than both of them.

She blocked the nightmare from her mind, shoved it inside a box and buried it deep. This man couldn't take anything from her. Others tried before him and failed. She'd defeated Kane. She was a survivor. She was better, stronger, braver. "I did."

He cocked his head, puzzled, like he didn't understand the joke. He wouldn't. Men like him only understood power and control, rulers and victims. Amelia was neither. She spat in his face.

He reared back, his placid expression contorting for a fraction of a second before the mask slid back into place. "That was unwise."

She jutted her chin. "Go to hell."

"See? That's the problem with the women of the world. They just don't know their proper place. Luckily for you, that world is gone. We're creating a new, better society. And we can teach you a better way." He raised his arm as if to strike her. "Your first lesson begins now."

"Not that one," Harmony called out.

"This is the girl, then?" Instead of hitting her, he tilted Amelia's chin up with his thumb. Her skin crawled at his touch. He leaned so close she could see the pores in his skin, the cruel gleam in his eyes. "Well, that's a damn shame. We could've had some fun. Still, for you, the Sanctuary will be quite generous."

"Let me go."

"How fascinating." Cerberus trailed a finger down the side of her cheek. "The girl who lived."

She flinched, jerking her face away. "Don't touch me."

He smiled wide, revealing canines sharpened like fangs. "Load her up with her mother."

35

WILLOW

Willow's heart beat wildly in her chest. Panic pressed in, threatening to overwhelm her. She sucked in ragged breaths, her entire body trembling with fear and adrenaline. She crouched on the ground where she fell, the stems and leaves of the plants around her bent and crushed.

The Headhunter named Scorpio towered over her, eclipsing the sun. He wore a cloak of fox-skin, bushy red tails dangling. The digital scorpion tattoo snaking up his neck flicked its venomous stinger. Huge and immensely muscled, he looked like he could pull a train with his teeth. His squinty eyes were hooded in his fleshy, shovel-shaped face.

He wasn't aware of her presence, his pulse gun aimed at Silas and Finn, the ones he viewed as a threat. She wasn't even a blip on his radar. Which was fine by her. She sucked the blood from her split lip, pretending to sit sweet and docile like a good little girl. But inside, she coiled tight as a snake, waiting, waiting for the right moment to strike.

Two men held Amelia by the arms, but she thrashed and shrieked like a wild animal, clawing at anything she could reach. Twice, one of the men cursed as she raked his face with her nails.

But they were careful with her. They knew she was the first

survivor. That's why they needed her. They didn't hit her back. They didn't have such qualms about the rest of their group.

Silas lunged at the closest Headhunter and received several gut-punches for the effort. He staggered, clutching his stomach. "Next time, we'll just waste a bullet on you," Razor said.

They chose Celeste and Nadira, too. Celeste didn't resist, but Nadira did. Razor struck her across the face. Her head bounced back. The sight of Nadira slumped between those brutes, her hair hanging exposed and limp around her shoulders, filled Willow with rage.

She wanted to fight with every fiber of her being. But she wasn't stupid. They carried knives, but what were knives against pulse guns? Even if she managed to kill this fox-tailed thug with her little blade, then what? She and Silas couldn't take out eleven more bastards on their own. It was impossible. They would lose.

But she wouldn't give up. There had to be an opening, somewhere. These monsters had a weakness. They needed to find it and—

A glimpse of movement snagged her gaze. She turned her head slowly as to not draw undue attention. Someone tore out of the woods to her left, racing full-tilt between the two residence halls. It was Gabriel. He sprinted toward the cafeteria and the garden, pumping his legs like pistons, a rifle in his hands.

Willow sucked in her breath, adrenaline spiking her veins. She stole a glance at Scorpio. He and the other Headhunters faced away from the residence halls, their attention on Silas and Finn and Amelia, who still fought and screamed like a wild thing. Anyone standing near the garden and driveway couldn't see Gabriel if he stayed behind the buildings.

Willow squinted. Something moved behind him. A huge streak of black came barreling between the trees, followed by smaller streaks of brown and gray and black. The dogs.

Gabriel was leading the infected pack right to the Headhunters. It was incredibly risky, incredibly dangerous, and brilliant as hell.

She recognized the streak of black—the wolf from the warehouse. She didn't know how or why he was here, but they needed any help they could get. She tensed, every muscle ready to spring, and watched them come with her heart in her throat.

Gabriel rounded the corner of the first residence hall and pressed himself against the wall. He swiftly assessed the situation, raised his gun, and squeezed off three shots. Two Headhunters standing near the cafeteria entrance dropped, blood oozing from their temples.

"Hey—!" a bald guy yelled. Gabriel's rifle jerked again. The Headhunter fell to his knees, then toppled sideways without another sound.

The black wolf snapped at the dogs' heels, almost like he was herding them. An instant later, more than a dozen dogs burst between the two buildings and careened into the fray like snarling demons from hell.

Distantly, she heard Silas groan. "Not the damn dogs."

The Headhunters' eyes widened in shock. They spun, guns wavering, unsure where to aim first. The dogs were everywhere, a rampaging whirlwind of savage fury and slavering fangs.

Gabriel whistled. From the south, the tow truck charged up the drive, Jericho leaning out the window and shooting as Micah drove, tires spinning, gravel spitting up dust.

Sweet Creek Farm erupted into chaos.

Willow twisted, searching desperately for Benjie. She glimpsed his neon green T-shirt against the wall of the cafeteria, where a Doberman cornered him, Gracie, and Harmony.

But before she could move, Finn lunged in front of Benjie, grabbed him by the waist, and thrust him over his shoulder. He backed away from the growling dog, shouting.

Out of the corner of her eye, she saw Celeste break free from the Headhunters and flee for the cafeteria. A large mutt charged toward her.

Before it could reach her, the black wolf surged in, barreling into the mutt and sending the creature sprawling.

But the Doberman still stalked Finn and Benjie.

"Get out of here!" Celeste screamed. In one fluid move, she bent down, grabbed one of the bricks edging the garden, and hurled it at the Doberman's head. The brick struck its snout. It yelped and skittered back.

It gave Finn time to dash for the cafeteria entrance.

Finn dumped Benjie safely inside. He held the door open as he seized Celeste's outstretched hand and jerked her to safety. Gracie and Harmony managed to dash in after them, with Horne following close behind.

It was over in a matter of seconds.

"What the hell!" Razor yelled, drawing Willow's gaze back to the battle at hand. Benjie and Finn were safe for the moment. That was all she needed to know.

Razor turned from Silas and aimed at a slavering stray, blood-streaked drool dripping from the dog's jowls. He discharged the pulse gun. A streak of red, crackling energy shot into the dog and bowled it backward, end over end. It didn't get up.

It was the opening Silas needed. He crouched, the blade he kept in his boot already in his hand, and launched himself at the Headhunter. He seized Razor by his skinny neck from behind and stabbed him.

Razor crumpled, Silas on top of him. Silas tore the pulse gun from the man's hands and leapt up, whirling, searching for the next threat.

Scorpio still stood only a foot from her. He raised his rifle and aimed it at Silas. It was too late to scream. Besides, Silas wouldn't hear it in the bedlam. Now was the time to fight.

Willow pulled her own blade from her boot with trembling fingers. Before she could think twice, she sliced her knife across the tendons along the backside of the Headhunter's knee.

He stumbled to his knees with a roar of pain, his gun wavering. He bent, feeling for the wound beneath the blood spurting down his leg.

Willow sprang to her feet and kicked the gun out of his hand. It went flying into the garden.

Scorpio cursed and spun, searching wildly for his attacker.

Willow darted a few feet away. A German shepherd raced past her, nearly bowling her over, but she kept her balance. She risked a second to check for the rest of her people.

Silas bolted across the yard, fleeing a Headhunter but heading for the tow truck, where Micah and Jericho could return fire. One of the thugs had Elise and was carrying her toward the bikes. In the center of the fray, Nadira fended off two mutts with the hoe. Beneath the apple trees, three Sweet Creek people were down, unmoving.

When she glanced back at Scorpio, he was staring straight at her.

He bared his teeth, his eyes glittering with pain and fury. "You little whore!"

Scorpio rose unsteadily to his feet and lurched toward her. He was huge, easily twice her weight and more than a foot taller. He was bigger and more powerful, but that didn't mean he couldn't be beaten.

She remembered Silas's lessons. She had to take away his power advantage by getting in close. *Close enough to feel him breathe.* Either that or dodge every punch he threw at her. One hit and she'd be out. Out and dead.

Scorpio swung at her head. She narrowly avoided it; the air from the force of the blow whizzed past her cheek. Her right foot tangled in a plant. She staggered, about to go down, but managed to right herself.

A terrier nipped at Scorpio's bloody leg. He swore and punched the dog in the head. It dropped to the ground, unconscious or dead. He met her gaze, so close she could see the network of broken blood vessels marring his cheeks. His lips peeled back from his teeth. "Your turn."

Fear speared through her. This needed to end fast. She wasn't good enough to defeat a powerful fighter, even a wounded one. If she ran, he'd find his gun and start shooting again. He'd kill her friends.

She couldn't let that happen. Every instinct screamed against it, but she forced herself to face him and stand her ground. Sound faded away. The world faded away.

Scorpio lunged. He swung his arm back and plowed his fist straight at her skull. His aim was high and hard.

And she was short. She ducked beneath it and darted in close. She inhaled the scent of sweat and blood, felt his soft belly against her hand. He swung so hard, the force of the missed blow sent his arm flailing across his body, exposing his right side.

That was where she plunged her knife, striking hard and fast straight into his vulnerable liver.

Scorpio screamed and jerked away. He stared at her in stunned disbelief, his eyes wide and startled, almost like a child's. He collapsed into a fetal position. He didn't move. A husky and a mutt sprang on him, growling and snapping at each other.

Willow staggered back, acid rising in her throat. The knife dripped. Her hands were trembling, streaked with warm blood.

She'd killed a man. A human being. He was breathing, alive, and then in a few moments, he wasn't.

She wanted to drop the knife, to fling it away like something foul and poisonous, but some instinctive part of her made her hold onto it. She wasn't done. She couldn't be done. They weren't safe.

The battle wasn't over yet.

36

GABRIEL

G abriel's heartbeat roared in his ears, but he was fearless. He sprinted into the fray with a bold and reckless fury.

Death would come for him, but whether it came now or later by his own hand didn't matter. Nothing mattered. The bullets whizzing by him didn't matter. The pain didn't matter. His life didn't matter.

Time slowed. He ran without ducking or seeking cover. Micah and Jericho crouched behind the tow truck parked at the top of the drive, aiming for the Headhunters fleeing for their motorcycles.

Several of them took cover behind trees and returned fire. Jericho was trying to get to Elise, who slumped across one of the bikes, her hands bound, a black bag over her head.

A skinny Headhunter in a black-furred pelt fled from a Labrador, twisting back to shoot wildly. Gabriel stepped into his path and clotheslined him with the rifle barrel. He went down like a bundle of twigs.

Gabriel stared down at the man, who clutched at his throat, gurgling and gasping for breath, his eyes frantically pleading for mercy.

You don't have to kill. Micah's voice echoed in his mind. But there was only darkness, no light, no mercy. He would never kill an innocent again, but these monsters weren't innocent.

He shot the man in the head and moved on.

He caught sight of Gonzales, kneeling around the corner of the cafeteria. Gonzales leaned out, fired a shot at a Headhunter, managed to hit the guy's thigh, then twisted and aimed a couple of shots at two dogs about to pounce on Anna, who'd fallen to the ground beneath a tree. Gonzales missed both times.

Gabriel leveled the rifle and took out the dogs. He glanced back at Gonzales. The man huddled against the wall, frantically reloading his pistol. A Headhunter—a tall, black-haired man draped in a leopard pelt—crept up on him from behind. Gabriel recognized him with a jolt —the bastard from the highway who'd shot the little girl. He'd somehow managed to sneak around the cafeteria so he could shoot Gonzales and the rest of them in the back.

Gabriel sighted the Headhunter's chest, about to pull the trigger when Gonzales jerked and crumpled. The Headhunter shot first. But his focus was still on his prey; he hadn't noticed he'd just become prey himself.

Gabriel slammed three bullets into the man's torso. He went down without a word.

The black wolf raced past him, chasing down a retriever. Gabriel dashed for Gonzales and knelt beside him, his gun still up, his gaze sweeping the area before darting back to the wounded man. "You okay?"

"I didn't know." Gonzales gasped as he pressed his hand against the bullet wound in his side. His black hair clung damply against his neck. "I swear to you."

"I believe you." It wouldn't be the first time someone like him had trusted the wrong person.

A scream rent the air. His heart surged in his chest. He knew that scream, knew that voice.

"Go," Gonzales wheezed. "I'll be fine."

Another scream. Gabriel whirled, searching for its source. He saw

Silas up and running, Nadira crouched, swinging at a dog with her hoe.

And a dozen yards away, a huge Headhunter draped in a wolf-skin backed toward the bikes, Amelia pressed close to his body, one burly arm around her neck, the other with an activated slasher rod held a few inches from her temple, the plasma crackling like blue fire. The bastard was using her as a human shield. Gabriel's gut knotted with rage and the first cold tangle of fear.

"Let her go!" he roared before he even knew he'd spoken.

The Headhunter spun toward him. "I'm afraid I can't do that."

Amelia whimpered, clawing at the man's arms, trying to kick at his shins behind her. But she was still weak from her illness, her skin pale, her legs trembling. He was incredibly strong, his muscles barely straining to hold her. She was no more than a mouse to him.

"I said let her go." Gabriel advanced across the garden until his feet hit gravel, three yards from Amelia. The tow truck was two dozen yards ahead and to the left. To the right, the parked motorcycles and the woods beyond.

Micah still fired at the Headhunters in the woods, but Jericho turned his attention to the one holding Amelia hostage. The muzzle of his gun poked out from behind the front fender.

"Cerberus!" Jericho called. "You're surrounded. Surrender!"

The man called Cerberus only smiled. His eyes glittered with malice. His tattoos seemed to slither over his arms and neck. "You can kill me, but I promise you this. You will lose something in the exchange."

Sweat dripped into Gabriel's eyes. He steadied his hands and kept his weapon trained on the spot between Cerberus's eyes. He could make the shot. Any day of the week, he could make that shot.

But maybe not today, when the stakes were so high. A single tap from that slasher would send electrified plasma melting through flesh and bone to fry her brain.

"This one is quite valuable," Cerberus continued. He took a step backward, toward the bikes, dragging Amelia with him. "I daresay she might be the most valuable human alive at this moment. Wouldn't you?"

"If she's so valuable, then you won't kill her." He kept his eyes on Cerberus. In his peripheral vision, Jericho crept out from behind the tow truck, Micah providing cover. If he could keep him talking, Jericho could sneak up behind him and take him out.

Cerberus's smile widened. "A resource only holds value if you're able to utilize it. What good is she to me if I'm dead?"

"She could be the key to the cure. She could save mankind."

Cerberus rolled his eyes. "A bit hyperbolic, don't you think? Besides, should mankind truly be saved? From what? Isn't it better this way? We're all free now to pursue our own desires. We can create this world anew and bend it to our own purpose. Isn't that the definition of liberty?"

Gabriel's jaw tightened. He kept his gaze on the Headhunter's face, but he saw Jericho out of the corner of his eye, slinking soundlessly behind Cerberus, a wicked blade held low in his right hand.

"You're full of crap," Gabriel said. "Her life is more important than your death, much as I'd like to put you down like the dog you are. Release her and I'll let you go."

Jericho crept within five steps when Cerberus tensed, somehow sensing a trap. He half-turned, jerking Amelia with him, the plasma crackling an inch from her skull. A few of her hairs curled and singed.

The Headhunter glared at Jericho. "Move any closer, and you can watch her brains turn to mush and leak out of her ears."

But he was distracted now, his attention torn between Gabriel and Jericho. He had none left for Amelia. And that would be his destruction.

Gabriel locked eyes with Amelia. Her eyes were scared, but they were not crazed or wild. She might be physically weak, but this was still the same girl who'd kept her head as a hostage, who'd faced her father and defeated Kane. Her eyes shone with the same focused strength he'd fallen for on the *Grand Voyager*.

For an instant, he was back in the Oceanarium, Amelia kneeling in front of him with a blade to his throat, her gaze spearing straight to his soul, completely undoing him. She'd been strong enough to spare him, to trust him.

He'd been the weak one. He still was. Gabriel couldn't do a thing to alter the past, but he'd be damned if he let her die now. He sent her an unspoken message with his eyes, willing her to understand. She did. She saw what he meant to do, and she nodded with the faintest tilt of her chin.

"Not a step closer!" Cerberus's grip on her neck slipped a bit, the slasher tilting a few inches away from the side of her head.

Amelia reached up behind her and clawed Cerberus's face. He grunted and tried to jerk free, but she was too close. Her nails dragged across his eyeballs.

Gabriel lunged, barreling into Amelia and knocking her from Cerberus's grasp. She fell to the ground and rolled frantically out of the way. Gabriel stumbled once, then he was on his feet again, crouching and spinning toward the Headhunter.

But Cerberus was faster.

Gabriel made a fatal error. He'd misjudged his attacker's speed based on his size. But Cerberus's movements were agile and lightning quick. He jerked the pulse gun from his holster and aimed it at Gabriel's skull.

He was too close to miss. Gabriel couldn't do a damn thing.

He froze, waiting for the pulse of the laser, for the explosion of boiling-hot pain, the bittersweet agony of death. Cerberus's lips curled into a cruel smile as he pulled the trigger.

A body hurled itself in front of Gabriel. He felt a heavy, warm weight. Something soft crumpled against him. They both collapsed to the ground.

Another shot fired at close range. His ears rang. Everything went dull and distant. As if in a daze, he saw Cerberus stumble, red blooming from his shoulder. Two more Headhunters ran up to protect their leader, their guns blazing, forcing Jericho to dive for cover.

The battle shifted away from Gabriel as the Headhunters fled for their bikes.

He turned to the form crumpled next to him, his heart in his throat. Gently, he rolled the body over. Nadira stared up at him, blood trickling from the corner of her mouth.

————

Gabriel lifted Nadira gingerly in his arms, cradling her, and ran for cover behind the wall of the first residence hall. He felt wetness on his arms. Blood dripped a trail in the grass.

A husky lurched at him, jowls dripping with red foam. It limped from a bullet wound to the hindquarters. Gabriel kicked it hard in its wounded leg. It slunk away, searching for easier prey.

Gabriel propped her up against the wall, his hands trembling. He gently tugged up her shirt. Blood leaked from the tiny hole in her chest. Tendrils of hair clung to her damp forehead. Her face was ashen, her lips tinged purple. In her right hand, she clutched her pale blue headscarf.

"Why?" he blurted, stunned.

She sucked in a shallow, ragged breath. "You needed help."

"You should've let me die!"

"When I die, I know where I am going."

"What does that matter?" He pressed his hands over her wet shirt, his fingers slick with blood. Even as he did it, he knew it wouldn't matter. Her wound was too severe, too deep. If they were near a hospital, with robotic surgeons and cell rejuvenation procedures and instant flesh grafts, maybe things would be different. But they weren't.

There was nothing to be done.

"I have peace, Gabriel." She coughed. Blood bubbled from her lips. "But you—you are lost."

He rocked back on his heels. "I am—not a good person. You know what I am."

"I know . . . that you deserve a chance . . . at redemption. Everyone does."

Far above him, vultures circled in the sky. The sun drifted behind a cloud. She gazed at him with those huge dark eyes. He felt his black heart cracking open. "I deserve nothing. I deserve death."

"Sometimes—we don't get what we deserve." She smiled weakly at him. "Sometimes, we get what we don't deserve."

He shook his head, his eyes burning. "This isn't right. It's not how things are supposed to be. You're—you're good. You're not supposed to die. You can't die. Not—not for me."

Nadira reached out and touched the side of his face. "I am not afraid."

The sun was shining, but all he saw was darkness. "No! Don't do this!"

But she was no longer listening.

After she died, he drew her into his arms, this girl he barely knew. She was light, her limbs soft and limp. Her head nestled against his chest and her dark hair spilled over his forearm. He held her, weeping for things he never even knew he'd lost.

MICAH

Micah stood inside the cafeteria kitchen's walk-in pantry. He stared down at Harmony, the woman who'd betrayed them. Jericho and Willow stood on one side of him, with Finn, Amelia, and Silas on the other. Silas trained a rifle on her, just in case.

The battle was over. Seven Headhunters were killed. Six had escaped, including Cerberus. After they'd put the remaining dogs down, he'd looked for the girl and the wolf to thank them. The girl spoke to Willow for a few moments, but then she faded back into the trees, her wolf becoming a shadow among shadows, like they'd never existed in the first place.

As much as he would have liked to, he didn't have the time or energy to search for them. Not after everything their group had just lost.

Gonzales hadn't made it. Three other Sweet Creek people were dead, two bitten by infected dogs, and two more wounded but likely to live. Horne was shot in the outer thigh, but the wound was shallow. The bullet exited cleanly. Mrs. Lee tended to him in the infirmary.

But the Headhunters had kidnapped Elise. And sweet, kind Nadira was dead.

Micah gazed down at Harmony, his eyes burning. His heart felt hollowed out. Part of him wanted to curl up and weep, but he couldn't. Not yet. This awful day hadn't ended yet.

After it was over, they'd found her cowering inside the walk-in pantry with Benjie and Gracie huddled beside her. In a surprising move, Celeste offered to watch the children without a single complaint. They didn't need to be a part of this.

Harmony sat stiffly on a large barrel, her spine straight, her hands folded in her lap. Her gray hair shone beneath the single bulb hung from the ceiling. The wooden shelves behind her were lined with bags of rice, clumps of dried herbs, jarred preserves, and baskets of onions and potatoes. The air smelled of flour and garlic.

Gabriel stormed in, blood on his hands and clothes, fury contorting his face. He held a pistol in one hand; in his other, he gripped Nadira's hijab, now only a limp scrap of fabric.

He leveled the pistol at Harmony's head. "*You*! You sold us out! Nadira is—she's dead—because of you!"

Harmony recoiled, her face blanching. "I didn't intend for anyone to die."

Gabriel's hand shook. But when he spoke, his voice was low and deadly calm. "I'm going to kill you now."

Micah pushed Gabriel aside and leapt in front of the woman. He turned and faced his brother, holding out his hands to block him. *Be good.* His mother's voice echoed in his mind. He couldn't allow any more killing. Not now, when there was no need. It was over. "No one else is dying today."

Gabriel's mouth twisted. "Get out of my way."

"No! This isn't justice."

"A life for a life is justice!"

"One more death on your hands isn't going to give you peace."

Gabriel seethed. "Who said anything about peace?"

Micah shot Jericho a look. "You aren't going to stop this?"

Jericho's eyes glimmered darkly. "Maybe we make our own justice, now."

"No! I don't believe that. You don't believe that, either. We have to be better. We *are* better!" Micah stared at each person in the group. He wasn't backing down this time. Sometimes violence was necessary. He understood that. He willingly accepted the cost. But this was different. "Defending ourselves is one thing. This is an execution."

"He's right," Finn said. "This is wrong."

"You don't get a say, pansy-ass," Silas spat. "You're a spineless coward, too weak to do what needs to be done."

"No." Micah's eyes never left his brother's face. "Mercy is not weakness. Compassion is not weakness. We don't have to turn into murderers, Gabriel. We have a choice!"

Jericho sighed and put his hand on Gabriel's arm. "Your brother is right. Stand down."

For a moment, Gabriel hovered on the razor edge of violence. Then the fight went out of his eyes. He lowered the gun, his shoulders slumping. "She just—she jumped in front of me," he said dully. "There was nothing I could do."

Grief and regret distorted his features. His eyes were glassy and unfocused, like he was watching a different, more terrible scene playing out in front of him.

Pity struck Micah with such force it stole his breath. Whatever sins his brother had committed, he felt genuine anguish over Nadira's death. Part of him wanted to wrap his brother in his arms and whisper, *Always*. "I know."

Jericho took Gabriel's gun from his limp hand and led Gabriel out of the pantry. At the door, Jericho glanced back at Micah and Silas. "You've got this."

Micah nodded, appreciating the trust and responsibility Jericho put in him. He turned to Harmony and shoved his glasses up the bridge of his nose. "It's time to talk."

"We need answers," Amelia said. "And you're going to give them to us."

"I'll tell you anything," Harmony blurted, her face ashen. "Please. My granddaughter needs me."

Willow stepped forward. She glared balefully at Harmony. "You stole my brother!"

Harmony's left eye twitched. "I could give him a good life here. He could grow up with another child his own age, a sister—"

"I'm his sister!" Willow shook, the tendons standing out on her neck.

"—He would be safe," Harmony finished.

"You mean safety bought and paid for by killers!"

The woman winced, but she did not look away. "I . . . I did what I had to do."

Willow made a strangled sound deep in her throat. Her blood-stained hands hung limply at her sides. She was exhausted and stressed.

"Willow," Micah said gently. "Do you need to be here right now?"

Finn put his arm around her shoulder. She tried to shrug him off at first, but he held on. "Benjie needs us, okay?"

She sagged against him and nodded. He led her out of the room.

Amelia looked at Micah, her expression tense, her eyes flashing. He'd never seen her so visibly angry. "Is it my turn yet?"

"Just don't kill her," he said grimly.

Amelia turned to Harmony. "Where the hell did they take my mother?"

"You can't go after her. They have hundreds more men."

"Where is she?"

"You need to leave. You aren't safe here."

"That's not what I asked you!"

"I don't know where their compounds are!" Harmony said. "No one knows. But they'll come back with even more men. They'll come for you."

Micah squatted in front of her. He forced his voice to remain calm. "We understand the danger, Harmony. But we need your help. I think you owe it to us, don't you?"

She hunched her shoulders, but her eyes were still defiant. "You were taking Amelia to a research facility to find a cure. The Headhunters were doing the same thing. They say the Sanctuary has the best surviving medical research team, made up of former members of the CDC. It's where she needs to go. But if I traded with the Head-hunters, we'd both win."

"What did you trade for us?" Amelia's hands balled into fists at her sides. "What was worth my mother? Nadira? Me?"

Harmony's eyes shone with unshed tears. She spread her hands and stared at her bright orange nail polish, still perfectly manicured, without a crack or blemish. "Antivirals for my nephew."

Micah narrowed his eyes. "Antivirals are useless against the Hydra Virus. The government even admitted that much on the newsfeeds."

She shook her head. "Not those. Different ones. Ones manufactured at the Sanctuary. It's not a cure, but it delays the spread of the disease."

Micah stared at her. "What are you talking about?"

"Why do you think most of the Headhunters don't wear personal protection gear or respiratory masks?"

"Because they're already infected," Micah said slowly as under-standing dawned on him. He and Amelia exchanged perplexed glances. What did that mean?

"A few are immune—I'm certain Cerberus is. That's how he took control of the gang so easily. Before the virus, he was only a hench-man. I know many of the others are infected. But the antivirals they trade for with the Sanctuary keep them asymptomatic—and alive. I don't know how long they last. Cerberus says indefinitely."

"And those are the ones you needed," Micah said.

"Yes." A single tear trickled down her lined cheek. "My nephew Carson is dying. Those antivirals could save his life, give us time until a real cure is found. I've lost my daughter, my husband, and my grand-son. I—I couldn't lose anyone else."

"You were willing to trade our lives for your own."

"When I realized what Amelia was, I knew the Headhunters would give me anything I needed. That's how it works now!" she exploded, her dark eyes defiant. "The Headhunters aren't anything new. They've controlled most of Northern Georgia—including Atlanta—for a decade. Now, they've spread into Tennessee and the Carolinas, too. The virus only solidified and increased their power. We've traded goods for protection for almost eight years. If you toe the line and do as they say, they don't hurt you."

"You're a monster," Amelia said.

Harmony wiped the tear away and sniffed. "I did what I had to in order to protect my family, just like everyone else."

Micah crossed his arms. "That's where you're wrong. Not everyone would trade an innocent life. Not everyone would sell out the people who trusted them—"

"Hate me all you want, but my people saved you. We took you in at great personal risk. We fed and clothed you. We provided expensive medical care to your sick. Who else would have done that?"

Silas snorted. "You took us in to betray us."

"No!" She glanced at Micah beseechingly. "Not until I knew what Amelia was—what she was worth. I know what the Headhunters do. They've always traded in synthetic drugs, illegal weapons, and people, when it suited them. Last month, Cerberus told me if I ever came across a survivor, he'd give me whatever I wanted. I never would've done it if I wasn't desperate. I'm sorry."

"Were the rest of your people in on it, then?"

Her mouth pinched. "Only Russell, I swear. And I didn't know they'd try to take the women, too."

"Yes, you did," Amelia said tightly. "That's why you made a deal to keep Benjie."

For a moment, Harmony said nothing. She couldn't. Her guilt was written all over her face. Her lower lip trembled. "I'm a good person."

Micah shook his head wearily. She was a good person, until she became desperate enough to cross that line. Everyone was desperate now, or else they soon would be. What would happen then? How many good people would resort to the most repugnant of acts?

Anyone could commit horrific crimes if they were desperate enough, if they felt justified in their desperation. Harmony had. Where was the line between doing what you must to protect those you love and yet still hold onto your soul, your humanity?

He didn't know. He didn't have all the answers. *Be good. Be brave.* There was a line. Maybe the key was never forgetting it was there. Maybe you had to make an intentional decision to stay true to yourself despite the harshness and cruelty surrounding you. If you didn't, you were one terrible decision away from becoming what you'd once loathed. If you were no different than the enemy, what was the point?

Amelia swayed on her feet. She looked far too pale. Before Micah could say anything, she waved him off, leaning against the doorframe to steady herself. "What is the Sanctuary?"

Harmony scrubbed her face with the palm of her hand and took a breath. "They've been building something up in the hills for years, preparing for something like this. They say it's a government-operated safe zone, like Raven Rock and Cheyenne Mountain and all the rest, only above ground. It's restricted to essential personnel, important officials and their families, and the richies who can buy their way in. But they have everything—power, communications, working utilities, research facilities, a hospital. Rumor is that's where they moved President Sloane and the surviving Unity Council members after Mount Weather fell."

Silas and Amelia exchange startled glances. Amelia grabbed Silas's hand and squeezed. Micah frowned, puzzled by their reaction. Had they heard of this Sanctuary place before?

"Why didn't you say something before?" Amelia asked.

Harmony stiffened. "You didn't ask. And it didn't seem important. What the government does in other parts doesn't matter here."

"Unless they find a cure—then it matters!" Amelia's face reddened, her hands balling into fists. She was usually in such control of her emotions, hardly letting her fear or anger show. But her mother was kidnapped, and Amelia nearly taken with her. She was upset, worried, and angry, but she still held her own. She was stronger than anyone Micah knew, other than his mom. "Is that where they're taking my mother?"

"I have no idea. I only know a bunch of them go every month to trade for their antivirals. They might try to sell Elise as a servant, a cook, or . . . something else."

Micah's stomach knotted at the woman's words, but Amelia didn't seem to register their meaning. She crossed her arms, her expression hardening. "Then that's where we go."

"We should try to track them down now, tonight," Silas said, "before they get too far."

"We don't know where their compound is. We'll be vastly outnumbered," Micah cautioned. He didn't want to risk anyone else. Not now, not even for Amelia's mother. "We need to be smart."

"That's why we have to go to the Sanctuary," Amelia insisted.

Micah stepped closer, careful not to touch Amelia, but hoping his presence would bring her a little comfort, at least. "Where is this Sanctuary?"

Harmony rubbed her eyes, her face lined with fatigue. "I'm not certain, exactly. I've never been there."

"Take a guess," Silas snapped.

"Please." Micah kept his voice even. "Try your best to be more helpful."

She refused to meet Micah's eyes. Her gaze drifted toward the shelves of sugar and flour beside her. "It's past Dahlonega, nestled at the base of the Blue Ridge Mountains, back there in the middle of nowhere."

Micah guesstimated it was around a hundred and fifty miles north. "We'll have to go through Atlanta."

"No one goes into the cities willingly, certainly not Atlanta. And not unless you're a Pyro. No one messes with them. No one. They make the Headhunters look like kittens. Add in the millions of diseased bodies, infected rats and dogs, the fires—Atlanta is burning. It's a death wish."

A chill ran down his spine. "What route do the Headhunters use?"

"They take the back roads around the greater Atlanta suburbs. It's four times as long, but your odds of survival are a hell of a lot better. I wouldn't attempt the city if I were you." She winced, as if thinking of something painful. "It's no place for a little boy."

Silas frowned. "We need to get there before the Headhunters if we're going to get Mother back. Our best bet is to surprise them and force them to reveal where she is."

"Then we cut through the city," Amelia said without hesitation.

"Amelia—"

"We're going!" She clutched her charm bracelet through her shirt. Her knuckles were white.

He knew she wouldn't budge, just as he knew he would give in despite his misgivings. "Okay," he said with a sigh. "I'll tell Jericho."

Amelia turned to Harmony. She lifted her chin, her eyes going hard. "And we're taking two of your trucks."

Silas gestured at Harmony with the muzzle of his gun. "What are we doing with her?"

"Blessed are the merciful, for they shall obtain mercy." One of the only Bible verses he remembered, and only because his mom hung a cheap digital art canvas over the towel rack, so he could always work on becoming a better person—even in the bathroom.

Silas's expression turned even more sour. "What the hell does that mean?"

"Leave her," Micah said. "She's no danger to us now. And we need to bury Nadira."

"Of course." Amelia's eyes softened. "Silas and I will help."

As Micah turned to follow the others out, Harmony seized his shirt sleeve.

"I am truly sorry about Nadira and Elise." Her voice was tinged with genuine sorrow. Her eyes glistened. In the overhead light, her face sagged, her sallow skin creased with age and grief. "Please forgive me."

He'd argued to spare her life, to grant her mercy. But forgiveness was too great a request, even for him. He turned his back and walked out, leaving her alone with her tears.

38

WILLOW

Willow sat on the ground, leaning against the wall of the residence hall. Her backpack lay beside her. She'd showered and dressed in the fresh clothes Anna gave her. She had to roll up the cargo pant legs so the ends wouldn't drag, but it worked well enough.

The moon shone, round and full, spilling pale white light over the hunched buildings of the Sweet Creek compound. The stars glittered like shards of ice. An owl hooted somewhere nearby.

Benjie is safe. She kept repeating it in her head, over and over. Celeste had saved him from that dog when she'd thrown the brick at it in a startlingly brave and selfless act.

Willow had thanked her profusely. They'd exchanged genuine smiles for the first time since they met on the *Grand Voyager*, both soaked to the skin and terrified as they huddled beneath that bridge.

She shivered in the cold night air. She wore a sweater and wrapped an auto-warming blanket around her shoulders, but she couldn't seem to get warm.

She'd managed to hold it together until now. After the chaos of the dogs and the fighting, she'd wanted to get as far away from the Headhunter's body as she could. She stumbled across the battered, bloodied ground to the tree line and bent double, vomiting up the contents of her stomach.

When she straightened, still sick and trembling, she caught sight of the girl and the wolf hovering on the edge of the clearing, as if undecided whether to stay or go. She walked toward them on shaky legs, half-expecting them to flee. But they didn't. "What's your name?" she asked.

The girl still held an old hoverboard beneath her arm. Her eyes roamed over Willow's face, dark and calculating. "Raven." She jabbed a thumb at her own chest. She pointed at the wolf sitting calmly on his haunches beside her, his ears pricked, blood matting his forelegs and muzzle. "Shadow."

"Thank you for saving me, for helping us."

She shrugged. "You needed it."

"Are you alone? Where are your parents?"

She merely shrugged again, her gaze hardening. "Dead." She looked a little younger than Willow, too young to be alone in the woods. Willow glanced at the wolf again. He was disconcertingly still, a breeze softly rippling his thick fur.

"Did you—did Shadow come from a wildlife refuge? A girl here told me there's one a few miles away."

Raven's eyes darted past Willow to the compound. She took a step backward and activated her hover board. The wolf rose soundlessly to his feet. "We have to go."

She wanted to ask more questions, but Raven seemed both simultaneously fearless and skittish. "You can come with us," Willow said in a rush, startled at her own forwardness. Jericho and Silas wouldn't be keen, but she didn't care.

Raven only pulled her hood back up, shielding her face, and jumped on her board. She whistled to Shadow. Before Willow could say or do anything, the girl disappeared through the trees, hovering a foot off the ground as she skimmed over leaves, roots, and low underbrush, easily maneuvering around trees and bushes, the wolf loping beside her like a silent shadow.

They'd gone as mysteriously as they'd come.

And now she was here, slumped against the residence hall in the middle of the night, waiting to flee to some new promise of shelter and safety. But appearances were deceiving, and sometimes promises turned out to be false as fool's gold.

She knew that better than anyone.

The cold of the ground seeped through her pants. She felt cold all the way to her bones. A weariness like she'd never felt descended over her. Her body ached. Her eyes burned. Her legs felt like they couldn't carry her weight any longer.

Her hands wouldn't stop shaking. She kept scrubbing her palms against her pants, trying to get all the blood off. But it was still there. She couldn't see it, but she felt it there, staining her skin, seeping into her cells.

She took a life. She knew in her head that it was necessary. She would do it again to protect Benjie and everyone else she cared for. But her heart—her soul—was a different story. Something deep inside her recoiled, repulsed at the thing she'd done.

She kept replaying the scene in her mind, over and over, the softness of his belly, how easily the knife slid through human flesh, the stunned look in his eyes as he collapsed, shocked that he wasn't exempt from death after all.

Like so many rites of passages in life, there was a 'before' and an 'after' now. She had killed. She was a killer. The word left a bitter taste on her tongue. What did that make her? Had she changed, even in ways she couldn't see? Did she want to change?

Silas exited the residence hall, caught sight of her, and strolled over, the nail-spiked baseball bat swinging at his side. His face was a shadow in the dim moonlight. She didn't say anything. She didn't know if she could.

He squatted on his haunches, forearms resting on his thighs. He stared at her for a long moment, his gaze drifting down to her trembling hands. "It doesn't last forever."

She didn't need to ask him what he meant. She knew. She remembered how she and Benjie were trapped in the bowels of the ship with a semi-automatic pointed at them. Silas had rounded the corner and shot the terrorist, saving their lives. She remembered how afterward, he'd been pale and shaken. It must've been his first kill.

He stood up and held out the bat, handle first. "We have a little time left."

She almost forced a smile, then realized she didn't have to. The one thing you never needed to be with Silas was fake. He simply didn't care. Tonight, that was exactly what she needed.

"You still have that thing?" she managed.

His teeth glimmered. "You could say I've taken a shine to it. You coming?"

She pulled herself to her feet. She curled her fingers into fists, then opened them again. The blood wasn't visible, but it was there. It always would be.

She took the bat. "Let's go, then."

39

GABRIEL

Gabriel slammed the shovel into the hard-packed earth. His hands were blistered, but he did not stop. His eyes stung, but he did not weep. He dug shovelful after shovelful, until the pit beneath the great spreading oak tree was deep and wide enough for its purpose.

Micah, Willow, and Amelia came to help. He sent them away with a litany of furious curses. Micah hesitated. "I saw what you did. You helped us. You saved Amelia."

"I couldn't save *her*," he said, his voice raw.

Micah nodded, his face contorting with conflicting emotions—sorrow, pity, and guilt. "I know. I'm sorry."

Only Micah stayed, standing guard a dozen yards away on the edge of the tree line. When Jericho came a few minutes later with handcuffs, Micah sent him away. "Let him be," Micah said. So Jericho did.

They left him alone with the body, the shovel in his hands, and the grave. The trees stood silent and still as sentinels all around him, their black shadows gnarled and twisting. The moonlight filtered through the branches above him, casting the world in a ghostly gloom. A mournful howl rose somewhere in the distance.

He lifted her body and placed her gently down into the earth.

Inside the pit, he squatted beside her. He carefully wrapped the head-scarf over her hair and smoothed the stray tendrils off her face. He crossed her arms over her chest and closed her dull, staring eyes with the pad of his thumb.

He had no faith and no words worth speaking.

He shoveled the dirt over her with great care, covering her face last. He dug until his blisters burst. His biceps burned. His heart beat inside his chest and refused to quit.

When he finished, he stood at her grave and didn't know what to do. His soul was black, and his heart was a hollow thing. He'd believed death would be his justice, and in a just death, he would find his peace.

Now, he knew he would have neither. This girl had died for him. He had not wanted it or asked for it. He had not deserved it. But she did it anyway. She was kind and good and innocent and he was none of those things. It made no sense to him.

He stood facing the darkness. It called to him, tugging at the dark inside his own soul. He was prepared to go. He was ready. He longed for it.

The mournful howl came again, much closer now. He peered into the darkness of the woods.

A pair of yellow eyes stared back at him. The shadows shifted, and he saw the great black wolf poised between two pine trees. The broad shoulders and chest rippled with muscles beneath its thick fur. The wolf raised his regal head, his muzzle long and narrow, his gaze intelligent, cunning.

He clutched the shovel handle, ignoring the sting of his blisters. Then he relaxed his fingers. He dropped the shovel to the ground with a dull thud. If the wolf came for him, so be it. He wouldn't fight his fate.

The wolf didn't attack.

"Come on!"

The wolf merely watched him with those yellow eyes.

"What are you waiting for!"

The wolf didn't move.

Gabriel didn't move. *Earn your redemption*, she said. He did not deserve it. But *she* did.

For the first time in a long time, Gabriel thought of his mother. It was Micah who'd been closest with their mother, Micah who took her faith and admonitions to heart.

Gabriel was more like their father—a knot of helpless grief and anger. But now Gabriel would give anything to talk to her again, to feel the warm security of her hug, to hear one last time the words always in her heart—*do the right thing, my son*. What would she think of what he'd become?

He'd lost his way. But maybe he could find it again.

He wouldn't run. He wouldn't die. He couldn't, not after what Nadira did for him. Death was the easy way out, wasn't it? It was so much harder to live with your sins. So much harder to stay, to atone, to earn what grace another had given, and at so great a cost.

He looked at the wolf again, meeting those yellow eyes that seemed to pierce his soul. After a long moment, the creature melted back into the trees, a shadow indistinguishable among shadows.

Gabriel picked up a handful of dirt and crumbled it between his fingers over Nadira's grave. He would stay. If there was such a thing as redemption—if it existed for someone like him—then he would find it. He had to. He would do everything in his power to earn it.

He would earn it for Nadira and the little girl in yellow.

He would earn it for Micah. His brother, his everything. It was his mother's last wish for Gabriel to take care of Micah, for her boys to be good and brave together. The world had fallen to pieces, but he wouldn't lose his brother, too. He would fight for Micah.

He would earn it for Amelia. She couldn't love him again; he knew that. He had no misconceptions, no false hopes. He'd betrayed her, nearly destroyed her. Nothing he could ever do would make him worthy of her love. But maybe, someday, she could forgive him.

He glanced through the trees to the dark shape of his brother at the edge of the clearing. Micah still waited for him. It was something.

It was a beginning.

40

AMELIA

Amelia stared up at the bowl of the night sky. She'd spent the last five hours lying on the back of the open truck bed, exhausted but sleepless. Too many anxious thoughts and endless questions hummed in her mind.

Silas drove, with Finn sitting shotgun. Amelia shared the back with Willow, Micah, and Benjie and a half-dozen blankets. Willow sat facing the way they'd come, a rifle on her lap as she guarded the rear. Benjie curled up like a kitten against her side. Jericho, Horne, and Celeste rode in the other truck, with Gabriel in handcuffs in the back.

They stopped at least a dozen times to clear a path, shoving dead cars and the occasional fallen tree branch out of the way. In five hours, they'd gone twenty-six miles, with another thirty to hit the city, and another hundred to go after that. Still, at least now they had a destination, a goal.

They were headed for the Sanctuary to save her mother and find a cure. It was a place that represented safety, law and order, and hope for everyone. Though for Amelia, it was so much more.

Beside her, Micah shifted. He didn't touch her, but she still felt his presence, his warmth. "Do you want to see something beautiful?"

She smiled in the dark. "Of course."

He pointed at the sky. "A falling star."

The night was clear. Without ambient light, the sky was a black like she'd never seen, rich and full of depth, limitless. The stars were sharp and bright, like tiny shards of ice or glass. She stared hard, straining her eyes until her vision blurred. And then she saw it: a streak of fire across black velvet.

"As long as you can still find beauty, you know you'll be all right," he said. "That's what hope is."

Did she have hope? She thought so, but the obstacles arrayed against her seemed insurmountable. For every enemy and fear she bested, two more rose in its place. Like the Hydra monster from the myths, she thought ruefully. The namesake of the virus that had destroyed the world as they knew it. "Sometimes, hope feels impossible."

He made a shape in the air with his fingers. "Hope is a thing with feathers."

She gave a half-smile. "I know that one. Emily Dickens."

"Good." He traced another star as it arced through the sky. "We can't give up. We won't. We've come this far. We'll figure out who the Headhunters trade with and find a way to rescue Elise. I know we will. And you'll help the scientists find a cure to put a stop to all this."

Her heart twinged at the thought of her mother. She'd just found her again, only to have her ripped away. "You think so?"

"I know so," he said, without a shred of doubt in his voice. She admired his faith, his belief that there was something bigger than all this, a meaning behind the things they couldn't see or understand.

"I don't get it."

"What?"

Another falling star streaked across the sky, a shot of brilliant fire. "Why I'm still alive."

"My mother was Catholic." Micah shifted again as the truck jolted over a pothole. "Her faith was everything to her. She would say that you have a purpose."

"But why me?" Why was she the only known survivor of the

Hydra Virus? How had she lived when no one else had? What made her special? Did it have something to do with the illegal epilepsy medication her father designed? Or was it something with the epilepsy itself, some aspect of her brain that the disease irrevocably changed that made her different? "Maybe it's just some freak improbability."

"Maybe. Or maybe it's more than that."

She didn't know if there was purpose or meaning to any of it. She did believe in beauty. She believed in music and art and literature and those things that awakened something deep inside her soul.

Micah folded his hands behind his head and gazed up at the sky. "If the rumors are true, then the Sanctuary is a safe place, Amelia. A safe place for you, for Benjie, for all of us."

"I hope so." But was it truly safe? More questions flared in her mind. Who was the real mastermind behind the bioterrorism attack that unleashed the Hydra Virus on the world? Her father helped design the bioweapon, but he wasn't the ringleader. Her mother had feared high-ranking government officials were involved. Could President Sloane have orchestrated the whole thing?

Amelia tugged the leather thong from beneath her shirt and rubbed her charm bracelet, her stomach tightening. She longed to talk to Micah about all this, but she couldn't. Her mother had warned her. *Trust no one.*

The Sanctuary might be even more perilous for Amelia and Silas than out here. They knew the New Patriots were used as patsies. They were targets for anyone desperate to cover up the truth.

But maybe the Sanctuary would live up to its name—an oasis in a desert of sickness, terror, and death. They would rescue her mother. And they could all make a new start and rebuild their lives.

Amelia didn't know which version was truth and which was fiction. But her instincts were clamoring, her gut telling her that some way, somehow, there were answers waiting at the Sanctuary.

And if the scientists there could use the antibodies in her blood to discover a vaccine or a cure, then she would do whatever it took to help them. She would do everything in her power to stop the Hydra Virus—but first, she had to live that long.

She pulled her bottle out of her backpack and dropped the remaining two pills into her palm—the only thing that stood between her and the seizures that could render her unconscious, brain-damaged, or dead.

Her emergency auto-injectors were gone. Without medication, the next seizure could come at any moment, in a day or three weeks or six months.

Beside her, Micah stiffened. "Is that the last one?"

She gulped down a single pill and placed the other one back inside the bottle. "I'm keeping one. In case I can find someone who can replicate the formula."

With every seizure, she would lose more and more of herself, her brain breaking into pieces as she forgot memories, forgot how to read, how to hold a fork, how to talk—how to be human. "My father might be the only person who can make more."

"Do you think he's alive?"

"I don't know." She wondered who'd created the antivirals that successfully delayed the onset of the disease. Was it someone with previous knowledge of the genetically engineered virus? Someone like her father? Could he still be alive? And if so, was he back in the States? The thought chilled her to the core.

Her mind warred against itself in the same old battle she'd fought since she was a child. The man she feared and loathed was also her savior. She wanted him dead. She needed him alive. She hated him. And there was that small, childish part of her that still desperately loved him.

He was her father. He was the man who'd introduced her to the violin, who'd glowed with pride at her concerts and competitions, who'd worked so hard to save her life. Things were not always black and white. Love and hate and grief and joy could all be tangled up together. She thought again of her mother, the choices she made, the sacrifices. Her heart ached in the hollow place beneath her breastbone. She missed her mother.

For most of her life, she'd believed her mother was weak. Only now did she realize how strong her mother was all along. There were different kinds of strength. Her mother had a quiet strength, a spine of steel hidden beneath her demure exterior. A strength that endured years of emotional abuse, all to protect Amelia.

Her mother's dauntless love saved her, and she hadn't even known it.

Even as she worried for her mother's safety at the hands of the Headhunters, she knew her mother would never give up. Declan Black hadn't broken her. The New Patriots hadn't, either. Her mother would survive. She would endure.

And this time, Amelia would save her mother.

A brisk wind rustled through the trees on either side of the road. She shivered. Micah untucked the blanket he'd rolled beneath his head and handed it to her.

"I can't steal your pillow."

"I can use my backpack. Take it, please." He flashed her a dimpled smile. "I insist."

She wrapped herself in the fleece blanket. She remembered how he sat with her for hours when she was sick, how she'd focused on his kind brown eyes to distract herself from the burning fever. "Thank you."

They fell silent as more falling stars cascaded across the sky. It was incredible. Micah was right. If there could be such beauty in the midst of so much chaos, fear, and uncertainty, then there must also be hope.

And with hope came life, came finding a new way to live, to be. She didn't want to be tough but alone, like Silas. Or strong but distrustful, like her mother. She refused to live in fear, afraid of touch, of connection. She wanted to rebuild herself, one block at a time.

She touched her shorn hair. And she would start with trust. *Tomorrow*, she thought wearily. She would start tomorrow.

They watched the sky for the next hour. Micah's body was warm next to hers. She snuggled into the blanket and felt herself drifting.

Exhaustion overtook her and she gave in to it, lulled to sleep by the hum of the truck and the songs of crickets and other creatures of the night. For the first time since the *Grand Voyager*, she did not dream.

In the early morning hours, she drifted in and out of consciousness, only half-awake. As the truck crested a hill, Silas slammed the breaks. Amelia jolted, rolling against Micah.

"Oh hell," Willow mumbled. Micah gasped. She sat up, rubbing her eyes.

The air seemed thicker. It smelled strange, like something charred or singed. "What is it?"

"Look," Micah said hoarsely.

In the distance, she could make out the skyline of downtown Atlanta. The sky over the city was ash gray, the skyscrapers barely visible beneath dark pillars of smoke.

Harmony had been right. Atlanta was burning.

To reach the Sanctuary, they would have to travel right through the heart of it.

The End

ACKNOWLEDGMENTS

As always, my deepest gratitude is to my readers. Without you, my books would only be snippets of thoughts, characters, and scenes swirling around in my head. You make the story come alive. Thank you for reading.

To my beta readers, who caught errors small and large and helped strengthen this story: Jazmin Cybulski, Kimberley Trembley, Lauren Nikkel, Jeremy Steinkraus, Barry and Derise Marden, and Leslie Spurrier, who has graciously read (and helped improve) all of my books.

To my developmental and line editor, Michelle Brown, for the time and attention you devoted to my characters and their emotional and physical journeys throughout the story. And finally, to Eliza Enriquez for her eagle eyes and ability to catch those last little errors.

To my children and husband, thank you always for your patience and encouragement. It means the world to me.

ABOUT THE AUTHOR

Kyla Stone is an emerging author of contemporary young adult fiction and suspense/dystopian novels. She lives in Atlanta, Georgia with her husband, two children, and two spoiled cats. When she's not writing or spending time with her family, she loves to read, hike, draw, travel, and play games. Her favorite food is dark chocolate.

Kyla loves to hear from her readers. For news and new releases, visit her at:

www.FaceBook.com/KylaStoneBooks

www.Amazon.com/author/kylaStone

Email her at KylaStone@yahoo.com

SNEAK PEEK OF BENEATH THE SKIN

1

"Sidney Shaw, please come to the principal's office." The intercom hiccups with static. "Sidney Shaw, you are needed immediately in the principal's office."

The whole AP Spanish III class stops mid verb conjugation and turns to stare at me.

My heart jolts in my chest. I didn't really expect to get away with it, but I guess hope springs eternal, even for a diehard cynic. Until now, anyway. I stuff my book and papers into my backpack as Mr. Primero orders everyone to refocus.

I walk through the empty halls to the principal's office, my stomach curdling with dread. The only sounds are the rustle and murmur of voices behind closed classroom doors and my sneakers scuffing the worn floor. The secretary buzzes me through the locked door into the office suite. She's in her twenties but wears old lady glasses. She peers at me over her cat eye frames like she knows everything, as if she's already formulating the gossip she's going to spread in the teacher's lounge during her next coffee break.

"Have a seat, Miss Shaw." She pops her gum and gestures at the parallel waiting room sofas covered in some swirly, floral pattern from the 90s. A frizzy-haired freshman curls up on one of the couches, her face an unfortunate shade of green.

I sit down on the cushion closest to the principal's office. I'm twitchy, jumpy. My fists clench and unclench in my lap.

Voices echo through the wooden door. Apparently, the meeting started without me.

"Honestly, I don't know that another suspension is even going to get through to her," the high-pitched voice of the principal, Mrs. Rittenburg, echoes through the door.

"Clearly, something must be done," says the vice-principal, Mr. Adeyemi, in his deep baritone.

There's a new voice, muffled, edgy, irate. "I've had enough! That girl is a menace to society. The seriousness of this offense warrants an arrest. I want her expelled."

Mrs. Rittenburg clears her throat. "Yes, Mr. Cole. We'll take your concern under advisement. Rest assured, we *will* take appropriate disciplinary action."

I stare at my rings. Red splotches fleck the cheap metal and plastic. My knuckles still sting. It hurt more than I thought it would, the shock waves traveling all the way up my arm. And the sound of it, the soft squelch of my fist hitting flesh. I wince.

I try not to think about expulsion, a possibility that grows stronger with every passing moment. I've had plenty of detentions and a few suspensions. Frank will go nuclear if I get expelled. He'll do more than that. Acid coats the back of my throat. I swallow hard.

My knee starts shaking. You can't exactly put expulsion on your college applications. And I can't stay here in this pathetic, Podunk town full of cornfields and morons. I can't.

There's a pause in the ranting through the door. I can barely hear a fourth voice. I tilt my head without overtly looking like I'm listening.

". . . calm down for a second."

"Calm down for a second?" Mr. Cole bellows.

". . . heat of the moment . . . overreacting . . . look at this from another angle."

The fourth voice belongs to the guidance counselor, Dr. Yang. I've had weekly appointments with him since October of junior year, when I decided to take a stand for feminism. I may have flipped off the P.E. teacher for forcing me to wear my too-short and too-tight uniform. I may have also suggested Coach Taylor was a pervert for insisting on required activewear for adolescent minors that showcased the female form. While I've been stuck with Dr. Yang for a year, I'm also allowed to wear my uniform sweatpants permanently.

I don't think I'm getting my way this time. My knee shakes harder. Green-faced girl opens her eyes, glares at me for a second, then flips on her side and turns her back.

Dr. Yang is still talking. I've missed a large chunk of it. ". . . gifted student . . . shame to lose . . ."

"How dare you?" Mr. Cole cuts in. "What about the malicious assault of my son?"

". . . not technically on school grounds . . . extenuating circumstances."

"You've got to be kidding me!"

Mrs. Rittenburg says something too softly for me to hear, something about, "your responsibility."

Mr. Cole slams opens the door and storms out. It's been four years since I last saw him, since I hung out with his step-daughter and my ex-best friend, Jasmine Cole. He looks at me and curls his upper lip in a snarl of rage, but he keeps on walking.

Mrs. Rittenburg calls me in. She stands behind her massive desk, all five feet, two inches of her, hands fisted on her hips. Vice Principal Adeyemi towers next to her.

"Sidney, I'm sure we don't need to tell you how upset Mr. Cole is." Mrs. Rittenburg proceeds to lecture me, her voice grating my ears. "We have a zero-tolerance bullying policy, do you understand? You need to seriously consider your future, young lady."

"Yes ma'am." I nod, acting concerned and adequately contrite. My pulse pounds in my ears. The lights are too bright. I'm dizzy and sick to my stomach.

Then it comes.

They're not going to expel me.

Relief floods through me, almost enough to wash the nausea away. Almost. I murmur, "Yes ma'am," whenever the principal pauses, keeping my gaze glued to the faded orange carpet. If I let myself meet her gaze, she'll realize I'm not sorry. I'm not sorry at all.

Dr. Yang taps my shoulder. "My office. Now."

I follow him out of the principal's office and down the hall without speaking. The counseling office is small and crowded with a laminate desk, some puke-green file cabinets, and a bulletin board stuffed with inspirational clichés like, "Genius is 10% inspiration and 90% perspiration," and, "Everyone is a Winner." There's a photo on his desk of a pretty Asian lady with a wide, laughing smile.

I sink into the navy blue La-Z-Boy across from his desk and cross my arms. "That guy has a major case of male PMS. Am I right?"

Dr. Yang clears his throat and smooths his slightly rumpled gray suit. He's Korean and somewhere north of forty, the first strands of gray threading through the black hair combed across his forehead. He rests his elbows on his desk and steeples his fingers under his chin. One finger taps against his jaw.

"Are you ready to talk?"

"What for?"

"You do realize you are teetering on the edge, don't you?" He pauses as if I'm supposed to reply. "You were almost expelled today. Mr. Cole wanted to file an assault report. He still might."

My breath hitches in my throat. "Yeah, I got that."

He adjusts his glasses, squinting at me like he's trying to analyze some foreign object for the first time. "Sidney. What in the world were you thinking, beating up a twelve-year-old boy?"

"I didn't beat him up. We were clearing up a little misunderstanding."

"You still have blood on your rings!"

I glance down at my hands, surprised he noticed. "Okay, fine. I might have hit him."

"Whatever for?"

"I'm pretty sure he's a demon spawn out to steal the souls of the impressionable young students of Brokewater Elementary."

"And I'm pretty sure he's not. Try again."

I twirl my gold ring with the blue flower around my middle finger. "Okay, fine. He's an alien in child-form sent to earth to gather intelligence on us. He must be destroyed before the mother ship returns."

"Sidney, I'm on your side. When are you going to start believing that?"

I snort. There's no one on my side. I'm on my own. Always have been, always will be. "I couldn't help myself. He's got a very punchable face."

Dr. Yang's finger keeps tapping his jaw. "What do you have to lose by telling me the truth?"

That one gets me. I don't have anything to lose. And Dr. Yang saved my ass just now, whether I want to admit it or not. He's been trying to save me for over a year. The fact that I'm beyond saving hasn't registered on his radar yet. "Okay, fine. Look, this isn't some adorable little kid we're talking about here, okay? That prick is a sociopath in training. He torments my little brother constantly."

Every day since school started three weeks ago, eight-year-old Aaron came home with red finger marks on his arms, bruised knees, rips in his shirt, and tiny pinpricks in his skin from the sharp jab of a mechanical pencil. Yesterday, a deep purple bruise pooled around his right eye. He finally admitted the bully is Jackson Cole, Jasmine's younger brother. When he spoke Jackson's name, something cold and dark slithered into my brain. There's no way in hell I was letting another Cole mess with this family. Not again.

"Okay." Dr. Yang nods emphatically. "I think I get it, but there are other ways to handle bullying."

"You don't understand. Aaron is—different. He can't defend himself. Someone has to." I tried to get Aaron to stand up for himself, but he couldn't. He's weak, soft in all the wrong places. He never fights back. Never. The world stomps all over him and he just lets it happen.

He's going to be someone's prey his entire life. I can't let that happen. I won't. He's good—innocent and pure in a way no one else is. I want him to stay that way.

"If bullying is an issue, one of your parents should contact the teacher or the elementary school administration."

I snort again. In what fantasy world would that ever happen? Ma and Frank barely even put food on the table half the time. They're either drunk or fighting or gone. It's my job to protect my brothers. No one else will. "Are you even serious right now?"

He sighs. "I do realize your parents aren't the most . . . reliable, but you can't just—"

"I had to take care of it myself, okay?"

And I did take care of it, just like I'd promised Aaron. The thought of Jasmine Cole's brother hurting him burned like a white flame in the center of my skull. I needed to make sure Jackson regretted ever messing with my family, just like I made Jasmine regret messing with me.

I skipped first period this morning and waited at the bus stop on the corner of Elm and Broadview in the only upscale neighborhood in Brokewater. Jackson rode the 709 bus, the same one Jasmine used to take before her step-daddy bought her a new Camaro junior year. A few younger kids milled around on the sidewalk, untucking their designer T-shirts and kicking at stray pebbles with their $80 shoes.

Jackson Cole slouched up to the bus stop in skater jeans and an over-sized orange shirt emblazoned with "Skate. Eat. Repeat." He exchanged fist bumps with a couple of lookalike twerps. Before he could do anything else, I was on him.

I spun him around and got right up in his face. His eyes widened.

"Look, you ferret-faced little monster. I'm going to say this once, and once only. You lay a hand on Aaron, or even look at him sideways, and I will come after you with a chainsaw and chop off those fancy shoes of yours. We clear?"

His surprise faded quickly. "Get your hands off me. My dad's a lawyer."

"That's a big fat lie. I happen to know he's a dentist. And a lousy one at that. Stay away from Aaron."

"And what if I don't?" He tossed his head, a fringe of highlighted blonde hair falling into his eyes.

I'd planned on just scaring some sense into him, not actually hurting him. But my anger zapped through me like an electrical current. I couldn't help myself. I grabbed his shoulders, and I shook him. "Don't test me, or I will rip out your insides and feed your entrails to you, piece by piece. Leave. Him. Alone."

"Get off me!"

I gritted my teeth. Where was the shy kid who used to spy on me and Jasmine through her bedroom door, who used to do cannon-balls into the pool right next to our lounge chairs? I pushed the images out of my mind. That boy was long gone.

The bus pulled up next to us. He glared at me in disgust. "That gay prick gets everything he's got coming to him."

That's when I punched Jackson Cole right in his smug little face.

He dropped to the pavement, grabbing his nose with both hands, blood spurting between his fingers. The rest of the kids stared at me in shock, like I'd just transformed into a sparkly vampire before their very eyes. The bus driver yelled, "Hey! Hey you! Get back here!"

I walked away, knuckles stinging. A fat, satisfied grin spread across my face.

I grin again just thinking about it.

"Sidney, you have to understand," Dr. Yang says. "One more situation involving violence, and we're beyond expulsion. We'll be having a conversation about arrest warrants and police records. Scratch that. *You'll* be having the conversation—or worse—with cops, lawyers, and judges. Do you understand?"

"Yes." And I do. Dread scrabbles up and down my spine. My knee starts shaking again, and I push it down with my hands. "Can I go now?"

Dr. Yang watches me for a long moment. "Sidney, your potential, your obvious intelligence—no one wants to see that go to waste. Your

PSAT scores were quite good. You could easily get into a decent college. It would make us all very happy to see you pursue your higher education."

I roll my eyes. "Well, if it'll make you happy, I'll definitely consider it."

"You have to turn things around, clean up your record. This is your senior year."

I know he's right, and I hate that about him. How often he's right, and I'm in the wrong. "Okay, fine. Whatever. I got it."

"And your Phys Ed grade. You have to bring it up. You already have a D in badminton. Really?"

"Coach Taylor hates me."

"Haven't you given him good reason? I'm not sure why you signed up for another class with him when Coach Puglisi offers alternative P.E. classes."

"Because I'm not a Zumba girl, okay? Can you really see me in a ponytail and spandex? And I'm pretty sure Pilates would kill me." I'm also a glutton for punishment, apparently. "Can I go now?"

"No. Not yet. Did you hear the part about being suspended? You looked like you were doing your zoning out thing in Mrs. Rittenburg's office."

He surprises me again. I debate whether to admit it or not, but there's no harm in coming clean now. I shrug. "I might have missed a few things."

Dr. Yang nods tiredly. "First, a three-day suspension. Second, a letter of apology to Jackson Cole. And third, twice-a-week counseling sessions."

Heat flushes through me. "Why should I apologize to a bully? No thanks. I pass."

"You can always choose expulsion."

I feel the walls closing in. I cannot be expelled. Not now, when it's finally senior year and escape is within sight, the red blinking EXIT sign that is graduation. And not when I know how Frank will react, what he'll do. My mouth goes dry. I hate every word of what

I'm about to say. I hate this feeling of capitulation, of defeat, of letting the bad guys win. "Okay fine. I'll write the stupid letter, but only under official protest. But why more counseling sessions? You know how much I love these weekly gab fests with you, but they interfere with my studies. It's my senior year, as you so graciously reminded me."

Dr. Yang writes something on a notepad. "We're going to try something a little different. Group counseling."

"That sounds horrifying. What is it?"

"You will continue to meet with me on Fridays during your free period at 10 a.m. But we're adding a session on Tuesdays at 9:30 a.m. You and at least one other student will meet with me as part of a small group therapy session."

I stare at him suspiciously. This is horrifying. "Who?"

"Arianna Torrès, for one."

I laugh out loud. He's got to be joking. "No effing way."

"Yes."

"What the hell do I have in common with miss Beauty Queen? Is she in grief therapy because she broke a nail?"

"We'll discuss things further at our next meeting. Your suspension is effective immediately. Counting today, tomorrow, and Monday, you'll be back just in time for Tuesday's session."

"Look, Doc. There's no way. I can't—"

He stands up and walks around his desk. He opens the office door. "You can, and you will. I have faith in you, Sidney Shaw."

"Damn it all to hell." I spit the words out. Arianna Torrès is one of the most popular girls in school, a firmly entrenched member of Jasmine Cole's platinum-haired Bitch Squad. She's on the student counsel, plays the flute, and worse, she's one of those goody-two-shoe Christians who meet at the flagpole to pray and plaster "Good Clean Fun Bible Study" posters all over the school every month. Panic lurches through me, like Dr. Yang's just told me I'll be locked in a cage with a prowling tiger for an hour every week.

"Please take care of yourself," he says pleasantly. If there's one thing I know about Dr. Yang, it's that he's solid as a rock once his mind's made up. There's no getting through to him.

I grab my backpack and stomp out of his office. I tried to help Aaron and things got more than a little out of control. As usual, all I've done is make things worse. How much worse, I'm afraid to even think about.

2

All around me, students are laughing, shrieking, slamming locker doors, dropping binders and notebooks into backpacks and messenger bags, shoving each other, hugging and flirting. They move like some huge, mindless organism. I ignore them all.

I grab *King Lear,* my English notebook, and my Spanish III workbook out of my locker and shove them into my backpack. At least I can get some actual homework done during this ridiculous suspension. I shut my locker and turn around, nearly slamming into Jasmine freakin' Cole.

"You bitch!" Jasmine's former frizzy, mouse-brown hair is dyed ice blonde and falls sleekly down her back. I can barely see the girl I used to know through her heavy pink blush, inky eyeliner, and spiky layers of mascara. She's wearing a white peasant shirt that skims her belly and perfectly frayed skinny jeans.

"What the hell do you want?" I say.

"Are you completely mental?"

My hands curl at my sides, my muscles tensing. "Looks like someone forgot to take her happy pills this morning."

A small crowd forms a ring around me, with Jasmine right in the center. On her left is Margot Hunter, the ultimate Queen Bee of Brokewater High. Margot is tall and slim, perpetually tanned, with honey-blonde locks tumbling down her back in big, bombshell curls. Though she looks like a cheerleader, she's into drama and musicals and lands the starring role in every school play. The teachers worship her. She's charming on the surface, but nasty in an underhanded, passive, unprovable way. Tearing girls apart is as much a pastime for Margot Hunter as painting her nails.

Jasmine steps into my personal space. "You beat the crap out of my baby brother!"

Peyton Daugherty and Isabel Gutierrez press in around us.

"Ugh. What a lard-ass," Peyton says with a sniff, flipping her flaxen, chin-length hair. She has Irish-pale skin and a penchant for spouting un-ironic nonsense like "Totes Amazeballs" and random letter configurations like "BFG."

"If you were any bigger, you'd have moons orbiting you," Isabel says. She's Hispanic, with huge dark eyes and curly black hair cut into a pixie and dyed Windex-blue. She and Peyton are both cheerleaders and rally girls. They bounce into classrooms and remind everyone of this rally or that football game, don't forget to cheer your heart out and gulp down the school spirit Kool-Aid.

What they don't understand, what they'll never understand, is that I don't care about the weight they seem to find so revolting. I wear my fat like armor. It's my shield and my weapon, a barricade against their puny barbs and useless arrows. They can't touch me. I'll bulldoze them to the ground.

"You're batshit crazy, you know that?" Jasmine jabs her finger at me.

I slap it away. "And your brother's a psycho. He got what he had coming to him. If only someone would sucker punch your whole family, you'd all be better off."

Margot puts her hand on Jasmine's arm. "She thinks she can hit a little kid and get away with it. Doesn't she know we strictly enforce anti-bullying polices?" Margot's voice is calm and silky. Her thing is talking about the unpopular girls like they aren't even here, like they're not even worth acknowledging. Either that, or they suddenly get disreputable reputations. They're sluts. They hooked up with the entire football team. They're cheaters, liars, freaks, backstabbing bitches. The rumors spread through the hallways and classrooms like poison gas. You breathe it in, and supposition, rumor, hearsay, and innuendo harden into concrete truth in your lungs. I know. She did it to me.

"You might want to step off that pedestal," I snap. "It's starting to crack under your weight."

Jasmine's upper lip curls. "Why am I even surprised? You've always been a psycho freak."

Pain splinters inside me. I can't help it. Out of all of them, she's the only one who can hurt me, whose words still slice to the bone. I pretend I don't care. I pretend I'm invincible. I clench my teeth and push out everything but my anger. "It must be hard to use your entire vocabulary in one pathetic sentence."

Jasmine glances at Margot, then steps closer. "Are you even for real right now?"

"Get out of my face. Your breath stinks so bad, I don't know whether to offer you gum or toilet paper."

Someone in the group snorts. Jasmine's eyes narrow to slits. "You think this is funny? My dad says you belong in jail."

"Do I look like I give a shit? Get out of my way." I glance past the ring of faces. Behind them, Arianna Torrès stands in the hallway, staring at me, one hand pressed against her stomach. Her perfect face is closed, unreadable. Does she already know about the stupid therapy group? Is she repulsed by the thought of being stuck with a loser like me? Why should I care? I don't. I don't give a rat's ass about her. I glare at her, and she ducks her head and keeps walking.

"Jazzy, make her apologize to you." Margot's voice is syrupy sweet.

"I'd rather boil myself alive in a vat of oil, *Jazzy*."

"That can be arranged." Isabel crosses her arms over her chest.

Eli Kusuma strolls up with Nyah Morales, a stunning black girl and a card-carrying member of Margot's squad. She glares at me from beneath a lush cloud of caramel-colored hair.

Eli slings his arm around Margot's shoulders. He's the captain of Brokewater High's loser football team, the Wildcats. Eli is one of those human specimens of nearly perfect dimensions. He has a strong, wide jaw, gorgeous amber eyes, and his body looks like it's been chiseled from granite.

"Hey, ladies." He flicks a strand of shaggy brown-black hair out of his eyes and flashes a megawatt grin. He's shallow and vain and oh so popular, but he's never been mean to me.

I turn to him. "Why do you hang out with these mentally deficient Barbie dolls?"

"Um, hello?" Nyah says, tossing her hair. "Because we're hot."

Eli just grins and shrugs at me, like he can't help himself.

"Jazzy, make her apologize before she regrets it," Margot says.

"You aren't pretty enough to be this stupid," I say. "Get the hell out of my way."

Margot's face hardens. Her eyes go dark and furious. She's used to girls withering beneath her gaze. She's not used to this, to me, and she's royally pissed.

She's not the only one. My pulse pounds against my skull. I want to claw their self-satisfied, judgmental eyes out with my fingernails. I would try it, too, if EXPULSION wasn't scrawled in red ink across my brain. "I'm warning you. Move or I'll go nuclear on your ass."

Jasmine hesitates. Her gaze flicks to Margot. "Let's go. I need a shower after being around this disease-infested slut."

They're going to leave. I should shut the hell up, but I can't help myself. "You need more than a shower to get rid of your diseases."

Jasmine's face blooms bright red. "You're a psycho-bitch. Just like your mother."

Anger mixes with the pain twisting my stomach. I blink back hot, stinging tears. I will not let them see me cry. "And you're a festering ass-wart, just like your brother."

I push past her before I completely lose it. The bell rings, and the rest of the crowd falls away, letting me through.

"Skank!" Margot mock-coughs.

"We're not done here!" Jasmine yells after me.

But I'm out of there before I start throwing punches. I want nothing more than to slap the smugness right off their shiny, starved faces. My eyes burn. My heart stutters in my chest. Dark, painful emotions threaten to boil right out of my skin.

I know what I need to do, what I have to do.

Made in United States
Troutdale, OR
04/28/2024

19508821R00184